This book is a work of fiction. Any resemblance to actual persons—living or dead—events, or locales, is entirely coincidental.

BEAUTY AND THE BASSIST

Copyright © 2020 The Real Sockwives of Utah Valley

All Rights Reserved.

No part of this publication may be reproduced, stored in or introduced into a retrieval system, or transmitted in any form or by any means, electronic, mechanical, printing, recording, or otherwise, without the prior permission of the author, except for use of brief quotations in a book review.

Cover Design by Melissa Williams Design

Guitar by migfoto Adobe Stock

Trophy by martialred Adobe Stock

Crown by lukpedclub Acobe Stock

Column by Alfmaler Adobe Stock

Rose by pandavector Adobe Stock

Lights by beaubelle Adobe Stock

Published by Garden Ninja Books

ExtraSeriesBooks.com

First Edition: July 2020

0 9 8 7 6 5 4 3 2 1

*For Dantzel Cherry,
a true beauty in every way*

ONE

Shane

When I get out of my car at the UCLA Medical Center in Santa Monica, I lock the car doors, then unlock them again before walking away. I used to yell at our lead singer, JT, for not locking the doors to the van, and he used to yell at me for locking them so obsessively when I knew he had a tendency to leave his keys inside.

God speed, buddy, I think as I walk through the automatic glass doors.

From behind me, I hear JT laughing. "Dude," he says. "I can walk through car doors now. I'm dead."

I don't look behind me, but I know he's there, wearing his ratty Sex Pistols t-shirt and the Converse shoes that fell apart back in high school. I know better than to react to him in public. No one else can see him. Instead, I smile at the cute nurse behind the reception desk and walk back to the rehabilitation center.

I've been on our lead guitarist, Kevin, for weeks to tell me how his physical therapy is coming. When the pickup truck crashed into our van two months ago, Kevin was driving. He was wearing his seatbelt, but that didn't stop the frame from crushing his left arm, metal and glass fully severing his tendons in three different places.

"Dude," JT says. "At least it wasn't his skull."

I put on my sunglasses as I walk beneath the fluorescent lights. They hurt my eyes these days; plus, I don't want to be recognized. Used to be I'd have girls hanging on my arm, whispering low in my ear, asking me to sign their arms and breasts and thighs. The only thing I'm going to be asked about if I'm recognized here is the accident.

I don't want to talk about it.

Kevin told the people in reception to expect me, and they clearly recognize me even with my glasses, because they wave me back to a room where Kevin is sitting on a long padded bench. His hands are held out in front of him, a hot girl with dark braids, a skin-tight shirt, and yoga pants sitting next to him.

"You think Kevin is banging his therapist?" JT asks. "I sure as hell would be."

He's not sleeping with her, unless he and Maya have eased up on their hardcore monogamy.

Kevin looks up at me as his therapist walks him through opening his left hand, then folding his fingers and thumb down and clenching them into a fist. Kevin's fingers don't straighten all the way, and his face contorts in pain as he goes through the motions.

"Okay, last rep," his therapist says. "Good! That's getting much better. Take a break, and then we'll work on range of motion."

Kevin groans and leans his head back against the wall. "Do we have to?"

"Oh, come *on*," JT says. "I could have turned that range of motion thing into a hundred different pick-up lines. I guess he's serious about hanging up his schlong. More for you, I guess."

Ha. Not that I've been taking advantage of it. Not since—

The therapist looks over at me. "Hey, I'm Tori. You must be Shane. Kevin told me you were coming. I've heard a lot about you."

Hey, today could be the day. I turn on my best charming smile, hoping Kevin has done me a solid and told her the good stuff, but then I notice that Kevin is wincing and shaking his hand. His fingers curl naturally, like he's got hardcore arthritis.

"Dude," I say. "How's it going?"

"How does it look like it's going? I've lost fifty percent of the feeling in my fingers, and that may never come back. My range of motion sucks, and I can barely straighten my fingers."

Tori looks between the two of us and stands. "I'll give you guys a couple minutes. Do a few more reps while I check the rest of my schedule, all right?"

She bounces out of the room, and JT takes a good look at her ass while she goes. "Dude. *Tight*."

JT was a lot of things, but not subtle.

Kevin takes a deep breath and does another rep of his exercise. "So, there you go. You've seen how it's going. Happy now?"

I stare at him. He obviously can't play like this. "Hell, no, I'm not happy. How long is it going to take for you to—"

Kevin glares at me. "I've told you, Shane. I'm not coming back. It's over. The band is done."

My palms start to sweat, and I cross my arms and wipe them on my shirt. "Come on, man" I say. "I know you're frustrated, but you can't give up. Do you think JT would have wanted—"

Kevin swears at me. "Who cares what JT would have wanted? JT is dead, okay?"

"Ha," JT says. "He's right. Who cares about me?"

Kevin, of course, doesn't hear him. "And Lando found another band already. He was halfway out the door *before* all this. I can't play, and I may never play again. Maya and I are thinking of moving out to Denver, you know? Going back to school."

"It's not going back if you've never been," I say.

"But I can still *go*," he says. "Maya's got her associate degree. We'll live on student loans and my royalties for a while until we figure it out." He points his good hand at me. "*You*, on the other hand, need to stop wasting time waiting on me and get your head back in the game. You always talked about building a solo career." He holds his arms out wide. "Now's your chance."

I drop my arms to my sides and try to look casual. I still have my sunglasses on, which I hope are hiding some of my frustration. "It's okay. I'll wait for—"

Kevin shakes his head. "No, man. I'm not coming back. We've been friends freaking forever, so I don't want to tell you to get lost, but if you can't stop trying to revive the band, just do me a favor and quit calling, okay?"

We stare at each other for a moment, and I want to punch Kevin in the face. Yeah, this is a setback, but it doesn't have to be the end. "We were going to be like Anthony Kiedis and Flea, remember? We were going to play together our whole lives."

"That was you and JT," Kevin says, "and I hadn't heard you talk like that since we were in high school. Come on, man. You're the one of us who walked away from this with hardly a scratch. You're Shane Beckstrom. Since we put out 'I'll Take You Back,' you're the one who gets all the press. There are a thousand guitar players who would jump at the chance to play in your band. Hell, you can keep the name, if you want, but as it was, Accidental Erotica is over."

The lights seem like they're getting brighter in here, even through my glasses.

"Keep it together," JT says.

"I don't want you to give up," I say. But I can already feel myself breaking out in a cold sweat. I can't stay here much longer.

"I'm not giving up," Kevin says. "I'm moving on, and so should you. You got a gift, man. And I don't mean your music."

I nod. I know what he means. JT is dead, Mikey washed up from drinking, Kevin can't play. Out of the four of us who started the band in high school, I'm the only one who made it to twenty-eight and still has a shot.

"Fine," I say. "But you know if you ever change your mind—"

"I'll call." Kevin winces, and I don't know if it's because of his hand, or because he feels bad. "And dude, don't be a stranger.

Just shut up about the band already, okay?"

"Okay." I back up toward the door, and give him a cursory "later," as I beat it out of there, blowing past Tori in the hallway. The lights are getting brighter and the cold sweat is starting to bead on my forehead and I'm starting to feel like I'm going to pass out.

I stumble out of the hospital by the nearest door and sit down on a bench outside the emergency area. I put my hands on my knees and try to breathe. I haven't smoked since high school, but these last two months, all I want is a damn cigarette. I also want to put my fist through the brick wall of the emergency room, though I know both ideas are bad for my health.

Instead I grit my teeth and muscle through. I don't know if this all has something to do with the whiplash or the concussion and the resulting headaches—the only injury I suffered in the crash—or if I'm just freaking out over the loss of my buddies and my band, but I damn well can't wait for this to stop fucking happening to me.

I wait until my head clears—it always does eventually—and find JT leaning against the brick wall with his arms crossed, staring at me with a crooked smile. "Dude," he says. "You're a mess. I mean, not like I was. Remember how my br—"

"Shut up," I say, and JT disappears.

I bury my face in my hands and wipe away sweat, then pull out my phone. I can't drive home like this. Last week a semi honked its horn next to me, and I swerved three lanes over. It was only dumb luck that no one was there. I'm about to pull up Lyft and come back for my car later—something I've been doing an embarrassing amount, but haven't been caught at yet—when I notice a missed call from Parker, our agent.

My agent.

I dial him back. "Park!" I say, with far more gusto than I feel. "What's up?"

"Shane," Parker says with equal enthusiasm. "How'd it go with Kevin?"

I take another deep breath. I do not want to go all soft in front of Parker. He's the only one left who's still on my team, and if he knew I was losing it under the pressure, he might decide I've peaked and find himself another bassist. One who isn't losing his goddamn mind.

"He says he's out," I say.

"Okay. You believe him this time?"

I lower my head into one hand, holding the phone with the other. "Yeah. Sounds like he and Maya have other plans."

"Right," Parker says. "So I heard. How about you and me get together for dinner, and we can plan a strategy. I know it's been rough since you lost JT, but—"

"Yeah," I say, before he can slip into platitudes about how it's time to move on and this is what JT would have wanted. It pisses me off, what I said to Kevin. He's right. What JT would have wanted is to headline our band with his kickass voice and our combined music and lyrics until he was as withered and wrinkled as friggin Mick Jagger.

God only knows what he wants with me now.

"Sounds good," I say. "Let's plan on it."

"One more thing." Parker's always got an agenda for these phone calls, which I'm grateful for, because unlike a lot of other people, he's not trying to pry about my feelings. "I think I mentioned this before, but JT was booked to emcee a competition next week."

"Oh, yeah!" JT says from over my shoulder. "I forgot about that." He may disappear, but he's never far away.

I snort. "The beauty pageant, you mean."

"Miss California Poppy," Parker says. "It's like a week's work. Shouldn't be a big deal. They're not going to hold him to it, god knows, but it might be good for PR if you'd do it. Plus, you know, you'd get to look at hot ladies, so I feel like it wouldn't be too big a sacrifice."

"That's why JT was doing it. I remember him going on and on about how serious he was going to take the swimsuit competition."

"Hell yes, I was," JT says.

"Can I tell them you're in?" Parker asks.

JT sits down next to me on the bench. I refuse to look directly at him, but I stare down at his shoes. "Dude, you have to do it. I want to stare at all the honeys."

"I'll think about it," I say.

Parker sighs. "Look, man, I'm going to level with you. You've turned into kind of a hermit, which people understood for a while. And you've got a bit of time left before the rumors start, but your window is limited. It's time to come out with your *Dark Side of The Moon*, you know? Your *Wish You Were Here*. You've always been good at capitalizing on what's going on in your life, and I know this will be no exception. But you've got to appear occasionally in public between now and then, or people are going to forget about you."

I ball my fists. The bright lights and cold sweats are fading now, and instead of the brick wall, now I want to punch Parker right in the face. He's right. I've always capitalized. JT was the singer, but I've always been the charismatic force pushing us forward. I've thrown everyone under the bus—girlfriends, groupies, other musicians.

But if Parker thinks I'm going to do that to my dead friend—

JT laughs. "Hey, man. I'm right here. You could ask me what I think about it."

"I'm working on the album," I say, in my best disarming tone. "It's one thing to churn out angry spurned boyfriend crap, but if you want Pink Floyd, you're going to have to give me time."

JT scoffs. "And you're going to have to remember how to play."

I give him a sideways look. He's the only one who knows it, but I haven't written a thing. I haven't touched my guitar since—

"I know, man," Parker says. "You got it. So you're in for the pageant?"

I've said no such thing, but he does have a point. I've been hermiting, and I don't have a single note to show for it, let alone this solo-sad-song album I'm supposed to be writing.

Plus, my dead friend appears to be glued to me, and far be it for me to deny him a little voyeurism.

"Fine," I say, and we hang up.

"Thanks, man," JT says. "You're doing me a solid."

"If you're a ghost, you could go by yourself."

JT shrugs. "You know what I am."

I turn away from him, thinking about what Parker said. I know I need to play. I need to write new material, give people the insight about what I'm feeling—or the fake-crap version that people want to identify with, anyway.

"Dude," JT says, "you can write fake crap in your sleep. Get on it already."

I shake myself and refuse to respond. It's only been a couple months. I'll get back on that horse. In the meantime, JT is right.

Beautiful women ought to make for a damn good distraction.

TWO

Shane

I show up at the auditorium where the pageant is taking place and have a hell of a time trying to drive the last couple of blocks. There's a carnival setting up down the street that's blocking off half the side roads so that all the cars coming in and out of the area have to take this one path, which in Orange County pretty much turns the neighborhood into a parking lot. I'm wearing dark reflective sunglasses, which will hopefully help me not be recognized, but I still don't want to hike in from blocks away.

I finally manage to make it to the theater parking lot. It's relatively empty, given that there's no audience today.

JT perks up in the back seat. "About time, man. Ready to scope out the honeys?"

"First, no one says 'honeys' like that anymore. And second, what we're going to find here is a bunch of desperate, scantily-clad girls and the pageant staff who are ready to parade them around to be judged on the size of their boobs."

"You say that like it's a bad thing. Or so different from our concert after-parties."

He has a point. I have been known to bang one or more desperate, scantily-clad groupies with low self-esteem on an after-concert high. I never used to think anything of it, and I probably shouldn't now.

I change my mind immediately when I walk into the auditorium. I'm about forty-five minutes late, only partly because of traffic. The auditorium seats are covered in dresses and swimsuits and enormous suitcases full of salon products. I'm not exactly shocked by that—I wear my share of makeup on stage, and I've performed with women who obviously wear even more.

What shocks me is the age of these girls. They're adults, but not one of them can be over the age of twenty.

"Dude," I whisper to JT. "I am not scamming on teenagers. I don't care if they are of age."

"Yeah, well," JT says. "I'm dead. I'm going to go look up some skirts." He saunters off and does just that, while I roll my eyes behind my sunglasses.

A woman approaches me from the direction of the stage. She's supermodel gorgeous, but she looks older than the rest of the girls, maybe close to my age. She's got dark hair that curls around her shoulders and skin so tan that I wonder if she might be Latina. She's wearing this dress that's half black and half white in this sort of off-center pattern, and it hugs her body—her very hot body—nicely.

She's also glaring at me. "You're late."

"Hi," I say, letting some of my annoyance show in my voice. "I'm Shane."

"Allison Mendez. And you're late."

"Yeah," I say. "I'm always late."

Her scowl grows deeper. "Great. We decided to get started without you, so we're about to run the opening sequence. You can use the time to read over the script." She thrusts a stapled stack of paper at me. "You can read, right?"

I look over at JT, who is lying on his back staring up the dresses of a couple of girls who are fussing over their evening wear. I shake my head slightly, and Allison's eyes narrow. "You can't read? Seriously?"

"I can read," I tell her.

"With your sunglasses on? Is this some kind of statement you're making? Are you too cool to let other people see your eyes?"

I snatch the script from her. "What's your problem?"

Allison puts her hands on her hips. She's hot, but seriously intense.

JT looks in my direction, and he smiles.

Okay, maybe I like intense. But there's normal intense and there's heinous bitch intense, and this is—

"My *problem*," she says, "is that despite agreeing to do this, you show up forty-five minutes late and don't care who you inconvenience."

I hold up my hands, one of them still containing the script. "Look. I didn't sign up for this. My buddy did. I'm just here covering for him. And you *just met me*, so I don't know what makes you think you know so much about me."

The girls in the room are starting to notice us, turning toward us and whispering to each other. Not a few of them are probably saying variations of "oh my god, there's Shane Beckstrom," which is something I normally encourage, but lately makes me sick to my stomach.

Allison, however, doesn't seem to care. "I know your type," she snaps. "You think that just because you've got this bad boy rock star thing going, you can do whatever you want. But I'm here to tell you to stay away from my girls."

"Your girls." I want to lift up the sunglasses and glare at her, but I don't want to give her the satisfaction. Plus, I wear them inside to avoid headaches from the fluorescent lights. I might have told her that, if she'd asked instead of just assuming I'm an asshole.

"Yes, *my girls*," she says. "I know why guys like you sign on to do this job. But you're not going to take advantage of them. Do you understand?"

"Yeah, I got it," I say sharply. "Some rock star broke your

heart, and now you have to take it out on everyone who happens along. Noted."

"For your information," Allison says, "I have never dated a musician. But I've worked for plenty of them, and I know how they think."

JT tires of looking up the skirts of the girls who are staring at us, and comes over to stand behind Allison. "Dude," he says. "She's hot. I can just see her in a leather corset." He mimes cracking a whip in my direction, and I laugh.

Allison does not appreciate this. "That's hilarious, is it?"

"No," I say. "I just figured out what you're so pissed about."

JT grins like he already knows what I'm going to say. Allison, on the other hand, doesn't. "Oh, really," she says.

"You're just mad because you want me so bad. But it's okay, sweetheart. I don't bite unless you want me to."

Allison looks like she wants to kill me, which is fair. It's an asshole thing to say, and I take way more glee out of her anger than I ought to.

I shrug. "What can I say? I'm a jerk. You've got me pegged."

She points down a hall the way that I came. "The green room is out there to the left. Go have a seat and read the script. I'll let you know when we need you."

I bite back a comment about how I can be anything she needs. But I do check her out from behind as she walks away, and damn, she's smoking hot.

"You," JT says, coming around behind me and checking out the view over my shoulder, "have a type."

I turn around and head into the hall before I answer him. "Can you blame me?"

"No," he says. "But you're right about her. She wants you bad."

"It doesn't matter. I'm just here to do the job you signed up for and get out."

"Aww," JT says, following me through the doors on the left. "Come on. I'm dead, so I can't get any. But there are some seriously hot honeys in there that you have got to see up close and personal, if you know what I mean."

The green room consists of a leather couch, a floor-length mirror, and a table covered in more makeup and a couple piles of papers. I sprawl out on the couch, flipping through the script. "Again," I tell JT, "no one says honeys. And yeah, I'm sure the contestants are hot. And also barely legal."

JT sits down on the table, right on top of a pile of papers, which don't move an inch. "Then do it with whip lady. It's been months, and you need to get laid."

I refuse to look at him. "You're only saying that because you think you get to watch."

"Hell, yes, I'm going to watch." He rolls his eyes when I glare at him over my glasses. "Okay, fine. I'll block out you, and just watch *her*, okay?" He holds up a hand in an approximation of him trying to do this, and I shake my head at him.

"Dude, if you insist on watching, I'm never having sex again."

"Fiiiiine," JT whines, in that way that he always did when he knew he was in the wrong but wasn't going to admit it. "I'll just listen."

I'm about to protest, but he cuts me off. "It's not like I've never heard you have sex before."

I laugh. "Yeah, okay. Remember me and that girl in the back of our van when Kevin was driving us up to San Francisco?"

"Dude, I wish I could forget. Those sounds you made are forever burned in my memory."

"Well, enjoy those, because they're all you're going to get for a while."

JT groans, walks over to the mirror, and starts cleaning his teeth, as if he's had anything to eat in the last three months. I flip through the first few pages of the script, which I can in fact read, and find that it's basically a bunch of corny jokes that sound like they would be better coming out of the mouth of William Shatner.

"No way am I sticking to this," I say.

As if summoned by my belligerence, the door swings open

while I'm still in the middle of the sentence. I'm struck again by how beautiful Allison is, but also how exhausted she looks.

I imagine I'm not helping that any.

"How's the script?" she asks. "And yes, you will stick to it."

I definitely won't, but I don't argue the point. She'll figure out soon enough. "Ready for my entrance?"

"No. But we have to put up with you sooner or later."

I smile. I respect a girl who can throw my shit right back at me. "You don't have to. If you don't want me to do this job, I can walk right out the door. Makes no difference to me."

She sneers at me. "You would, wouldn't you? Commit to doing something and then walk out and never look back."

"Hey, you're the one who doesn't want me here."

"I don't," she says. "But I do need you here."

My smile widens. "Ah. She admits it. I knew you were hot for me."

"Whatever. You're clearly the one who wants me."

I scoff. "Right. That'll happen."

Her face hardens, like this actually bothers her. And I think it might. "Whatever. Get off your ass, and bring the script with you. And please try not to be a total nightmare on stage, okay? We have a show to put on."

"It doesn't matter. You're going to hate what I do no matter what it is. Are you a bitch to every guy you want to bang, or am I just special?"

"Maybe you're special," she says, and then hesitates, like she's just now realizing that isn't an insult. "And maybe I know Anna-Marie."

That settles over me like a lead blanket. "Oh," I say. "That would explain it." My ex-girlfriend, Anna-Marie, decided to completely ignore me in favor of some tool from LA on the one weekend she came back to Wyoming after four years away. I might have reacted to this by writing a song all about how I was still in love with her just to get back at her and her rich, city-boy boyfriend.

Then they got married and the world decided they were the cutest couple ever, so the joke was on me. But hey, I got two hit albums out of the deal, supposedly all about how she broke my heart, so I made out all right.

Long story short, Anna-Marie hates my guts.

"Really?" Allison says. "That's it? You're not going to defend yourself?"

"What's to defend? You've already made up your mind about me. Besides, what do I care what you think?" I know I should stop there, but I'm starting to get mad, the way I do whenever I think about the way Anna-Marie ignored me like I was nothing the minute her now-husband showed up. I mean, she and I were way over. But we'd been a big part of each other's lives back in the day, and I'd thought we'd be the kind of old friends who were in and out of each other's lives, even if the romantic part was over.

The joke, again, was on me.

"You say you know my type," I continue, "but believe me, I know yours. You're a man-hating crazy cat lady who feels the need to take her own sexual frustration out on every guy within shouting range. So just go home, cuddle your cat, and leave me alone."

"Leave Lord Shelldon out of this," she says. But she seems less angry now. More . . . amused.

And she *is* a cat person. I'm kind of proud of myself for getting that right.

"How do you know Anna-Marie, anyway?" I ask.

She shrugs. "I don't actually *know* her. I used to work with Jenna Rollins, so most of what I know about you I heard from her."

She says this like it should make sense, but I'm not getting the connection. "Anna-Marie knows Jenna Rollins? The pop star?"

Allison looks startled, like she thinks I should know all about the social life of the girl who has barely spoken to me since she left town without saying goodbye back when we were twenty. "Oh. Anna-Marie is friends with Jenna. Because Anna-Marie's best friend is the sister of Felix Mays, who's married to—"

"I know who Felix Mays is," I say. "I was there at the VMAs the night he pushed Alec Andreas off of that stage onto Kanye West."

Allison smiles. "So was I. And it was glorious."

It *was* glorious. As is Allison's smile. "Anna-Marie has a friend who's a girl?"

Allison laughs. "Yeah, a couple of them. I've only met her once, but I thought she was cool."

Which explains why she hates me. Still, I'm glad we're not yelling at each other anymore. "Do you really have a cat named, what was it? Sir Snugglesworth?"

She laughs. "No, but clearly I need a second cat so that I can name him *that*. Mine's named Lord Shelldon."

"Maybe I should get a cat," I say. I've never had this desire before, but sitting across the room from this gorgeous woman, who I have no intention of taking home with me tonight . . . it reminds me that I'm the crazy person who lacks for human affection, not her.

"Oh, then you keep the name," Allison says. "It would be way better knowing that *Shane Beckstrom* has a cat named Sir Snugglesworth."

"What? I can't like cute cat names?"

Allison holds up her hands. "Oh, no. You definitely can. *Should*, even."

I smile and she smiles, and for a moment I regret being as defensive as I've been. It's not like she's said anything about me that isn't true.

"I have a concussion," I say.

Her smile slips. "What?"

"From the accident. It's why I wear the sunglasses inside. I get headaches from the fluorescent lights. They say it'll go away, but it might be months before it does."

"Oh," Allison says, her voice softening. She's quiet for a moment. "Maybe we should start over. I think we got off on the wrong foot."

I bristle at that. There's nothing that makes me feel angrier since the accident than people looking at me like I'm some wounded puppy. I'm the lucky one. I'm the one who got out of that van alive. "No, thanks. I don't need your pity."

"It's not pity," Allison says. "It's possible that I'm legitimately sorry about what happened to you, and I think maybe I shouldn't have been so hard on you."

I shake my head. "You have a thing for bad boys, don't you?"

She looks surprised. "What?"

"You do. First you're angry about what a jerk I am, and now you're deciding that I must be some wounded soul underneath. Well, I have news for you. I'm not wounded, just an asshole. I'm everything that Anna-Marie said, so there's nothing to start over. You were right about me. You were right about everything."

And with that I get up and stalk back into the auditorium, ridiculous script in hand, Allison and JT following after me.

If I'm going to do this job, might as well get it over with. The sooner the show is done, the sooner I can go back to the dark cave of my apartment and resume pretending that the rest of the world doesn't exist.

THREE

Shane

The next day I'm standing in front of a microphone on an empty stage as women in high cut bathing suits parade in front of me. Their ass cheeks undulate as they practice not falling off the apron stage while sauntering and turning. The auditorium lights are on, so even through my sunglasses I can see Allison glaring at me each time one of them passes me. She's wearing a tight red dress today and a pair of high-heeled boots to match, and if anything, she looks even hotter than she did yesterday.

I smirk back at her. It's not my fault that most of these girls have chosen swimsuits that ride halfway up their butt cracks. Out in the audience, a busty dark-haired girl is eyeing me hungrily. And while I'm not entirely certain, I think the lips of her vulva may be hanging out of either side of the crotch of her swimsuit.

I lift my glasses. Yep. That's definitely what's happening there. JT sits in the row in front of her, staring openly. That swimsuit reeks of more desperation than I've encountered since the last time I saw Anna-Marie's cousin Lily.

Allison follows my eyeline and throws her hands in the air. "Carmen!" she says, "I told you not to wear that swimsuit until you make some alterations." She rushes over to Carmen, who looks at me knowingly. When Allison returns from ushering Carmen to the dressing room, she sits down next to one of the girls—Collette, I think? She's got bleached blond hair and wide blue eyes and a boyfriend who keeps skulking around. I don't see him at this moment, but Allison says something to her, and Collette holds out a palm and does a wax-on, wax off gesture at the general area of my crotch.

"Can I help you ladies with something?" I ask into the microphone.

All eyes turn toward me. The girl in the string bikini currently walking the stage stops mid-stride to turn around, and Collette grins. "I was just reading your aura!"

"Ah," I say. "Is that what the kids are calling it?"

Allison smiles at that, but stifles it quickly so that she can glower. I grin at her, which only makes her glare harder. It's kind of adorable.

"Yep," Collette says, turning to Allison. "He clearly wants you."

Allison's mouth falls open, and she shushes Collette. It's too late, though, as giggles travel through the room.

I smile. "Oh, really?"

"I think you two were married in a past life."

Allison looks less than pleased by this news, which is hilarious.

Collette's eyebrows hug together, like she's concentrating. "Yes. And then you killed him."

That sounds about right.

"All right," Allison says. "Back to work." She moves over and starts helping one of the girls get her bikini straps crossed correctly over her back while Carlyle, the director, calls for me to take it from the top.

I read from the script, because I don't have it memorized yet. Carlyle has some kind of yard stick up his butt, because he snaps at me anytime I off-road it. I've decided to keep my asides to myself. He won't be able to snap anymore once we have an audience, and if he doesn't like the way I announce the girls, he can get out here and do it himself.

As we move through the script, I watch Allison work. She rotates from girl to girl, smiling at something this one says, helping that one with the pins in her hair. JT is following Allison around trying to look down the front of her dress, which makes me want to smack him upside the head. I vow to do this at my earliest opportunity that won't make me look like a psycho. Carmen comes back looking all kinds of pissy that her swimsuit didn't pass inspection. She's got on a crop-top number that I think must be borrowed because the bra part looks like it's one size too small, and she's popping out the top. Allison walks over and gives her a hug, then looks as if she's saying something reassuring.

This job sounds like hell to me, but I can tell she's good at it. Even if from the way one of the girls, in a red bikini, keeps turning around and licking her lips at me, I think she ought to be protecting me from them and not the other way around.

"All right!" Carlyle calls. He's a gay dude in a three piece suit with a hairstyle that looks like he's trying to simulate the perfect wave. It makes me want to buy him a little surfboard barrette and glue on one of those tiny ninjas you can get out of vending machines. Little dude would be rocking out up there. "Let's take a break, and then we'll move on to talents. We'll save the full showcase for tomorrow, but I want to make sure we can get all your props on and off the stage."

Girls start scrambling like they don't know the definition of "break," and I hop down off the stage and walk over to Allison. She's standing next to a seat over which are draped several garment bags, frowning at her phone. "Hey," I say. "How's it going?"

Allison looks up from her phone and almost smiles. It's a good look for her. "Well, I haven't murdered any husbands today, so that's something."

"I could see you as the black widow type."

JT walks up behind her. "This is dark, even for you," he says.

I ignore him. The corners of Allison's mouth turn up a little more, and I decide I'm going to make it my mission today to get her to give me a real smile. I've seen her smile at several of the girls, and it's dazzling.

"Did Collette have any idea how many other past-life husbands you've killed?"

Closer still. "I think you might be a special case."

"I usually am." Next to the row of auditorium seats, someone has left a makeup case folded open to reveal a row of flesh-colored fake breasts. JT kneels beside it, poking at one, though he doesn't have any effect on it. I bend down and take it away from him, tossing it in the air with one hand.

Allison's smile disappears, probably because I've touched an intimate prop belonging to one of the girls she's trying to shelter from me. "So these talents," I say before she can snap at me. "What can I expect? Yodeling? Will anyone be demonstrating tax preparation?"

Allison reaches out and snaps the fake breast from me mid-toss. "While I'm sure you could use the financial advice," she says, "I don't think we have anyone scheduled to do that this year."

"Dude," JT says, now sitting sprawled across the aisle, so that anyone who passes is likely to walk through him. "You should tell her about those IRAs you made us all get. She's wound so tight that'll probably turn her on."

I shake my head. I'm doing just fine financially, but I don't like to advertise it. It goes against my irresponsible, fuck-em-all image to tell people I have half a year's income socked away and investment accounts in excess of that.

I reach down and pick up the opposite breast, pinching it between two fingers and wiggling it at Allison. "What's the point of these, anyway?" I ask. "Are they supposed to be attractive? They're false advertising, if you ask me."

Allison snatches it out of my fingers before I've even finished my sentence. "Which no one did," she says, more harshly than is warranted. I fold my arms and roll my eyes behind my glasses.

So much for making her smile.

"Get back on stage," she says. "When Carlyle says we're taking a break, he means get ready for what's next."

Down on the floor, JT is making whipping motions again. I don't exactly want to do what she says, and Carlyle is using his break to yell at someone over the phone about scones, which makes me wonder if there's a breakfast table around here I've missed. So instead I take a leisurely walk over to the guys manning the sound equipment. At least those guys will probably be able to carry on a conversation about something other than swimsuit cuts and my general lack of redeeming qualities.

I don't make it as far as the sound table before Carlyle is off the phone and shouting about why he doesn't see any props on the stage. I use the stage door and walk through the wings. I'm not sure if I'm going to be announcing these props, but either way, this ought to be good, and I want a front-stage seat.

Back in the wings, one of the girls—a redhead whose name I originally thought might be Diva, but the script tells me is Deena—is gathering up a collection of scarves. I'm going to need popcorn for this. I lean against the side of the proscenium.

Allison heads backstage as scarf-girl comes out, trailing the scarves behind her in long sweeping movements. Someone backstage is yelling about the amount of space required for her marimba to roll out through the wings. Scarf-girl is still wearing her swimsuit, but wraps the scarves around her arms and begins to dance, the scarves flying in all directions like long-feathered wings.

It's kind of impressive, actually, and I stand at the microphone and watch her, while backstage someone starts wailing about the marimba squishing her camellias. There's no music, and I look down at the sound people, wondering if they've missed their cue. But no, Carlyle said he wanted to practice getting the props on and off, and that they'd run through the talent numbers later.

Deena swoops through her dance moves, and I begin to understand why she's doing this. As she does, she sheds scarves and then picks them up again in a whirling melee that begins to match the rise of the fight breaking out backstage. I can hear someone screaming that her prize-winning camellias are now permanently bruised, and someone else screaming that her marimba hasn't been within a mile of those camellias, which is obviously not true if the marimba is anywhere in the building.

A headache is starting to build behind my eyes, despite the sunglasses, and JT comes over and slings an arm around me. "Come on," he says. "It's not so bad. Not like that time we—"

JT is interrupted by a loud crash backstage that sounds vaguely like something huge slamming into a marimba. The sound rattles through my bones, and I jump, knocking over the mic stand. The sound guys glare at me, and my headache sharpens, pounding like an ice pick to the back of my eyeballs. I bend down and pick up the mic stand, hoping that no one will notice the cold sweat beading on my forehead. JT is gone, but I swear I can smell his blood, dripping across the seat, soaking my shirt so much that the paramedics will search for the wound in my side that isn't mine. My hands feel slick and sticky.

"Hey, man," one of the sound guys says over the shouting backstage. "Are you okay?"

I'm standing in front of the upright microphone, and I can hear my own breathing through the speakers in front of the stage.

I have to get out of here, but for all I know there's a cell phone somewhere and it's taking a video that will spread over the internet, and everyone will know that I'm clearly unhinged. It feels hot in here, but my palms are ice cold. I grab the mic.

"I can't work like this!" I shout into it. Then I jump down from the stage and storm off toward the green room like I'm having a diva fit.

It's what they expect of me anyway, and it's better than them knowing I'm losing my fucking mind.

FOUR

Allison

"Look at these! Look at them!" Becky shrieks, waving a vase of flowers in my face. "My camellias are permanently bruised, and it's all her fault! Her and her stupid, huge-ass marimba!"

I'm pretty sure she's going to be bringing a fresh cut of camellias on the actual pageant day, so I doubt it matters how bruised these ones get. Honestly, the camellias look perfectly fine to me anyway, but I know nothing about gardening. I do, however, know very well how stressful the rehearsals only days before the pageant can be. I open my mouth to try to calm her down with soothing assurances—it's not unlike being the Horse Whisperer, this pageant coordinator role of mine—but Sherry jumps in.

"Please don't yell like that," she begs. "It's making my babies nervous." She's crouched down, furiously petting the back of one of her three white miniature poodles, while in the other hand she holds the rings they'll jump through as part of her dog-trainer talent.

Gwen gives Sherry a disdainful look before turning her death glare back to Becky.

"My marimba hasn't been within a mile of your camellias," Gwen growls, even though her marimba is quite literally right there next to them. "And maybe you should look in a mirror before you start throwing around the words 'huge ass.'"

Becky gasps and Gwen smirks, folding her arms and turning back to her instrument, and I hold in a groan and make sure I'm standing between them in case Becky decides to lunge. It wouldn't be the first time in my many years at this job that I've had to physically keep a girl from using her new French-manicured tips to do some face scratching.

I should be grateful for having to head off a possible cat fight; this *should* be the perfect excuse to stop checking out Shane Beckstrom. Which is ridiculous, because no matter how incredibly hot he is—and damn, he is—he's also a self-centered jerk, and I have better things to do with my time than ogle some entitled rock star who knows all too well how good-looking he is.

But I find my eyes drifting back to him anyway.

He's out on the stage, turned toward Deena, who's twirling with her scarves—she has all of them now, thank god, because there was almost another cat fight yesterday when one went missing and it turned out Heather had taken it to use as a chic head wrap. One among many crises I was in the middle of dealing with when our emcee decided to show up forty-five minutes late, which didn't help my admittedly already-formed opinion of him.

He's facing Deena like he's watching her, but his head dips down and he grimaces slightly. Like maybe he's in pain.

I remember him telling me he had a concussion, and about the headaches.

But when I tried to be a decent person and maybe revisit some of those opinions—because I recognize that snap-judgments of people aren't always fair, and he *was* kind of cute there for a second, talking about cat names—he accused me of having a thing for bad boys and stormed off.

I flush, turning back to the girls, my irritation peaking again for reasons that have little to do with the marimba/camellia feud. "Look," I say firmly. "First, you know my feelings on women tearing each other down, especially with insults meant to body shame." This with a hard look at Gwen, who purses her lips and frowns at the ground. She's a bit hot-headed, but she has a sister with Down syndrome who she loves like crazy and would defend to the ends of the earth, so I know she gets my stance on this. "And second," I continue, turning to Becky, who clearly already knows what I'm going to say, "I know how stressed out we all are, but if you have a problem with another contestant, the respectful thing to do is—"

My long-suffering pageant-mother rant is interrupted by a loud, jangling crash that makes me jump and Gwen shriek.

Angelica cringes at the cart of sound equipment she just shoved into Gwen's marimba. A speaker from the top of the equipment tower is now on the ground, hopefully not broken. "Sorry," she says. "I—"

Whatever else Angelica was going to say is cut off by the clatter and then shrill squeal of a microphone as it hits the stage, and I spin back around. Deena's covering her ears with her scarves, and Shane's picking up the mic stand he must have knocked down.

He straightens, and he seems paler than he did a moment ago. The microphone stand shakes in his hand.

"My marimba!" Gwen yells, practically throwing herself bodily over the instrument as if to prevent future assaults by sound equipment.

"I'm sorry," Angelica starts again, "but the cart was in my way, and I needed to move it to get to my paints."

I should be heading this off now, but I can't tear my eyes from Shane. His rapid, shallow breathing near the microphone echoes through the auditorium.

I'm not the only one who notices something's wrong.

"Hey, man," Trevor, one of the assistant sound guys, calls to him while Henry, his boss, dashes up the stage left stairs to the sound cart Angelica shoved over. "Are you okay?"

Gwen's chewing out Angelica now, and Becky's trying to defend her, but I can't tear my eyes from Shane, whose mouth opens and closes, his Adam's apple bobbing, the mic in his hand trembling.

"I can't work like this!" he shouts into the mic, and that, at least, shuts the girls up. He jumps down off the stage and stomps off.

There's a beat of silence as everyone stares after him.

What the hell was *that*?

"Oh my god, what a drama queen," Angelica says, wrinkling her nose. I'm inclined to agree with her, and more than that, to chew him out for it. Showing up late when we're on a tight schedule is bad enough, like his time is so much more important than the rest of ours, but throwing fits and refusing to work . . .

Except I don't think that's what actually happened there.

"Maybe," Becky says, clutching her vase of flowers to her chest. "But I'd still ride that so hard he'd—" She cuts off when I give her a look. A few other girls snicker.

The girls think I'm a prude, and hell, Shane probably does too. But I've been doing this pageant coordinator thing for a long time, and sure, flirting with the cute host seems like it's all fun and games. Until it goes too far and word gets out and a girl gets dropped from the pageant last minute for breach of contract and disgraced in pageant circles ever after. And the smarmy guy walks away with another locker-room story to tell.

I've seen it happen, to one of my friends back when I was competing myself, and then again my second year as coordinator, when I was still too new to do anything about it. Not that I think I could even now—there's no way Shane Beckstrom's career would suffer for banging a nineteen-year-old pageant girl, and he's made it clear he doesn't care about the actual pageant.

The thought of him skeeving on these girls raises my hackles more than is probably warranted, given that he hasn't, to my knowledge, done so—at least not yet. But still.

Collette appears next to me suddenly, and I startle. Sometimes I feel like maybe her real talent is teleportation. She's got this sort of ethereal quality and not just because she claims to be psychic. "I wonder if he was like that when you were married to him." She tilts her head and squints, like she's trying to see into my supposed past life with Shane. My body flushes, just like it did the first time she said that. She smiles at me. "Maybe that's why you murdered him."

"I probably had lots of reasons," I mutter.

"Enough about him," Gwen says. "Carlyle! Come look at what Angelica did to—!" Then she gasps. "Oh my god, Sherry, did your dog just piss on my marimba?"

We all gape for a second. There is indeed a puddle of urine right beneath the marimba leg, and a cowering poodle beside it.

Becky's nose wrinkles. "Isn't he supposed to be trained?"

"The noise scared him!" Sherry shouts, ignoring her own previous anti-yelling pleas. "Orville Redenbarker has a nervous bladder!"

"My marimba," Gwen wails.

Henry inspects the small speaker that dropped. "I've got thousands of dollars worth of sound equipment here. If that's damaged . . ."

Carlyle, who was watching from the back of the auditorium and has now scrambled his way to the front, looks just as stunned by Shane's rapid departure and all of this chaos as everyone else, and infinitely more pissed—especially at Shane, is my guess—and I don't think either Gwen or Henry's hissy fit will help that.

Poor Angelica looks like she might cry. "I'm so sorry, about your marimba and the speaker tower and—" Then her tear-filled eyes widen as she looks at Collette. "The tarot reading you gave me! I drew the upside-down tower card, and you said it was a fallen tower and that meant destruction—"

"It better not mean destruction," Henry grouses, while the other contestants gasp at this supposed fulfillment of prophecy, and Collette nods, her expression full of knowing sympathy.

"Hey, all of you, it was an *accident*," I say, and I squeeze Angelica's hand. "Why don't you and Collette go over and help Yvonne with her costume—it looks like her feathers keep falling off." I personally hope they don't do anything that makes it more difficult for me later when I promised to help her *actually* fix it, but for right now I just need to defuse the situation. "And Collette, no more tarot readings, okay?" I don't believe in that stuff, but I know how easy it is to get superstitious right before a pageant. I don't need anyone fueling that fire.

They nod and scurry off, but even with everything going on, even though I should probably be much more worried about my girls and their nervous-bladdered dogs and their desecrated instruments, I find my gaze drifting back to the doors where Shane left.

"Did you see that?" Carlyle demands, storming up the stage steps, and I'm not sure which part of all of this he's referring to, until he gestures back to those very same doors. "He just ran off! In the middle of practice, like—"

"How about I go yell at him?" I say, and that looks like it satisfies Carlyle, at least until Gwen and Henry start hounding him about their speaker and marimba. But I'm already walking to the auditorium doors by then and just barely catch Carlyle yelling, "Practice is over! *Over*, I tell you!"

I don't blame him for calling it there. No one's going to be able to focus now.

I certainly don't seem to be able to, which irritates me even more.

But even though I told Carlyle I'd yell at Shane—and there's definitely part of me that wants to—I can't ignore what I saw on his face, even under those dark sunglasses.

It reminded me of myself, sitting in my car alone, staring at the entrance to the oncology wing of the hospital. Willing myself to go in. Telling myself it was just a checkup, what are the odds it'd be back, especially so soon? Breathing rapidly. Clutching my purse with white knuckles.

And yeah, maybe he's an asshole, like I've heard he is, like even *he* said he is. And yeah, maybe I'm a little pissed that he's acting like he's not attracted to me, like he's too good for me or something, even though he was clearly checking me out. And maybe I'm more than a little annoyed at myself for caring at all, especially after that awful, shallow comment about the fake breasts.

Bad boy rock stars *aren't* my type—I've designed for enough of them. I should know.

But against my better judgment, I find myself wanting to talk to him. Wanting to see if he'll be open with me again like that bare moment when he told me about his concussion, and why he wears his sunglasses.

Wanting to see if maybe his claim that he's nothing but an asshole is just another faked diva-fit to cover up the panic underneath.

FIVE

SHANE

JT is waiting for me in the green room. I slam the door behind me and brush past him, sitting against the wall next to the couch with my knees pulled up to my chest." Hey," JT says. "Come on. The accident wasn't that bad."

"You don't remember. You were dead." The lights are so bright they feel like they're boring into my skull, and I get up and turn them off.

"Yeah, okay," JT says. "Good plan. Have whip girl find you in here all pathetic and shivering. Girls love that wounded soul shit."

"Shut up," I tell him. "And leave her alone."

"Whaaaaaat," JT says. "That's just cold, dude. It's not like I'm competition anymore. You don't need to call dibs when I'm dead."

I should have told Parker I wouldn't do this gig. I should have stayed in my cave of an apartment with all the lights off and a mounting pile of pizza boxes and Chinese takeout cartons and never emerged.

"But damn, have you checked out Allison's ass?" JT says. "I copped a feel when she was backstage checking this girl's hem to see if it was even, and *damn*—"

"Shut *up*!" I say.

The door swings open, and Allison stands there, back lit by

the hallway lights. "I didn't say anything," she says.

Shit.

"Oh," I say. "Sorry." I'm not going to try to explain who I was talking to, and there's nothing I can say that will adequately address why I'm sitting on the floor next to the couch in a corner with the lights off. I briefly consider unzipping my pants and making her think I've been jacking off in here.

That would be less embarrassing than the truth.

"Are you okay?" Allison asks.

I shrug. Let her think what she wants about me. I don't think she's the type to go to the press with it. "What do you want? Here to make fun of me some more?"

She steps in and closes the door behind her. In the crack of light under the door I can see her pacing to the couch and sitting down on it. She's just a silhouette in the dark, so I can't read her face. "I was going to yell at you for being such a diva."

"Go ahead."

She hesitates, and I want to repeat my rant from yesterday about how I don't need her pity. Whatever JT says, I've never found being a wounded soul to be a particularly great way to get women. Sure, it works, but then you've got girls following you around, thinking they've seen deep into your soul or some such shit. It's easier if everyone knows the score from the very beginning.

"It was the noise, wasn't it?" Allison asks.

My face gets hot. "Yeah, so?"

"Is it because of the accident?"

I shrug again, even though I'm not sure she can see it. "What's it to you?"

She hesitates. "I've had my share of days spent sitting in the dark."

I'm not sure where JT has gone. Probably feeling her up again while I can't see and chew him out for it later. He's right. I didn't generally care who he copped a feel with when he was alive; I should care even less now that he's dead.

She's quiet, and I can't help but wonder what could have happened to her to make her hide in a dark room like this.

"Why?" I ask.

"I had cancer."

My stomach drops. I never would have guessed that, though it's not like cancer doesn't happen to people of all ages. She doesn't elaborate, and I don't ask her what kind it was. I knew a girl in a band we used to tour with who had cervical cancer, and she was always saying what happened with her lady parts was nobody's damn business.

"That sucks," I say. "Are you okay?"

"Physically, yeah. For now, anyway."

I can see her profile in the dark, her hair falling down over her shoulders. I'm suddenly scared that she's dying or something, and I've been an ass to her because I didn't even know it.

"Was it treatable?"

"Yeah," she says. "And it was a couple years ago. But it could always come back."

I lean my head against the wall. That must be hard, always knowing there's that chance. Though I guess it could happen to any of us at any time.

Before the accident, I never gave much thought to my own mortality. Now it's fucking terrifying.

"I'm sorry about your friend," Allison says.

"Me, too."

I expect her to say one of the idiotic platitudes people tend to launch at me. He's in a better place. It was meant to be. He didn't feel any pain.

I saw the twisted angle of his neck, the lacerations that slit him open on his arms and throat. I marinated in his blood for over an hour before the paramedics finally got us all out of the van.

Even if it kills you, that shit's gotta hurt.

"You said you had a concussion," she says. "Do you remember the accident?"

"Yeah. I was conscious the whole time."

Allison's voice is quiet. "Did you know he was dead?"

"I knew. I thought Kevin was dead, too. He was unconscious, and he didn't make any noise until the paramedics were dragging him out. Took a long time. The van rolled off the road when the truck hit us, and it was pretty thrashed. We were all wearing our seat belts. Not great for our image, and now I've got road safety people trying to get me to do public service commercials."

I shiver, and Allison must notice, because she moves to the floor next to the couch. Having her so close, in the dark . . . it makes me even more aware of her than I usually am. I haven't been alone in a dark room with a woman since the accident. Logically, I know I should get out of here.

But I don't want to.

"You're opposed to being a spokesperson?" she asks.

"What am I going to say? Wear your seat belts, kids, and you have a one-in-three chance of walking away. Your best friend will be dead and your band will be done and your other buddy won't ever be able to play again, but you'll get to live through it all. Maybe. If you're lucky."

I say that last bit with more irritation than I ought to, and Allison shifts closer to me. "It sounds like no one in that situation was lucky."

I shake my head. "I know it's unfair of me to whine." JT reminds me of that often enough. "But I've always been a whiny son of a bitch, so I don't see why that should change now."

"What about your image? You're the bad boy with the charming smile. The devilish rogue. Isn't that your thing?"

"Not anymore," I say. Damn it. If I were trying to pull this wounded soul crap, I would be doing a good job. "Don't imagine that there's anything underneath, though. I used to be a charming asshole, and now I'm just an asshole. I'm not an onion. I don't have layers."

"Hmmm. Are you sure? You do act like quite the ogre."

"Right. And that's all you need to know about me."

"I get being different after, though. The cancer . . . it changed me. It's supposed to make you realize what's important in life, you know? Closer to family and all that. But it just made me more focused. More driven. Made me realize how little time I might have left to accomplish the things that I want to."

"What do you want to accomplish? The costuming thing?"

"No," she says. "I mean, I enjoy costuming, but I'm a serious designer. I'd like to have my own fashion line."

I can see it. Allison clearly works hard and cares about what she does. "Not trying to make a career of the pageant thing?"

"God, no. It's how I got my start, so I come back every year to help out the girls. I had some mentors in my pageant days who really helped me, made me think about what I wanted beyond winning, you know? You get so focused, you forget that there's life afterward. I want to help the girls figure out what they want out of this, besides the sash and tiara. The pageant can be a springboard into lots of fields, if you know what you want."

"And you know exactly what you want." It comes out sounding more suggestive than I meant it, but I don't mind. Allison's hand shifts next to mine, just inches away, and I gather that she doesn't either.

"They must be looking for us." I say. Not that I want to go back out there into the chaos, but I am wondering if we're going to get walked in on.

"Angelica pushed a cart full of sound equipment into Gwendolyn's marimba. When I left them, both Gwen and the sound people were threatening to sue. Carlyle got fed up and sent them all home. He's probably wondering where I am, though. I'll catch it from him tomorrow."

"He's not wondering where you are," I say. "Word is going to get around that you're in here with me, and they'll all think we had sex in the green room."

"Sorry about that. Wouldn't want anyone to think you were into me."

She says this at once like she half believes I'm not, which is crazy, and like she's testing me to see if I am, which is hot.

But I don't bite. Not yet. "Wouldn't want them to think you're into the guy who's off-limits, right?"

"For them," Allison says. "Not me. Not that it matters, since you'd never date someone like me."

"I don't think I said that."

"Oh, it was pretty clear."

Yeah, she's definitely baiting me. "Yeah, well, you told me quite clearly that you're not into . . . what was it? My *type*? Entitled rock stars? It's the hair isn't it? I've been told it makes me look like I'm trying to be Kurt Cobain."

"Really? I thought you were just trying to get girls to run their fingers through it."

I shrug. "Hey. You can run your fingers through my hair anytime."

Allison shakes her head at me. "I'm sorry I said that."

"That you want to run your fingers through my hair?"

"About your type."

"Why? It's not like it's not true."

"Really?" Allison says. "Is everything they say about you true?"

"Probably. What do they say about me?"

"That you get around, for one."

"Ha." She's scoping out the territory, trying to figure out if I'm as big a player as I seem. "Yeah, that's definitely true. Or it was, anyway."

"Not big on commitment."

"I don't have a problem with commitment. With the right person."

"Did you have a girlfriend at the time of the accident?" she asks.

"No," I say. "I haven't had a girlfriend since high school."

"So Anna-Marie is the only girl you've ever committed to."

"Yeah," I say. "And that went so well I was *super eager* to get into another relationship, let me tell you."

"You guys weren't good together?"

I pause and look at her over my glasses. My eyes have adjusted sufficiently that without the shades I can see her face.

She's watching me earnestly, with no trace of annoyance. My heart picks up pace.

"We were kind of a train wreck. And that was before I wrote those albums about her."

"About lies you made up about her?"

She's asking like she wants to know if it's true what Anna-Marie says. "Yeah. Exactly."

Allison's quiet, and I hope she's cataloging the million reasons for not getting involved with me. "I'm hardly one to talk about having very many relationships. The last boyfriend I had was the one I was dating when I got diagnosed with cancer."

"Ouch," I say. "That probably wasn't good for the relationship."

"No kidding. We were in this awkward place where we weren't serious enough to go through it together, but he still didn't want to leave the girl with cancer."

"So what happened?"

"I broke up with him. I didn't want to be this burden, you know?"

"Yeah," I say. "I know."

"Ha. You're Shane Beckstrom. You've probably got girls lining up to console you in your hour of need."

That's true, or it was. It's one of the things I was hiding from, the expectation that I was going to drown my sorrows in liquor and parties and girls.

Maybe if JT were still around, I would have. That was always our scene.

"Not really. I haven't been with anyone since the accident."

Allison looks surprised. "I thought your reputation was true. The internet would have me believe you had a different girl every night of the week."

"The internet was right, more or less." My throat constricts, but I keep going. "But what it won't tell you is that Shane Beckstrom died in that accident. I don't know who I am, but I'm not him."

The weight of that hangs in the air, and Allison puts her hand over mine. I want to pull away and tell her again that I don't need her pity, but it feels so damn good to be touched by her that I can't move. I don't dare.

"Whoever you are," she says, "you're not as bad as you think."

"Please. You were right about me. I am a rich, womanizing, entitled rock star who can't be trusted to show up on time or show anybody any respect. I'm all the things you hate and more."

"I thought that guy died," Allison says. "Isn't that what you just said? Besides, I'm a workaholic, uptight bitch who doesn't know how to have fun. So I guess we're even."

I look up at the ceiling. "I'm sorry. I shouldn't have called you a bitch. That was out of line."

"But the rest of it you agree with."

There's a note of humor in her voice, and I turn my hand over, taking hers in mine. Her skin is soft and warm, and holding her hand feels a whole lot more intimate than most of the sex I've had. "I'm willing to bet that you do know how to have fun."

"Really?" Allison says. "This is what you've learned about me in our two days working together?"

"Yes. Because no one who mocks me as mercilessly as you do is totally without a sense of humor."

"Maybe I like to mess with you."

"Maybe you do. Maybe I like it."

Her hand squeezes mine, and our eyes meet. Hers are barely a gleam in the dark, but they're locked on mine and my heart is in my throat and suddenly my mouth is dry and her lips are just inches from mine.

"Yeah?" Allison says, her lips parting just slightly. "Like this?"

Just as my chin dips toward hers she reaches up with her free hand and musses it through my hair, sending it in all directions.

I laugh and duck away, and somewhere in the process she lets go of my hand. "Yes," I tell her. "Exactly like that."

We're both laughing, and her hand is still in my hair. She runs it through, smoothing it down to my shoulders. The hairs rise on the back of my neck.

"It's so soft," she says. "What do you use on it?"

"Um, shampoo. We're comparing hair products now? That's what we're doing?"

"You condition." Her hands are still in my hair, and I have a powerful urge to move up against her and take her in my arms and press my mouth against hers.

Except, what would be the point? I'm losing my mind, and the minute she gets wind of my particular brand of crazy, she's going to go running. Even if she didn't, it's not like I can have someone in my life right now. I'm shit at relationships at the best of times, and now I'm goddamned certifiable.

"Careful," I say finally. "If I walk out of here with sex hair, don't think I'm going to go out of my way to disabuse people of the notion that you banged me."

Allison snickers, but she does drop her hand. "Have you heard that song, 'Sex Hair'? From *Parks and Recreation*?"

"Have I heard it? I've *covered* that song."

"Are you serious?" she asks. "You've covered Mouserat?"

"Oh my god, I was Andy Dwyer in high school. I mean, smarter. And meaner. But when it comes to musical ability, that was pretty much me."

Allison laughs like she can picture this, and I find myself smiling. I take off my shades to see her better.

God, she's so beautiful. And not just because I've been out of the game for a while, either. It blows me away that she hasn't had a relationship in years. There must be guys lining up, begging to take her out.

"Why don't you have a boyfriend?" I ask.

"Ha," Allison says. "That's what I'd like to know."

"Don't give me that. No way you don't have offers."

She arches an eyebrow at me. "Are you suggesting that you find me attractive?"

I roll my eyes at her. "You know you're gorgeous. So how come the only man in your life is . . . god, I can't remember your cat's name."

Allison smiles at me. She's not going to bail me out.

"Sir . . . it's not Snugglesworth. Snelgrove?"

Allison giggles. "You come up with the best cat names. It's Lord Shelldon. Which is no 'Orville Redenbarker' but . . ." She trails off with a shrug.

"Who the hell is—oh, that's one of those obnoxious dancing poodles, isn't it?"

"It is. And it pissed on Gwen's marimba."

I chuckle. That does improve my opinion of them somewhat. "Whatever. I like Lord Shelldon better. But now I need to get a cat named Snelgrove. Or I could give you that one."

"Oh, no. I wouldn't dream of taking it from you."

The idea of cats is sounding better and better—it would be nice to have a single living being that notices if I'm alive or dead from day to day. If I could be trusted to remember to feed them. They meow when they're hungry, don't they? "Think the humane society is still open?" I ask. "Or maybe someone has kittens available on Craigslist."

"You're really going to do that? Adopt kittens and give them those names?"

"Maybe. But this isn't a layer."

"Oh, no. Definitely not. Shane Beckstrom doesn't have layers."

"Exactly."

"Do you want to get a drink?" she says.

I emit a noise that sounds vaguely like I'm being strangled. I shut my mouth, but it's far, far too late. "You don't want to date me."

"Right." She moves her hands to her knees. "You mean you don't want to date me. Because I'm not attractive, is that it?"

"Oh my god. I said you were beautiful."

"You said that I know I'm gorgeous. It's not exactly the same thing."

I haven't had a girl work this hard to get me to compliment her in forever, and I'm loving it. "Fine. You're sexy. And I want to date you. But you're going to regret it. Trust me."

"Noted." Allison says. "So we're going out, then?"

"Fine."

"Fine."

We sit there, staring at each other in the dark, and while I'm not sure if I won or lost that argument, I'm back to feeling terrified. But we can't just sit here all night. I'm going to have to face the world again sometime. "You want to go to that carnival down the street?"

Allison looks confused. "The carnival?"

She can't have missed it. "Oh," I say. "You were thinking of something classier."

"Yes. But the carnival could be fun."

Shit. I am ruining my chance with this girl. "You don't have to say that if you don't want to. We could just go get those drinks."

She pauses. "Are you sure you'll be okay at a carnival? It's been a long time since I've been to one, but I remember there being lights and people and loud noises."

"Yeah," I say. "I know. But I just want to do something that feels normal."

She laughs. "And a carnival feels normal to you? I don't think I've been to one since I was in junior high."

I throw up my hands. "I grew up in Everett, Wyoming. A place with so little to do that every time some big blockbuster movie comes out—something other than Pixar or westerns, because we did have a tiny theater that played those—the town rents a bus, and we all carpool over to the only-slightly-larger theater forty minutes away. So yeah, I went to the carnival every year. It was our first big venue with the band, and until just a couple years ago, we went back and played it every year after that."

"Oh," Allison says. And I'm sure she's going to tell me what a loser I am for thinking that someone like her would be interested in something like that, but instead she smiles. "Was this where you took girls to impress them?"

I grin. "No. To impress girls I took them cow tipping. Until this one time Mikey and I snuck up on this cow, all quiet like, and I counted down but Mikey pushed first and his hands went right through."

Allison looks horrified. "Through the *cow*?"

"Yes, through the cow. Damn thing was out there all alone because it had gotten loose, then died and rotted right there on its feet. And I about died laughing and Mikey got so pissed that he chased after me with liquified cow all over his arms. The girls ran off, and I made Mikey walk home while I drove the van alongside him slowly, and he kept running and trying to hitch a ride on the bumper, but I stayed just out of his reach."

"Okay, yeah. In absence of cows, the carnival. Should we get food first? Or maybe after?"

"Um, we will eat at the carnival," I say. "It's mandatory. Plus, I saw they have food trucks."

Allison looks stricken. "You want to eat at a food truck?"

"Are you religiously opposed?"

"My family would tell you I am."

I look at her, and she looks at me. There's a story here, and I'm determined to wait it out.

"It's just," she says, "food trucks are kind of skeezy, aren't they? They just drive up and sell you food and then drive away. How do you know if they're legit?"

"Um," I say, "I think they have food handler's permits."

"How do you know? Have you ever seen one?"

"I can't say I've been looking." I'm smiling, but Allison is dead serious.

"I mean, really. It's like, hello, dude in a serial killer van who has shown up to sell me tacos. Are you running a prostitution ring out of the back? Is your van also used to transport the rats you catch and slaughter for meat?"

By the time she finishes this rant, I'm leaning back against the wall and cracking up. "Oh my god, Ally. You are unreal."

She looks up at me, like she's surprised. "No one's called me that in a really long time."

"Unreal?"

"Ally."

"It's short for Allison, right?"

She nods like this means something, but before I can ask, she takes my hand again and pulls me to my feet. "Let's hit that carnival."

"Okay." I feel vaguely like I have whiplash, only not real whiplash, because I can tell you from experience that royally sucks. This feels more like being on one of those theme park rides that cruises along in one direction, then abruptly changes course when you're turned around and can't see where you're going. As we step back into the hallway and I put my glasses back on, JT slaps me on the back.

"Dude," he says. "That was perfect."

I shoot him a dirty look, because I wasn't playing any of that for sympathy.

But as Allison checks to make sure Carlyle didn't change his mind about canceling practice, I lean against the wall outside the auditorium.

For the first time since the accident, I feel like I'm lucky.

SIX

Shane

The carnival is actually decently impressive for one of those pop-up deals that close down streets. They've brought in rides and dozens of vendor booths. An enormous network of bounce houses takes up half the neighborhood block.

I take off my sunglasses, and Allison looks up at me in surprise. "I thought you needed those," she says. Her eyes get caught in mine, and I smile at her knowingly before she quickly looks away.

"No," I say. "It's the fluorescents that give me a headache. I'll be okay on stage, too. The stage lights are incandescent."

She steals a look at me again, and I smirk at her.

"Okay," she says. "So you also know you're gorgeous."

I laugh. The real danger of going without my sunglasses is getting recognized, but it's early enough in the afternoon that the place isn't crazy busy, so hopefully it won't be too bad. Plus, I feel more confident being out with Allison, less like I'm going to get cornered alone. It's weird how claustrophobic the world can feel when you run the constant risk of people wanting to photograph you on the street. It's another thing I should feel lucky for.

Once upon a time I did.

We approach the carnival along a line of food trucks, Allison still in her red dress and high-heeled boots, which I assured her were appropriate carnival attire. "So," I ask. "What are you having?"

Allison eyes each as if it's more dubious than the last. "Hmm. Linguisa Forever. Fajita Mia. Sushi Taquito. This definitely inspires confidence."

"You don't have to have any," I say. "We could go somewhere for food when we're done."

Allison looks the trucks over with determination. "No, I'm going to try one of these. As long as you're paying, of course."

I smile. "Of course. Pleasure's mine."

She looks like she's not sure if I meant that to be an innuendo, and I give her an innocent expression in return. Not that I meant it like that, but it's my policy never to deny a double entendre, and it's served me well.

"Okay," I tell her. "The carnival tradition is you have to walk from one end to the other and survey the whole place before deciding what to do first."

"Oh, really. In these boots. Which you were so sure were appropriate." She looks around at everyone else in their flip flops and cargo shorts and t-shirts.

"Looking like that," I say, openly checking her out, "is always appropriate. Plus, it's going to be hilarious when I talk you into going in the bounce house." I indicate over her shoulder at the enormous bounce house that's big enough for adult occupants. Allison whirls around and then turns back to me, looking mildly horrified.

I laugh. "Come on. I'll let you mess up my hair as much as you want."

Allison smiles and plays with the ends of my hair, resting her hand lightly on my shoulder. Another few inches and we'd be touching down the length of our bodies, and I can already feel this heat coming from her, this stirring of something I haven't experienced since long before the accident.

"Oh my god, this ass," JT says, coming up behind Allison and putting his hand on her butt. "You have got to feel this, dude. She's keeping it tight."

I want to glare at him, but Allison's looking right up into my eyes, so instead I just step away, taking her hand and leading her across the carnival. JT walks way too close behind Allison, and it's all I can do to keep from wheeling around and punching him in the face.

Allison's right about the lights and sounds, but the late afternoon daylight is better on my headache, and the noise is spread out evenly, though I'm not in a big hurry to stand right next to the game with the big hammer and the lighted ball that shoots up with an air-pressured whizzing sound. Even that is drowned out amidst the whirring and humming of the rides and the murmur of people talking, punctuated occasionally by shouts.

It's loud, but not loud like the accident. That was the quiet of tires on the road, followed by the loudest sound you've ever heard in your life, followed by minute after minute of silence, with only a few voices reaching through.

Hey, are you alive?
Are you okay in there? Can you move?
Oh my god, that's Shane Beckstrom.

"Okay, you also have to try that one," I say, pointing to a spinning ride. "It's just like the tea cups at Disneyland, only—" I squint at it "—something vaguely more phallic shaped."

Allison eyes what appear to be various colors of spinning cucumbers with suspicion. "Yeah, what are they? Gourds? Dildos?"

"Clearly we cannot miss that. Unless we find something even better." I lead her all the way to the other end, where we find a square of tents full of carnival games.

"Okay," Allison says. "You have to win me something."

"Ha. These games are all rigged. You can't win."

"I know. Which is why you definitely have to."

"I'd probably spend less if I just bribed the person running the game to sell me one."

Allison shakes her head. "Have you no honor?"

"None," I tell her flatly. "Absolutely none."

Allison giggles. "Those game people are vicious, though. When I was thirteen, I wanted a giraffe from one of those, and I offered them all of my babysitting money for it. They wouldn't sell it to me, so I played away all my money and I still didn't win one."

"Damn," I say. "A giraffe, huh?"

Allison looks embarrassed. "Yeah. I might have a thing for giraffes."

God, this girl is adorable. "Please tell me your apartment is full of them."

"It used to be. I got rid of most of them a while ago. But I still have a set I've had since I was a kid—these little porcelain giraffes wearing different outfits."

"Well, clearly we have to see if they have a giraffe," I tell her, and we begin circling. "Have you ever thought about going to Africa? To see giraffes in the wild?"

"Definitely. I may have done some research into it."

I cock an eyebrow at her. "But you've never been? What happened to realizing how little time you might have to accomplish things?"

"That's it exactly," Allison says. "It's a lot of time to take off work when I've got so much to do. I have an opportunity to possibly get my line into Nordstrom, which would be huge, but first I need to make sure that my manufacturing is in place and that my investors are all on board and the designs are perfect, and I've still got to do the costuming and this pageant thing to pay the bills in the meantime—"

"Yeah, okay, that's a lot. But still. It seems like you should take that safari if you've researched it so much. Please tell me you at least go to the zoo."

"I have a membership," she says. "But I don't make it as much as I'd like to. Do you travel much?"

"I've been all over with the band. Not Africa, but a lot of places in Europe and a couple in South America."

"Nice," she says. "But tours are crazy. Did you get to really see places?"

"I did. We didn't sleep as much as we should have, but every city we went to, I got online and figured out what was best to see and then dragged Kevin and JT along with me. They'd whine the whole way, but every once in a while we'd get to talking about all the cool places we'd been—three idiots from redneck Wyoming, you know? I think they were glad we did it."

"Anywhere you always wanted to go but have never been?"

I shrug. "I'm not picky. Everywhere's better than Wyoming. Africa would be cool."

I bite down on my tongue. That sounded like I was suggesting she would go with me, which is obviously not happening, because I've probably got a maximum of thirty minutes before she realizes that A) I am bat-shit crazy or B) she is way out of my league.

We reach the end of our loop through the games. "No giraffes," Allison says. "But don't think that gets you out of winning me something."

"I maintain it would be better to try to buy one. You were refused, but I'm guessing your thirteen-year-old babysitting money wasn't terribly impressive. Am I right?"

"I have three younger siblings," Allison says. "I babysat a lot."

"Fifty dollars?"

"Sixty three."

"Right," I say, snapping my fingers. "I was thinking of starting the bidding around two hundred and going up from there."

"Two hundred dollars," Allison says. "Are you serious? For a carnival animal?"

"Two hundred to start, to *impress a girl* with a carnival animal. You saying you aren't worth it?"

Allison narrows her eyes at me, but I'm dead serious. "Hey," I say. "I recognize a good investment when I see one."

She flushes a little and smiles. "Okay, we've seen everything. Let's ride the dildos."

I grin and follow her back to the spinning ride, where I buy some tickets and Allison selects us a bright pink phallus, and we climb in. Allison buckles one of the seatbelts around her waist, even though I'm pretty sure those things are mostly to keep kids from feeling like they can climb out. She grips the wheel in the center. "Oh my god, what have I done?"

I laugh. "You've boarded the train and there's no getting off."

She cocks her head at me. "Is that your prediction for the evening?"

"No, actually. It's Sylvia Plath."

The operator is circling, making sure everyone's dildo doors are secure, while Allison stares at me. "Sylvia Plath," she says.

"Yeah." I smile at her. "The poet."

"I know who Sylvia Plath is. Why are you quoting her?"

I shrug. "I told you I can read. It's a poem about pregnancy, actually. Seems appropriate for riding in a phallus."

A bell dings and the ride starts to spin. Allison clings to the steering wheel so tight I think she's afraid I'm going to spin it as fast as it can go. I scoot around on the bench and put an arm around her, leaning back and enjoying the ride.

"You read poetry," Allison says.

This is not something I generally share with people, which is basically the theme for the day. "I do. I write most of our music. But I used to suck at it, so when I wanted to move beyond Mouserat, I started reading poetry. It's awesome. And it helps."

Allison leans into me as we spin, and her hair smells like rose petals and fabric softener, and that, more than the spinning, makes me dizzy. "So in the absence of cows, you quote poetry to impress girls?" She looks up at me, her hair blowing back from her face in the spinning breeze, and I push it over her ear.

"No," I tell her. "No one knows about that but the guys in the band."

Kevin. It's just Kevin, now that JT is gone.

Speaking of, where has he gone? I look around and see him standing with one sneaker on each side of a nearby spinning dildo, straddling the air over the heads of a couple who are clinging to each other in the vessel beneath. He gives me a thumbs up and grins as he goes round and round, and the operator doesn't stop the ride like the one at the carnival back in Wyoming did every time JT and I would try that stunt.

"What are you looking at?" Allison asks, and I snap my attention back to her.

"Nothing. Just thinking." The ride ends, and I help Allison out of the dildo. We're both walking a little crooked, but we manage to stay upright. JT leaps off of the car and bounds after us, whooping about how this time was his record. And it was, by a long shot.

He comes up behind Allison and presses himself all up her back. "Daaaaamn," JT says. "You have got to get some of this."

He starts humping her from behind, and I've finally had enough. "I'll get us tickets for the bounce house," I say, and I give JT a flick of my head to indicate that he follow me, which he does.

I stalk over to the ticket booth by the bounce house, muttering under my breath at JT. "Back. Off."

"What?" JT says. "Come on, dude. You need to chill out."

"Do not disrespect her," I tell him. "Do you understand me? Or I swear to god I will start playing the Spice Girls night and day just to shut you up."

JT holds up his hands. "That's cold."

Maybe it is, but if JT wasn't dead, I would punch him in the face right now like I did to Mikey when he tried to get with Anna-Marie just because we happened to be broken up. "Back off," I say again, and manage to keep from looking like I'm talking to myself while I buy the tickets.

Allison catches up to me at the bounce house. "Are you sure about this?"

"Definitely," I tell her, and we both take off our shoes and climb up the inflatable ramp and into the enormous structure. The roar of the air pumps makes it so we have to shout to be heard, and we bounce across the entrance and into a room filled with large inflatable bubbles that pop out of the floor. I jump on top of one of the bubbles, which deflates slowly underneath me until I'm lying on my back on the mat. Allison bounces experimentally up and down next to me.

"I can do this carnival thing," she says. "I can eat at a food truck. Look at me, being carefree."

I laugh. "Your feet aren't leaving the mat."

Allison gives me an offended look and then launches herself at me, messing up my hair again. I flip off the deflated bubble and pin her to the mat. Her fingers leave little electric pulses behind, and not just because all this bouncing has charged us both with static that makes our hair float on end. "You really like touching my hair."

She looks up at me, breathless. "Yes, I do."

My full body rush comes with an added dose of terror that I'm going to do something to ruin everything. I shift off of her to let her up, but she grabs me by the shoulders, shoving me down again and landing on top of me. I can hear the shrieks of other bouncers off in other parts of the structure, but none of them are right here. My whole body aches for want of her, and I can't take it anymore.

I reach my hand into her hair and pull her mouth down to mine. I kiss her and kiss her, and she responds in kind, our bodies communicating this perfect storm of longing and desire. The static crackles around us, and I groan against her lips, pulling her tighter against me—

"Hey!" someone shouts from outside. "Knock it off, you two. This is a family establishment."

We break apart, staring at each other wide-eyed. She's breathing as fast as I am, and I can't help but grin at her.

"Damn," I say, and she smiles back and nods.

"Yeah," she says. "Damn."

I laugh and scoop her onto her feet, then lead her out of the bounce house before we get into any more trouble. JT has disappeared somewhere—probably creeping on some girl who can't see him look up her skirt or else sulking that I won't let him dry hump this girl that I'm somehow on a date with. JT tried a lot of stupid things when he was alive, but that one is new.

"All right," I tell her. "I know there aren't any giraffes, but you still need to pick which animal I'm going to try to buy for you."

Allison looks at me uncertainly. "Are you really going to pay two hundred dollars for one of those animals?"

"It's a point of pride now. Let's make a bet out of it. I say I'm going to have to pay three hundred and fifty before they'll decide it's worth getting fired over and give it to me. You pick a different number, and whoever's closer to the actual amount wins."

"And what do we win?" Allison asks.

I hesitate. "I don't know. What do you want to win?"

"I'm not going to bet going home with you tonight, if that's what you're thinking."

It seems obvious, but it wasn't what I was thinking. I can barely stand to spend the night with myself, much less drag anyone else into it. "Noted. So what do you want to play for?"

"Winner picks where we eat dinner," Allison says. "Anywhere. Food truck or otherwise."

"Done," I tell her. "Pick a number."

"Four hundred."

"You're on."

We circle the games again, and Allison chooses a stuffed bulldog wearing a spiky plush cactus costume. There's a teenage girl working the game, which is one of those ball tosses where the balls are clearly too large to fit inside the pipes that win you prizes beyond wristbands and lollipops. Allison hangs back while I step up and lean on the counter between me and the girl. She doesn't appear to recognize me. I think most people at this carnival are outside our target demographic. "Hey," I say. "See that gorgeous girl in the red dress behind me?"

The girl nods.

"I need a favor." I pull out my wallet and a couple of big bills. "I'll pay you two hundred dollars for that stuffed animal right there."

She turns around and looks at the cactus-clad dog, then at me. "I'm not supposed to do that."

I drop another bill. "Two fifty." I'm prepared to go up to seven hundred dollars for this thing. I may be generally fiscally responsible, but part of being financially healthy is knowing what's worth spending money on.

This is it.

The girl looks around at the other booths uneasily. "You have to play," she says. "But I can make sure you win."

I smile. "Done." I hand her the cash, which she pockets in her carnival apron. She hands me three balls and goes to stand behind the bunch of pipes.

I make one toss, and she catches the ball on the rebound and drops it in a hole toward the center. "Winner!" she says, and grabs the bulldog and hands it to me.

"So he really won that, huh?" Allison asks, walking up to the booth. She's fighting a smile.

"Oh, yeah," the girl says. "Definitely. And you should totally date him."

Allison raises her eyebrows. "Why exactly is that?"

"Ummmm," the girl says, and I surreptitiously push another fifty dollar bill across the counter to her. I'm sure Allison notices, but I don't care.

"Because . . . he's cool," the girl says. "And like, old, but not, like, a creeper."

Allison grins at me. "Oh, yes. Not being a creeper is one of his finer qualities."

I link my arm through hers and hand her the improbably-dressed dog. "Come on. I paid two fifty, which means I won. And the Sushi Taquito place is clearly the sketchiest of all food trucks, so that's what we're eating. My treat."

Allison winces at the thought of food truck sushi, but as she trots along to keep up with me, she squeezes the dog tight.

That two-hundred-and-fifty dollar carnival animal was worth every penny.

SEVEN

Shane

We sit on a bench across from the carousel and eat our questionable sushi. I got the spicy tuna, and Allison picked the California roll, possibly because it doesn't contain raw fish, but hey. I respect a good vegetable.

"You don't have to eat that," I say as she unwraps her taquito. "We can go somewhere else if you think it's gross."

"No way," Allison says. "I'm being adventurous today."

I look down at my own sushi. I wonder if that's all this is for her—some adventure she's having before she goes back to her serious, well-ordered, and psycho-free life. I don't know what else she would be doing. I'm clearly not fit to be dating anyone, let alone someone like her. But she scoots close to me, her stuffed dog still tucked under her arm, and the last thing I want is to walk away.

"Tell me about your family," she says. "Are they still back in Wyoming?"

"JT and Kevin are my family."

Allison nods. "They're like your brothers."

I appreciate that she doesn't talk about JT in the past tense. He's sitting on the bench across from us, eating cotton candy that he got from who knows where. Given that no one is looking askance at the cotton candy floating in mid-air, I assume that it, like him, is visible only to me. "Closer than brothers."

"I have twin brothers who would argue that's impossible," Allison says.

"Younger brothers, right?"

"Yeah," she says. "Much younger. Joel and Julian are still in high school."

"And one more sibling, right?"

"My sister Nicole. We call her Nix. She's also younger than me, but we're still close."

"You call her Nix," I say, "but no one calls you Ally?"

Allison chews a bite of her sushi. "They did when I was younger. But when I got to be a teenager, I wanted to be taken seriously, so I made everyone start calling me Allison."

"Oh," I say, "hey, if you don't like it—"

"No, I do. I like it when you say it."

I like being the guy she likes saying it. More than I probably should. "Ally."

She grins back at me, and I realize I've surpassed my day's goal of making her smile by the dozens. Even if I don't have anything else in my life together, I'm proud of that.

"So why the gap?" I ask. "Between you and your siblings."

"They're technically my half siblings," she says. "My mom was a single mother. She married my dad, and he adopted me. They had Nix pretty much immediately and the boys several years later."

"Were you ever jealous of them? For being your dad's biological kids?"

She shakes her head. "Nah. My parents treated us all the same. If anything, I got away with more, because I was the oldest, so I was left in charge a lot."

"I bet you liked that," I say.

She laughs. "I did!"

"Are your parents Mexican?" I'm guessing by the last name of Mendez, mostly.

"Yeah," she says. "I'm half, though. My biological father was white, I think, but my mom is Chicana."

"You think. So he's not in the picture."

She shakes her head, but she doesn't seem upset about it. "My biological father was out of the picture before I was born. I'm not a hundred percent sure he even knew he had a kid. But it's fine. My dad is my father, and I wouldn't ever want him to doubt that." She lowers her sushi taquito. "What about your parents?"

I take a deep breath. This is more stuff I don't talk about, especially publicly. "My dad is back in Everett. I don't know where my mom is. She travels around a lot. Last I heard she was up near San Francisco, but that was a while ago."

"You haven't talked to her since the accident?"

"I have," I say. "For a minute. She just wanted to make sure I was okay. She read about it in the news."

Allison's starting to look sorry for me again, which I hate. "So, not a big part of your life, then?"

"Nah," I say. "She left when I was four. She's been in and out of my life since. Mostly out, but since I left Everett she'll show up every once in a while. Sometimes needing a place to stay, sometimes wanting tickets to one of my concerts or something."

Allison nods. "Are you and your dad close?"

I shake my head. "No. He's an alcoholic and a first-class asshole. We don't get along." I pick at my sushi. "He came out for the funeral, though. Complained we weren't having it in Everett, but at least he was there."

"Nice," Allison says. She's being sarcastic, and that reaction I do appreciate. She pauses then, turning serious. "That must have been really hard. Losing a friend you were that close to."

I can feel tears burning behind my eyes, and I nod quickly. Too quickly. "It was. Are you close to your family?"

"Yeah, I am." I'm pretty sure she notices the change of subject, but she doesn't call me on it. "Though not as close as my mom would like me to be. They're always bugging me to come home more. I should, because they don't live far, but I just get so busy."

"How often do you see them?"

She looks embarrassed. "I go home for dinner about once a month."

I shrug. "That's not so bad."

"No," Allison says. "But Nix still lives there, and the boys obviously. My mom would rather I was there for dinner every night, or at least once a week. Do you ever go home and see your dad?"

"Yeah," I say. "About every six months. His health's not great, and he doesn't have anyone else, so if I don't go check in on him, nobody's going to."

Allison doesn't ask me why I do that when my dad is such a dick to me, and I'm grateful. I don't know how to explain it.

"Dude," JT yells through a mouthful of cotton candy, "it's because you're messed up."

That, above all other things, is true.

"So what other poetry do you like?" Allison asks. "Besides Sylvia Plath."

I smile. "I like a lot of stuff. Hopkins, especially. And Robert Frost, even though that's a cliché. It's with good reason. Billy Collins, of course."

She shakes her head. "I don't know who that is."

"No way," I say. "Hang on." I balance my taquitos on my knee and dig out my phone. I look up "Litany," which is my favorite of his. It's basically a sarcastic deconstruction of love poems, but in this concise, hilarious way. All of Collins is like that, which is what I love about it.

I read the poem to her and put my phone away. Allison is staring at me, and I feel my face get hot. "I swear this isn't a thing I do to impress girls. If it were, I'd have read you the one by Adrienne Rich about having sex with a doorknob."

Allison laughs. "You totally have layers."

"No!" I say, further unwrapping my sushi. "I don't, I swear.

I'm a musician. People used to read poetry, you know? Like, for fun. And then T. S. Elliot killed fun, but people still like poetry. It's just all the poets now are song writers. The ones people actually pay attention to, anyway."

"I'd never thought of it that way," Allison says. "Elliot is the Prufrock guy, right?"

"Yep. Tied for most overrated poet with Walt Whitman. He celebrates himself and he sings himself and he's definitely way too impressed with himself."

"I don't know anyone like that," Allison says.

I smile. "Guilty."

She looks at me like she's considering something.

"What?" I ask.

"What I'm trying to reconcile," she says, "is this guy I'm talking to being the same person as the guy who told all those lies about Anna-Marie."

My mouth goes dry. "I am the same person. I told you I'm an asshole."

"But you also told me you died, and you're not the same person anymore."

"That part hasn't changed." I don't like the look of doubt in her eyes. It's only going to make it hurt all the more when she figures out what I am.

"Why'd you do it? Why did you camp on to Ryan Lansing's story and lie to the press about her?"

"First," I say, "I didn't know about Ryan's story until after I'd already done the interview. They came out hours apart, and I was up all night writing that song."

"Okay." Her voice is even, like she's suspending judgment until she's heard the whole story, but she shouldn't. What she thought of me originally . . . it was all true.

"And second, I didn't so much lie to the press. I more implied."

"Really," Allison says. "When you said that you guys had been doing the long distance thing and you had no idea she was seeing other people and you'd been in love with her since you were kids and would never love anyone but her, that was an implication."

I elbow her. "You've been Googling me."

She holds up a finger. "Not the point."

Maybe not, but I like it. "And third, Anna-Marie didn't care what I did. Sure, I hurt her pride, but it's not like she gave a shit about me, and she hadn't for a long time." She made it very clear how little she cared when Josh Rios showed up in town. I've always found it special that she can be so pissed at me for hurting her, but she didn't care enough to give me the time of day before that, and hadn't for five years. It's bullshit. She's just worried about her image.

"You'd just had sex with her, hadn't you?" she says.

Ah, yes. The footage where Anna-Marie and I got caught naked in the hot springs by a group of horny boy scouts. "You've seen the video?"

Allison shrugs. "Everyone with internet access has seen that video."

Something about the too-casual way she says it makes me think it's not just that.

"You watched it again," I say. "Recently."

Her cheeks turn pink and I smile. It's never bothered me much that everyone in the world has seen me naked, and it definitely doesn't bother me with her.

"So, yes," I say. "We'd just had sex. Not great sex, mind you, because we were interrupted by a creepy old man and a troop of Boy Scouts and then later a fateful bat."

"A bat? Seriously?"

"Yes. But regardless, the sex didn't mean anything to me, and it definitely didn't mean anything to Anna-Marie."

Allison looks uncomfortable with that. "I just think I would be really hurt if someone did that to me. Especially if they'd just slept with me."

"Okay, but really. This was not all romance and candles.

After the disaster at the hot springs, we went back to her house, and . . ."

She smiles. "Right. I got it. You can spare me the details."

"But we get interrupted by this bat that flew in her window. And she's like, 'Shane! Get it out! Get it out!' And I'm like, 'Believe me. It's out.'"

Allison laughs, and I'm glad to have changed the tone of the conversation.

"Then her whole extended family appears in the doorway and her dad has a baseball bat, and I'm standing there wearing nothing but a condom—"

"Oh my god," Allison says. "You're lucky there's not video of that."

"And her dad, who is not my biggest fan, is like 'Shane! Put your damn pants on and help me catch this bat.'"

"I imagine this wasn't the first time he caught you with her."

"Far from it. I don't think he ever expected that to happen *again* after all those years. But after that, I went home. That's the whole sordid encounter. It wasn't anything special. We were over each other long before then."

"But even if it isn't romantic, there's a certain amount of trust that you have to have in a person to be with them like that. Letting them in. Being vulnerable."

Oh. It didn't even occur to me that that's what she'd have a problem with. "Yeah, I don't think sex means the same thing to me as it does to you. And it definitely didn't to Anna-Marie."

Allison shrugs, and I can tell she's unsettled about it. I finish my sushi and ball the wrapper in my hands. "Does that bother you?"

She shrugs again. "No. It just reveals a certain callousness toward sex, that's all."

"Yeah, well. I told you I'm an asshole."

"Why do you do that?"

I use the wrapper as an excuse to get up, and after I throw it away, I sit a little farther from her. "Do what?"

"Keep telling me I shouldn't want to be around you."

"Because it's true. And you're going to figure it out eventually. Sooner seems better than later."

"You did a shitty thing to Anna-Marie," she says. "But I don't think that's all you are."

I sigh. She does seem to be under the impression that I have layers, but I was telling the truth when I said that I didn't. "Let me spare you the mystery. It is."

She looks down at the dog, and I wish I'd brushed her off back in the green room. I wish we'd never come here, that I'd never told her all this shit. What was I thinking? Now she's done with me, and I'm going to go back to being alone all the time, which is really just karma, after what a jerk I've been. To everyone. God, even Kevin doesn't want to—

"Well, you clearly have good taste in food," she says, holding up the remains of her taquito. "So you have that going for you. Even if your affection for food trucks is questionable."

She reaches over and takes my hand, and I'm desperate not to let her go. Even if I know I'll have to, I can't do it yet. Not when she's granting me this reprieve from the inevitable.

"Want to make out in the photo booth?" I ask, and she laughs.

"I thought you'd never ask." And moments later we're behind the velvet curtain, and Allison has crawled into my lap, and her mouth is pressed against mine, and all thoughts have left my head beyond the desperate need for her. Her hands are in my hair, and mine are around her waist, and we're kissing like this is our last moment on earth. I wish that it was, because I just want to disappear inside her. I haven't felt like this about anyone in years and years, probably ever, and I'm so scared about what's going to happen when it ends.

Allison shifts on my lap and it sets my body buzzing. I run my hands up her sides, enjoying the way she feels in my arms, delicious and right and like we fit together in this weird, unexpected way that scares the hell out of me.

When my hands reach the bottom of her rib cage, Allison

jerks back, pushing me away from her. I put my hands on her forearms as she leans back on the console of the photo booth.

"Hey," I say. "I'm sorry. Did I do something wrong?"

She shakes her head. "No, it's fine. It's fine."

But it's clearly not fine. I expect her to flee out of the photo booth, but she doesn't. She stays there, sitting on my knees, breathing every bit as hard as I am.

"I need to get home," she says.

The burning feeling is back behind my eyes. I knew this was coming. It's not like I'm capable of anything else right now, but that doesn't make it suck any less. "Yeah, okay. I get it."

She cringes. "I'm not sure that you do."

"Nah, whatever," I say. "It's cool. I'll see you later."

She doesn't move off my lap, and I'm wishing now that I had somewhere to escape. "This isn't a brush off," she says. "I'm just not ready to have sex with you."

My heart stops. "Yeah, no, I know that. I didn't think that's what was going to happen. You made it pretty clear that sex isn't super casual for you, and—" And what? And I'm afraid to fall asleep because of the nightmares, and the last thing I want is for anyone else to see how truly messed up I am? "I know that wasn't where this was going."

"Really?" she says, like she can't imagine what else I would be here for, and that's fair. That's fine. That's who I am, and it's a good thing she's finally realizing it. "I guess I just don't want to get too worked up, you know? Kissing is fine, but I don't want to do anything else."

I nod. I'm pretty sure we weren't doing anything else, so she must mean that she doesn't want to do anything at all. Which is better, really. No need for *me* to get all worked up, either. Not about a girl who'll be gone and out of my life when the show is over, and maybe even before then. "Whatever. That's fine."

"Shane," she says. "I'm not brushing you off. Really." She looks upset about something, and I'm starting to wonder if that reaction to me running my hands up her body is really about something else. Maybe she's been through something traumatic.

"You could tell me if you were."

"I know," Allison says. "I would. But it's getting late, and I'm just so behind with work, and the pageant is delaying me even more, and I really need to get home."

Right. Sure she does. That's definitely what was on her mind a moment ago. "Can I walk you back?" I ask, and she nods.

"Sure, that would be nice."

But it isn't nice. It's awkward, and our conversation is stilted, and all the easiness is gone between us. By the time I get into my car back at the auditorium and drive home, I'm wishing I'd never met Allison.

I know this about people: sooner or later, they all leave. While I'm usually glad when it's sooner rather than later, it seems that Allison is an exception to that, too.

EIGHT

Allison

The whole drive home my thoughts are pinballing faster than I can keep up, ricocheting around my brain and setting off triumphant dings and warning buzzers, one after the other.

Did I really just have a date with Shane Beckstrom, bad boy rock star and guy who I was ready to murder for being late to rehearsal yesterday? Did I just have that date at a *carnival?*

I did, and it felt fun and free in a way I haven't felt in a long, long time. Before the cancer, definitely. I glance over at the stuffed dog in the passenger seat next to me. It eyes me back impassively.

Nix would be thrilled. She's been trying to get me to start dating again for . . . well, a long, long time. Dating or, really, doing *anything* that isn't work related.

You need some fun in your life, Allison, she's said on more than one occasion. I usually brush her off, telling her I can start having fun again when the costuming for this tour is done, or this pageant is over, or when my line is launched.

I heard her voice in my head when I asked Shane out. Her voice in my head, and my hands in that incredible hair of his, both of which combined to make me dangerously impulsive.

Impulsive isn't something I've ever been accused of being.

And no one in my family would ever imagine me enjoying a date at a carnival, or, dear god above, eating from a food truck. Let alone going on a date with *Shane Beckstrom*.

But something about that date made me feel more myself than I have been in years. Maybe Nix was right, maybe I did need to get back into dating again. Maybe I needed to get back the flirtatious Allison who could see a guy she wanted, whether for a relationship or just a few fun nights, and go for it. Maybe I needed a hot guy to kiss me like *that*, like all he wanted in the world was me.

But I think more of it had to do with Shane himself, and I don't just mean because of how incredible that kiss was.

Though, damn, that kiss . . . My body aches just thinking about it. The intense heat of his lips on mine, the static of the bounce house and the even more electric charge between us. And again in the photo booth, sitting on his lap, feeling him hard through his jeans, his hands moving up my body . . .

My throat goes dry, thinking of how quickly I went from this rising fire to feeling like a pail of ice water had been dumped on me. Then my awkward attempts to smooth it over and the even more awkward walk back to my car.

There's that warning buzzer again.

What was I thinking, doing all this?

I was thinking that there's something about Shane that keeps drawing me in. Something more than that hair and those blue eyes and that body. Something definitely more than his fame or playboy reputation—both of which, honestly, are drawbacks. There's something about being near him that makes me feel like I see parts of him no one else does, parts even he can't see.

I cringe as I pull into the parking garage of my apartment and get out. God, I sound like the girl in one of those novels about broody vampire boys, convinced I'm somehow the exception, and I'm not going to be just another in the body count.

I fumble with my purse and the stuffed dog and my keys as I unlock my front door.

Is it ridiculous to think that I *am* the exception? Because the things he told me, the way he was so open . . .

I walk in my apartment and see all my lights on and a shadow moving in my kitchen that's way too big to be Lord Shelldon. My heart jumps in my throat, and I clutch the stuffed animal like the world's most ineffective shield—and then my sister Nix pops her head out from the kitchen.

"Hey!" she says, and I almost lob the dog at her.

"Oh my god, you scared me to death. What are you—wait, it's not Wednesday already, right?" Nix always comes to stay with me a few days before the pageant. She likes seeing the prep, and I like having someone on hand to vent to when things get *really* stressful. But she wasn't coming until tomorrow, I thought. Did Shane make me lose track of the day of the week? What the hell kind of effect does he have on—

"Nope, still Tuesday." She leans against the wall, with a plate of what I think is my leftover Thai food, speaking around a mouthful of noodles. "I decided to come over a night early. Mom was driving me crazy."

That happens often enough. I love our mom, but she can be a bit smothering. Which isn't a problem for me anymore but definitely is for Nix. My sister's twenty-three, and an incredibly talented dancer with a specialty in ballroom, in which she competes internationally and very successfully. But ballroom competitions aren't exactly moneymakers, and her dream is to open her own studio someday, so she's living at home to save up money. I respect her dedication to her goals, but I'm also happy as hell it's not me still living there.

"I texted you a couple hours ago." She raises an eyebrow. "Though maybe you didn't see it because you were too busy . . . at the toy store?"

I ease my grip on the ridiculously cute cactus dog and set it down on the love seat. "Something like that." I start taking off my boots; my feet are seriously killing me after walking all over that carnival, though I didn't notice it much until now.

"Hey, if tonight doesn't work for you, I can go," she says, though she's eyeing me suspiciously. Because, really, why wouldn't tonight work? It's not like I'm having a guy over, and she knows it.

"No, that's fine, I'm just—Today was strange." It was also many other things, but I haven't sorted them all out yet. "By the way, how did you know those leftovers were even still good? You know how truly terrible I am at remembering to clean out my fridge."

Nix shrugs. "It didn't *smell* like it was going to kill me." She takes another big bite and brings the plate over to the couch, flopping down onto it. She's wearing a ratty old dance t-shirt and sweatpants, her dark hair up in a messy bun. She never hesitates to make herself at home here, which I often mock but actually adore. I'd always wanted a sister as a kid, but there's a pretty big age difference between Nix and me—seven years—and as I got older I thought that maybe we'd never get to be close friends, that there would always be too big a gap there. But in the last few years, she's become my best friend, closer to me than anyone.

That doesn't mean I'm eager to dissect this whole Shane thing with her, though. I've never really been an over-sharer when it comes to my dating life. But Nix is, and despite my reluctance to hear what a total idiot I'm being, the truth is, I could really use some perspective on this.

And there's no way I'm going to be able to hide it from her now. I can tell by the way she's eyeing me. She already knows something's up.

I slump on the love seat across from her and put my aching feet up on the coffee table, on top of a pile of fabric scraps I should probably clean up at some point.

"So, the stuffed animal you got there," Nix says, right on cue. "I take it there's a story behind this?"

"You could say so." I let out a breath. "I was on a date."

"You went on a date!"

"That's not the shocking part."

"Are you sure about that?" She gives me a teasing grin over the Pad Thai.

I glare at her. "Do you want this story or not?"

"I really do. Please continue." She gestures with the fork like royalty granting me permission to speak.

"I was on a date. At a carnival, actually." I pause because Nix looks like she's about to choke on her noodles. Which is probably an appropriate response. God, when did I stop being someone that anyone could imagine having fun? I've always been more on the serious side, sure, and spontaneity isn't exactly my strong suit, but—

"That's awesome!" she finally says when she can speak again. "A guy took you to a *carnival*? And you agreed to go? I love him already." She's the one pausing now. "Unless he was a jerk or something, and I'm supposed to hate him. In which case, done."

I rub my forehead. Maybe talking about this is a bad idea.

But I'm in too deep now.

"It was Shane Beckstrom," I blurt out.

She sits up so quickly she almost drops her plate. Her dark eyes are comically wide. "Shane Beckstrom. Accidental Erotica Shane Beckstrom? You went on a *date* with him?"

I'm guessing it's that last part that's causing the most shock. Nix is very aware that I know lots of famous people, particularly musicians, in my line of work. She is also very aware that I, as a general rule, don't date them. And that was before I stopped dating at all.

"I did."

"At a carnival."

"Yep."

"Oh my god, Allison. How in the world—you went out with *Shane Beckstrom*?" She leans forward and draws her long legs up under her, the food totally forgotten on my coffee table. "Isn't he, like, a hermit since that accident? But he's dating now?"

"I don't know. I mean, I guess he has at least now gone on

a date—"

She continues on before I've even finished. "Is he awesome? Is he a jerk? Do you like him?"

I could give her one blunt answer of yes to all of these, but I think I'll give her a heart attack if I don't explain things a little more. And really, it's a whole lot more complicated than one simple answer.

"I definitely thought he was a jerk at first. He's the emcee of the pageant, and we didn't exactly hit it off right away. He was super late, for one—"

"Oooh." Nix knows my issues with punctuality.

"—And he also had an attitude about it. To be fair, I was kind of stressed out and bitchy to him. But you know I always have issues with the guys they bring on to host these things. It's always some douchy B-lister who's only there to try to sleep with the contestants, you know? Or make asshole jokes about the swimsuit competition."

"Right."

"And above and beyond his general reputation in the press, I'd heard some stuff from Jenna about him a while ago that wasn't great."

"Really? Like what?"

"Well, you know how their first two albums are all about this girl he was super in love with, who cheated on him—"

"Yeah, the soap opera actress, right? The one who was in that hot springs video."

It does not thrill me to remember that, along with the rest of the world, my *little sister* has seen Shane naked. "Right. Well, she's Jenna's good friend. And apparently all the stuff from the albums is bullshit. They'd slept together, yeah, but they hadn't been *together* together in five years. He made up this whole story to capitalize on Anna-Marie's fame and on the internet video that got leaked, and according to Jenna, it really hurt Anna-Marie."

Not professionally, I don't think. But I could see how it would be painful, being used like that by someone you'd considered a friend, branded as this cheating bitch who broke his heart. She and Josh went public a few years back about how it was all a lie, and from what I can tell, some people believe them, and others believe Shane, but the press isn't going to let a juicy story die—especially when more and more hit singles were being released.

Shane says he hurt her pride, nothing more, but I'm not sure that's all that's going on. I don't know Anna-Marie very well, though, so it's not like I can say for sure.

And I definitely think there's something more behind why he acted that way in the first place.

"Did you tell Jenna that you actually have a bunch of their songs?" Nix teases. "That you're an Accidental Erotica fan girl?"

"I am not a *fan girl*. They have some catchy songs." I can only imagine the look on Shane's face if he heard Nix call me that. There's a fluttery feeling in my chest, imagining his smug smile. "Besides, they're huge. Who doesn't have at least one of their songs?"

"Probably Anna-Marie," Nix says.

She's got a point there.

"*Anyway*," I continue, "when Carlyle told me Shane was going to be the emcee, I didn't have high hopes he'd be any different than the others."

"But he is, right? That's where this story is going, clearly, since you went on a date with him." Nix has never been the patient type. I don't think she's ever read a book that she didn't flip to the ending first to find out whether it was happy or sad. Not that she won't read the latter—she just likes to be prepared.

I definitely can't give her the ending here; *I* have no idea where the hell this is going. And that makes me more nervous than I can bring myself to admit.

I guess I like to know the ending, too—even though if there's one thing that my cancer diagnosis taught me, it's that none of us get to know, not really.

"I mean, I think he's been a total playboy and kind of an

opportunistic asshole. Even he admits to that." I tug my lower lip between my teeth, thinking about all the things he told me today, both in the dark of the green room and then the flashing lights of the carnival. About his family, and about the accident. His love for poetry—though not Elliot or Whitman, that was clear—and how songs are the poetry of the present, and people don't even know that's what they're enjoying.

I am pretty positive he doesn't often tell people these things, and he definitely hasn't been telling the press. None of it was in any of the articles I read about him last night (because fine, yes, I *did* Google him a bit extensively. And rewatch the hot springs video a time or three).

So why did he tell me? Was it the same indefinable reason that I asked him out, when I haven't even wanted to go on a date in two years?

"But . . ." Nix prompts, raising her eyebrows.

"I don't know, I think he might be more, too. I just—I wanted to get to know him."

"*Really*," she says with a suggestive tone. "Like, on a purely intellectual level."

"Oh my god, Nix," I say, rolling my eyes. "Yes, he's crazy hot. And yes, I wanted to jump him." I kind of did jump him in that bounce house, but I'm not going to tell her that yet. But I definitely liked that there is an intellectual level, too. He's smart and he's got a sharp wit that's sexy, even if it pissed me off at first. He may deny it, but there are depths there, and reckless though it may be, I want to explore those. "But I also wanted to get to actually know him more. Are you happy?"

She gives me a smug smile. "I just want to make sure we're being totally honest here." She digs back into the food. "So you decided to get to know him at a *carnival?*"

I chuckle. "The carnival, as you can imagine, was his idea. And we went on rides, and he paid an insane amount of money to 'win' me this dog, and oh my god, he even got me to eat from a food truck and it was all . . . kind of amazing." I realize I've got a dopey smile on my face, and I try to tone it down by the end, but Nix's own smile tells me I'm too late.

"That does sound like an epic date," she says, and I can tell she means it. That actually sounds like a perfect date for Nix—my sister has always been the fun and carefree one of us, the charismatic one. The kind of girl who will jump into a pool at a party fully clothed, or will shamelessly sing impromptu, terrible karaoke and still somehow get the whole bar singing along with her like she's the second coming of Beyoncé.

I can feel the anxiety starting to congeal in my stomach. Because yeah, it was an amazing, fun date, but I'm not really that person, at least not all the time. I'm still the girl who gets uptight about deadlines and contracts. The girl who, if she stays up all night, it's not partying, it's hand-beading a designer gown while on speaker-phone with a fabric supplier in Indonesia.

I doubt that's the girl he'd really want.

"Honestly," I say, trying to make my voice sound casual. "You and him would probably be a better fit. I think you'd have a great time, and—"

"Are you trying to set me up with Shane Beckstrom? Who you just had a date with?"

"You do like rock stars," I say, in an admittedly weak defense. "Remember how much you begged me to set you up with Alec Andreas?"

"Which you didn't, and now he's married, so thanks for that." Nix gives me a mock glare, but she's not really upset. She doesn't have much trouble finding guys to date on her own—too bad they all turn out to be total douchebags. "And no, that's a terrible idea. I'm not going out with a guy who my sister is super into."

"I never said I—"

"Besides, he's kind of old, yeah? I don't do guys over thirty. No offense to the thirty-year-olds in the room."

I toss a throw pillow at her. "He's twenty-eight," I say, too quickly. Revealing another little tidbit I gleaned from Google.

"Well, in that case . . ." Nix pretends to consider. "Nope, still a terrible idea." She hops up and heads over to the kitchen, and I hear her open the fridge. "So when *are* you going to jump him?" she calls back, and I hear her take a can of soda out and pop the top. "Do I need to not be around this week?"

"You say this like it's a certainty." My body is heating up again, though, just thinking about it. His lips on mine, his hands on my skin, in my hair. That energy charging the air around us.

"I'm saying it like it should be. You clearly want to." She comes back in and hands me a cold Dr. Pepper, then sits back down on the couch with her own soda.

I'm happy to take a drink. I need something to cool me down. "Let me guess. You think he's perfect for this, because if he's been this total player who's been with hundreds of girls, then he's probably pretty great at sex." I say this lightly, and really, I know it shouldn't bother me—why should it? Of course rock stars get around—but the pit in my stomach grows.

Nix makes a face. "I think sometimes guys like that are actually worse. Like, they get so many girls anyway, they're not exactly concerned about getting a five-star review, you know?"

"Greg?" I say, raising an eyebrow. Greg was a back-up dancer for Cardi B, Pink, and a bunch of other A-list musicians, and Nix dated him briefly. Brief being a theme of many things involving Greg, from what I recall.

"Yep." She emphasizes the 'p' with a loud pop and takes a drink. "But they aren't *all* that way."

I can already tell Shane wouldn't be. God, that kiss alone was so intense, so perfect and electric—I can only imagine what the rest would be like.

Except.

I think about my panic moment again, as his hands moved higher up my sides.

"And you definitely like him," she says.

She's right, but I can't bring myself to admit it out loud to her yet. I trail my finger down a line of condensation on my Dr. Pepper and take another drink.

"Are you worried he's just playing you?" she asks. "Like all that stuff he was telling you was just to get you to sleep with him, and then he'll never speak to you again or something?"

I force myself to consider this. Everything I've heard about Shane Beckstrom points to the possibility. But.

"He said that the guy he was died in that accident," I say slowly, "and I get that—you know, how something like that can make you feel like a totally different person afterwards."

Nix nods, but her eyes are narrowed slightly, considering.

"Go ahead and say it. It sounds like a line, doesn't it?"

"But you don't think it was."

My heartbeat feels uneven in my chest. "No. I think maybe there's been more to him all along, things he's always been covering up with the asshole rock star shtick, and the accident is actually making him start to face that. I bet that's scary as hell."

There's a long stretch of silence, which is unusual in any conversation with Nix, and I close my eyes. "I probably sound like an idiot groupie, huh?"

She tilts her head, studying me. "Maybe from someone else, it would sound that way. But you've always had a way of being able to see through people to who they really are."

I let out a breath. It's such a relief to hear that from her, that maybe my intuition isn't completely failing me because of how long I've been out of the game, and how gorgeous his smile is, and the way it feels when he calls me "Ally"—like maybe I can be the serious girl *and* the fun one, and maybe he'd actually want—

I cut my own thoughts off, swallowing past a throat that feels too tight. "Not that it matters. He's Shane Beckstrom. Which, yeah, is more than what he's letting on, and I don't think he's actively playing me, no. But he's obviously not looking for anything serious. And I'm—"

I'm what?

"Scared to look at all?" Nix ventures quietly. She worries her lower lip between her teeth, like she thinks she may have gone too far with that.

But she's right.

I am scared. Especially with him.

Because I do like him, more than I want to admit to myself, let alone anyone else. And I think he likes me, more than as just some groupie conquest.

But that doesn't mean he'd still want me if he knew the truth.

False advertising, if you ask me, I can still hear him say, flipping the breast enhancement. A dick statement, for sure, even if he didn't have any idea of the way it would cut me. Of the way it would hone in on all my worst fears about letting someone close to me like that again.

Even if he didn't know that I was wearing one of those myself, only not to make my breasts seem bigger. But to seem like I have two breasts at all, when in reality, I now only have the one.

"Maybe," I say, equally quietly, and Nix comes over and throws her arms around me. She doesn't say anything about what a dick he'd be if he had problems with my mastectomy, or how I need to just get over my fear and take my libido out of cryogenic storage at some point. She just sits there and hugs me, and I hug her back, and then later we say goodnight and she makes up her usual bed on the couch, and I take my new stuffed animal and head into my room.

Lord Shelldon greets me as I walk in, rubbing his fat cat body against my ankles, like he's been dying to see me, even though he could have come out into the living room at any time to do so. I pet him, smiling to myself as I think of Shane with cats of his own, named Snugglesworth and Snelgrove. Tossing little toys with them and letting them crawl on his shoulders while he plays guitar.

Maybe with me sitting next to them all on the couch, like it's some normal day.

The panic clenches like a fist in my chest, and I force the

image away. I strip down out of the red dress and pull off my bra, the prosthetic coming off with it, and for the first time in a while, I stare at my bare chest in the mirror. I see my right breast and the place where the left one used to be, now a flat expanse of skin marred by a puckered scar.

I used to make myself look at it every day. Used to make myself say affirmations about how beautiful my body is. How strong it is, to have gone through what it did and come out the other side. I said them again and again until I believed them.

Or believed them enough, I suppose. Because while I could look at myself and value my experience and value myself with or without a perfect pair of breasts, I still can't help but be afraid of the look on a guy's face when he sees it—even though I would definitely tell him first, to prepare him.

But if it took me months to become used to it, to value it, how can I expect some guy to not have a problem with it? To not look at me and wish I had that model-perfect body he thought he was getting?

Shane's seen his share of model-perfect bodies, I'm sure. And the thought of him looking at me with disgust, even disgust he'd try to hide—it guts me.

I pull on my t-shirt, angry at myself and sad, feeling like the world's biggest hypocrite. Here I am, doing my best to teach these pageant girls to love their bodies, even the imperfections (and believe me, beauty queen girls can win prizes in hating on their bodies), while also trying to teach them that they are so much more than their looks. I preach empowerment to these girls like I know so damn much about it. Overcome your fears and go out and get what you want, rah rah rah.

But when it comes down to it, I'm a bigger coward than any of them.

NINE

Shane

When I get home to my empty, dark apartment, I seriously think about finding someone with kittens they want to give away. I also seriously think about calling Kevin and spilling my guts. But Kevin has Maya, and I'm still not confident in my ability to keep a houseplant alive, let alone two cats.

Besides, they're only going to remind me of her.

Instead I tear through the apartment, actually throwing away the remains of all the food I've ordered in over the last month. There isn't much else left out—I haven't touched my guitar or recording equipment in months. My guitars and amps all sit in the corner on stands, reminding me of that album I'm supposed to be working on.

I don't want to play. I definitely don't want to write. And there's only so much longer I'm going to be able to put Parker off, pretending that I am. When that's over, when everyone knows that I'm not holed up planning my solo career but have gone completely out of my mind . . . that'll be the final nail in the coffin that contains my life. Every part of me will be dead except my body.

I should have died in that van with JT.

"Cheer up," JT says. "There's still all those pageant contestants you could bang."

I actually do spin around and throw a punch at him, but he dodges. "Whoa," he says. "I was just testing you. You want this girl. You've got it *bad*."

I shake my head. "It doesn't matter. Someone like me does not get someone like her."

"Dude. That's why we became rocks stars. To get girls that are too good for us."

"First," I say, "that is not why we became rock stars. And second, this girl is different. She's . . . *responsible*. She has her life together and shit. She would never go out with me."

"She *did* go out with you."

"Because she felt sorry for me. It won't happen again."

"Awww," JT says. "Come on. Work that Shane charm on her. You know you want her all snuggled up next to you in bed, that dark hair on the pillow, that fine body all pressed up against yours."

Ahhh. I *do* want that. But it isn't possible. "Dude. Shut up."

JT just smirks at me. I collapse on the couch and find myself wishing I was the kind of guy who could end up with someone like her.

I arrive at pageant rehearsal the next morning both later than usual and somewhat annoyed. I'm barely sleeping, so dragging myself out of the house at any time of day is a Herculean effort. Coming here is worse. I'm not sure why we need a full week's worth of practice for the girls to get used to filing on and off the stage and doing one single act that is somehow supposed to constitute talent. I feel like we could have made do with one dress rehearsal and called it good.

I storm into the green room, figuring I'll hang out there until someone realizes I'm here and drags me on stage. I'm really not looking forward to seeing Allison—

But there's a girl I haven't seen before, sitting in the green room. She's got chestnut brown hair that looks like it's been chemically lightened and skin darker than Allison's. She's younger than me, for sure, but not quite young enough to be a contestant.

"Hi," she says, looking up at me. "You must be Shane."

God, she has Allison's eyes. "And you must be Allison's sister."

She brightens. "Guilty as charged. I'm Nicole, but you can call me Nix if you want."

I don't want to call her anything, but I collapse onto the couch next to her. "What are you doing here?"

Nix shrugs. "Allison invited me to check out the pageant."

By the way she looks me, it's pretty clear it's me she was sent to check out. That shouldn't make me feel better, but it does a little.

"So," Nix says. "Tell me what you think about Allison."

"Not a chance. Anything I say to you is going directly to her."

Nix smiles. "Yep. But you know you want to spill your guts to me anyway."

"Um, your sister is hot. And kind of awesome. And that's all you're getting out of me."

Nix appraises me again, and I suddenly realize what she's here for.

"I know I'm not good enough for her," I say. "So don't worry about that."

Nix looks surprised and opens her mouth to say something, but closes it again when Allison appears in the doorway. "Hey!" she says, sounding far too excited to see me, given how late I showed up and how much that bothers her. "I'm glad you guys have met."

I bet she is.

"I just knew you guys would get along," Allison continues. "We're going to need you up on stage in a minute, but why don't you spend more time getting to know each other?"

Nix frowns down at the floor, and Allison smiles, but it's stiff and fake. I'm still trying to piece together what's happening, when Allison goes on, like she's somehow compelled to keep babbling to fill the silence.

"I just think you two have a lot in common," she says, and my stomach sinks. She gets through a couple more sentences about how much she thinks Nix and I will like each other before I finally cut her off.

"Are you trying to set me up with your *sister*?" I ask.

Allison stutters a bit, and Nix looks decidedly uncomfortable. I want to entirely disappear. "Oh my god. What the *fuck*, Allison? Seriously. What the actual fuck?"

Allison squeezes her eyes closed. "I'm sorry," she says. "I'm sorry." Then she all but runs out of the room.

JT steps into the empty doorway. "Dude," he says. "That was cold."

I hope he's talking about Allison and not me, because I feel fully justified in stewing in my own resentment. If she doesn't want me, she could just say so. Despite her insistence that she wasn't brushing me off, I've already got the message. I don't need her pity and I sure as hell don't need—

Nix sighs. "I told her that was a bad idea."

"Yeah, well. Whatever. I get the message."

Nix shakes her head. "She likes you. She's just scared."

I look at her out of the corner of my eye. "She told you that?"

"Not exactly. But she's my sister. I can tell."

She's probably right to be scared, but I still wonder if there isn't more to it. "Has she . . . is there some kind of trauma in her past that makes her uncomfortable about sex?"

Nix looks up at the ceiling. "Yes. But not like you're thinking."

I watch her. Nix has no loyalty to me, but she's clearly not happy with the way Allison is handling . . . whatever the hell this is. "Want to fill me in?"

"Yes," Nix says. "And since Allison won't, I think I'm going to. It's for her own good."

"Works for me."

Nix makes a little whining sound, like she's not sure if she's going to regret this or maybe if Allison is going to murder her, which might be a real possibility. But I'm sick of being jerked around by this girl, and I need to know what the hell is going on.

"Allison had breast cancer," Nix says. "She's uncomfortable about sex because she had a mastectomy."

I blink at her. "She had a—"

"She's missing a boob! And she's kind of paranoid about it, so she hasn't been with anyone since."

"Oh," I say. And I'm remembering now, her not telling me what kind of cancer she had, freaking out when I ran my hands anywhere near her breasts, though I wasn't going to, like, grope her or anything. Telling me she just wanted to kiss.

Oh, god, those things I said yesterday about the fake boobs the girls use for the pageant.

"Shit," I say. "I'm an asshole."

Nix raises her eyebrows. "What?"

I groan and slouch down on the couch, leaning my head against the back. "Yesterday, I was joking around with her about all the fake breasts lying around the auditorium. And I might have said—" I cringe. "I called them false advertising and asked if they were supposed to be attractive."

Nix blinks at me, wide eyed. "Okay, yeah. That would do it."

Shit. "I need to apologize to her."

Nix squirms. "Look, you probably do. But you should also think about what you want. I mean it when I say she really likes you. She totally fell asleep cuddling that weird stuffed dog you got her."

That news makes me unreasonably happy, and I try to smother a grin and fail.

"But if the mastectomy thing is a problem . . ." Nix shrugs. "Just don't lead her on. I don't want her to get hurt."

I'm still so stunned by the news that I'm not sure how to process it. "I don't think that's a problem. Should it be?"

"I don't know," Nix says. "I think it probably would be for some guys."

"Aren't you concerned about the idea of me dating your sister? I'm assuming you know who I am."

"I do," Nix says. "And yeah, I'm concerned. But I don't know how much of your reputation is real, so I'm withholding judgment."

I roll my eyes. "You mean how much of it is true, or how much of that's really me?"

"Both."

"It's all true. All the stuff in the mainstream press, anyway. It's really who I am, but it's not, like, everything I am." Shit. That sounded a lot like admitting to having layers. "Don't tell your sister I said that."

Nix looks confused. "Don't tell my sister you're more than your reputation?"

"Exactly."

"Okay, I guess. But if you're really serious about her, you should probably tell her that."

I should. But I can't see how that would be fair to her. "I don't know. I'm pretty messed up. She'd be better off if I just left her alone."

"It's a little late for that," Nix says.

And deep down, I know she's right.

TEN

Shane

I find Allison talking to Carmen in the hallway. "It can't be adjusted!" Carmen is saying. "The swimsuit fabric is all one piece. I'll use butt glue, I promise."

"Butt glue doesn't work without *fabric* to glue to your *butt*," Allison says firmly. "I'm sorry, Carmen. You're going to need a new swimsuit."

Carmen looks horrified. "But I only have four days—"

They both look up at me as I approach, and I'm not sure whether Carmen or Allison looks more distraught.

"Talk to your wardrobe person," Allison says. "If you need someone to help you track down a store-bought swimsuit, I can—"

"Ugh," Carmen says. "*Fine.*" She stalks off down the hallway.

"God, Ally," I say. "I'm so sorry about those things I said yesterday."

Allison hesitates. "What things?"

"About the fake breasts. I was just messing around. I didn't mean anything by it."

Her mouth presses into a grim line. "Nix told you."

"Yeah. And I'm really sorry. I didn't know."

Allison looks down at her shoes. They're platform heels,

which she's paired with a purple and blue patterned dress that hugs her body just right. I wonder how much of her wardrobe she designs herself. If the stuff she wears is hers, she clearly rocks at it. But I notice that the neckline is just high enough to cover her cleavage. I think that's been true of all of the dresses she wears, and now I understand why.

There's a long silence, and I realize she's waiting for me to say something about this. I put a hand on her arm. "Hey," I say. "It doesn't matter. At least, I don't think it does." I realize I have no idea what a mastectomy scar looks like, so I guess I can't guarantee it won't bother me.

But being so close to her, I feel magnetically drawn to her, in a way that has nothing to do with her chest.

Allison shakes her head. "Yeah, you can't know, right? And I get it. It's not attractive, and I understand if you can't—"

"Ally," I say. "You're beautiful, and I'm crazy attracted to you. It's not a problem."

She looks up at me, her lips still pressed together. "Yeah, well. I'm kind of crazy attracted to you, too."

There's this heat building between us again, but I'm scared to let it ignite, afraid of what else might be holding her back. "So how much of what you said yesterday was true?" I ask. "Are you really not ready for, like, physical stuff? Or was that the only problem?"

"Oh," Allison says. "No, that was pretty much it."

I run a hand through my hair. "What the hell was that with your sister?"

Allison cringes. "I'm sorry. I was just scared. And she's a lot more fun than I am. She's a ballroom dancer, like, professionally, and I just thought—"

"Ally," I say. "I had fun with *you* yesterday."

"Yeah?" Her whole body relaxes, though I'm not sure why this is news.

"Yeah. Your sister seems cool and all, but I'm not interested in her."

Allison looks up at me, and her eyes meet mine, and I feel myself rock toward her. I put my hands on her hips and draw her body closer. We're standing in the hallway just outside the auditorium, and anyone could walk out here at any time, but I don't care. I just want to be near her.

"I'm scared, too," I tell her.

She nods. "But this doesn't have to be anything serious, right? We can just go out and see how it goes."

I feel like the floor has dropped out from under me, and I nod, too quickly. "Yeah," I say. "Yeah, that's fine. If that's what you want." I should want that. I don't get serious, because I learned a long time ago that, for me, it's a recipe for heartbreak.

No way is any woman going to stick around and put up with my shit, especially someone like Allison.

She's studying me, like she sees more of how I feel than I want her to.

"Did I just make it better or worse?" she asks.

"Worse. But it's fine. I'm not trying to pressure you, and I get how lucky I am that you're even willing to give me a chance."

I sound desperate, in no small measure because that's how I feel.

Allison shakes her head. "I thought that's what you would want. To keep things casual."

I should. But the way I feel about her—it's anything but casual. "What do you want?"

"Well," she says slowly. "I want to date you. And in an ideal world, neither of us would be dating other people."

I smile. "You know there's a word for that, right?"

Allison looks like she's about to hyperventilate. "I mean," she says, "I don't, you know, I—"

I lift my hands, about to tell her that I don't expect any kind of commitment, but she finally stumbles over the words.

"Would you be okay with that?"

I laugh. "With you being my girlfriend? Yeah. I'd like that."

"Okay," Allison says. "I'd like that, too."

We blink at each other, and I'm not sure how this could

possibly have happened. I'm a mess, and she's going to find out, and she's going to leave me, and it's going to hurt like hell.

But she reaches up and brushes my hair out of my face, and I feel like there's a forest fire happening between us. Like I could easily fall into her arms and lose all control. The point of no return is behind me. I'm not going to walk away from this girl. I don't want to.

Carlyle yells something in the auditorium, and Allison winces. I can do this. I can be responsible when I need to be. "We need to get to work," I say. "But practice is over at four, right?"

"Right," Allison says.

"So, what should we say, four-fifteen in the green room? You and I are going to make out like crazy."

"Yes," Allison says. "Please."

I smile and press my lips to her forehead. Her body is so close to mine, and all I want is to draw her closer, to be with her.

Damn. It doesn't feel like I've had enough time with her to already be in it this deep. "I may also have admitted to your sister that I have at least one layer," I say against her skin. "But it's a very shallow layer, and there aren't any more underneath."

"Mmmm." Allison presses her face against my chest. "You have more layers than you think."

I lay a hand on her back, holding her gently, as if she might break. "Isn't that what girls tell themselves to justify dating bad guys?"

"Maybe," she says.

I close my eyes and wonder how long that justification is going to last.

T wenty minutes later I'm up on stage, listening to Carlyle harass the girls about the way they bring their props on and off the stage. Turns out it was a good day to be late; after the disaster yesterday, Carlyle has started the day trying to get the girls to run props without anyone threatening to litigate. The marimba is massive but looks unharmed from yesterday's debacle, and the chick with the camellias only throws shade, not any props or pieces of set. I see the dog trainer girl, but not her dogs. Probably she wisely decided to keep them kenneled backstage until it's her turn.

Carmen keeps looking suspiciously from me to Allison, like she thinks something's going on between us. That's when I remember that both contestants and crew probably think we took a sex break yesterday, especially given how obvious it was that the lights were off in the green room.

In fact, several of the girls are sitting close to Allison and whispering, while nearby, Collette sits next to her boyfriend—a wiry guy with a buzz cut and a sour look on his face—and doing her wax on move at my genitals again.

"How's my aura today, Collette?" I call as Speed-painting Girl moves her canvas (still blank, because she's not actually doing the painting today) off the stage.

"Healthy," Collette responds. I'm not sure what exactly that means—am I virus-free, or is she referring to my libido? Because that's sure as hell roaring after being in the hall with Allison.

"Thanks," I say.

Her boyfriend looks from her to me. "What the hell are you talking about?" he asks.

"His aura," Collette says.

"Well, I don't like the way you're looking at him."

"I'm not looking at him like anything," Collette says. "I'm just reading his aura."

"I don't want you touching his aura," the boyfriend says.

Allison glares over at the guy. I know he bothers her because he keeps hanging around where he isn't supposed to be, but listening to him bitch at Collette, I wonder if there might be more to it.

The girl with the camellias is on stage now, arranging her flowers in vases and running through her lecture on what it takes to grow, care for, and arrange prize-winning flowers. She's not supposed to be running through her whole talent, but Carlyle doesn't seem inclined to interrupt her, so I wonder if he's given up on the idea of doing a quick prop run and just wants to let each of them have their time so they'll all calm the hell down about whose props are touching whose.

"Why do you get to date him?" Marimba Girl says. I'm trying to remember if her name is Becky or Gwendolyn.

"Because I'm not a contestant," Allison says. "And what's going on between me and Shane is none of your business."

"You're *dating* him?" Collette asks. "Oh my god, I knew you guys were going to reunite. That's so romantic."

Collette's boyfriend scowls at her while the rest of the girls crowd around Allison, asking a cloud of questions. Allison looks like she's about to hyperventilate at the center, so I grab the mic stand and pull the microphone close to my mouth.

"Hey," I say. "Back away from my girlfriend."

The girls all look up at me, and a wave of giggles spreads through the crowd. Then they all scatter to their various cell phones.

"Ladies!" Carlyle calls. "Quiet, please." Allison fends off the last of the girls and gives me a beleaguered look. Girls are tapping their phones all over the room, and one of them lifts her phone, clearly taking my picture.

Oh. They're putting this all over the internet. Of course they are.

Three minutes later, Carlyle and Camellia Girl—whose name is Becky, making Marimba Girl Gwendolyn—are arguing about how long it takes to get her flowers safely off the stage after her talent. Carmen, now wearing a long robe that drags on the ground as she walks, prepares to come on stage to perform an aria from *Die Zauberflöte*. Becky is most of the way off the stage when Nix comes storming into the auditorium, holding out her phone.

"I was like ten feet away!" she says to Allison. "How did I find out about this on Facebook?"

"Sorry, Nix," I say into the microphone. "That was my fault."

"Mr. Beckstrom," Carlyle says. "Is it possible for you to refrain from using this public forum for your personal drama?"

I raise an eyebrow at the idea of *me* being the main source of drama in this room, but Allison shakes her head at me, so for her sake, I don't start anything. I announce Carmen like I'm supposed to, then climb down off the stage and walk over to Allison and Nix.

"Sorry," I say to Allison. "You're going to learn this about me, but I don't generally think before I speak."

"It's okay," Allison says, and she really looks like it is, which makes me want to scoop her up and spin her around right here and kiss her in front of everyone.

"Oh my god," Nix says. "Mom put a shocked emoji on it. She must have learned how to do that just for this post."

Oh, shit. I hadn't thought about Allison's family seeing it. Sure, the press will get a hold of it, but that doesn't really have consequences for *me*. We didn't actually talk about whether or not we were being public, although she didn't ask me to keep it a secret.

Allison reaches over and turns off her phone.

"Um," I say. "How much are your parents going to hate me?"

"They're not going to hate you," Allison says, at the same time Nix says, "Probably a lot."

I groan. "I'm sorry." I remember now how much time I spent apologizing in my last relationship. Obviously nothing has changed, and I wonder if Allison is already regretting this.

"Hate is a strong word," Allison says, glaring at Nix. "They're going to be concerned."

"How concerned?" I ask. "On a scale of one to ten."

Nix wobbles a hand. "Mom like a seven. Dad, probably nine."

I take a deep breath. Right. They're going to hate me. Why shouldn't they? No parent is going to want their daughter dating me. And Allison's pretty close to her family, close enough to value their opinions, so—

"I think it's the other way around," Allison says. "Dad trusts me more than he trusts you, but since the cancer Mom is always acting like any little thing will break me."

Nix considers this. "That might be true."

"Oh, god," I say, sinking into my seat next to Allison. This aria appears to be fairly lengthy, and I'm grateful for that. I'm not ready to get back up on stage.

Though I realize now that I'm not sure where JT is. He seems to have disappeared, possibly stalking the women's bathroom, and as guilty as this makes me feel, I'm glad. There's only so much heckling I can handle while feeling like I'm already screwing up the only good thing I have in my life right now.

Allison puts a hand on my arm. "You're really worried about this, aren't you?"

I'm conscious that a couple of the girls are taking pictures of us, but I nod. "Yeah, I am."

She smiles like she finds this adorable, and I hope that means she's not desperately regretting her decision to date me. "It'll be okay. They're going to be freaked out at first, but it doesn't matter. They don't get a say."

Maybe they should, I think.

But I keep that to myself.

I'm late to my four-fifteen makeout appointment because while I'm waiting for Allison to finish working out a swimsuit plan with Carmen, I get a phone call from Parker. I think about letting it go to voice mail, but I figure he's seen the news online about me and Allison, and I'd like to get ahead of that before he settles on some ridiculous spin to exploit our relationship for my professional gain.

"Park!" I say. "What's up?"

"Shane!" he says back with equal gusto. "What's this I'm reading about you and Allison Mendez?"

"I'm dating her. I'm hoping that's what you read."

"It is. Hey, I'm calling because I got you two tickets to the benefit tomorrow night. You remember me telling you about it?"

I do now. Vaguely. "Look, Parker, I don't know if I'm ready for—"

"It's benefiting Syrian refugees," Parker says, "and half the music industry is going to be there. I've met Allison, and she's exactly the kind of girl you want on your arm at a thing like this. I'm going to send those tickets over, okay? Tell me you'll be there."

I grit my teeth, wanting to tell him to stop being an asshole and trying to turn my relationship into a career opportunity. But the idea of going to something like that with Allison, dressing up and dancing with her . . . it sounds normal. Nice, even.

"I'll think about it," I tell him.

"Shane," he says. "You're going to get through this. You just have to put one foot in front of the other and walk into the gala tomorrow and remember who you are."

"Okay, I will."

"You should tell him," JT says after I hang up. I turn around to find him leaning against the front doors of the building. Now that I think about it, JT was always leaning somewhere. He used to knock things over all the time—pencil jars and soda cans and, half the time, our instruments.

"Tell him what?" I say.

"That you're not coming back."

I shuffle my feet. "Maybe I am."

"No," JT says. "You're not. Besides, Parker was always kind of a dick. Even if you stay in music, you're not going to stay with him."

"I'm not going to tell him that. He's the last person who cares what's going on with me."

"That's not true," JT says. "Parker doesn't care about you."

I glare at JT, even though I know he's right. "Whatever," I say, and I stalk off to find Allison.

JT doesn't follow.

ELEVEN

Allison

Carmen waltzes out in a new purple swimsuit with large, asymmetrical cutouts in the side. She does a little turn, and I give her a pointed look. She rolls her eyes and poses in a way so I can confirm that all her crotch is indeed adequately covered and we can keep this pageant family-friendly.

She's unhappy about this, but I can't imagine she's surprised. After all, this isn't her first pageant. This being a regional pageant, all the girls had to win in both their hometown and county to be here. And there's no way Miss Sweet Orange let her flash her vag.

"That's perfect," I say. "Thank you." I should be thanking her pageant coach, who ran out this afternoon to find a handful of swimsuits, all of which Carmen has systematically rejected for one reason or another.

"I still like my first one better," she says.

"Awesome. Keep it for Drake's next pool party. But you can't wear it here." I'm snappish and sounding frustrated—which I am—but not because I'm in a bad mood. I'm actually in a very, very good mood.

Shane's my *boyfriend*.

I'm his *girlfriend*.

These words, surreal though they may be, keep circling

through my head, and I'm so giddy with them it's hard not to bounce on my feet. I feel like some high school girl who just got asked out by the star quarterback or something—actually, I feel way better than that, because I *did* get asked out by the star quarterback in high school, and I wasn't nearly this excited. Or stunned. Or nervous.

If we don't finish this swimsuit situation right now, I'm going to be late for my make-out session with said new boyfriend.

And he of all people knows how much I hate to be late.

"I just don't know if this color washes me out, you know?" Carmen asks, striking another pose in front of the mirror. "Maybe I should try the red one aga—"

"Well, I don't like him hovering around the dressing room door!" a contestant named Wendy says loudly, cutting Carmen off. "It's pervy."

Both Carmen and I—and about a dozen other girls—turn to see Wendy chewing out a red-faced Collette.

I sigh. I already can tell what this is about, and I don't like it, either.

"He's not trying to look at any of you guys," Collette says, fidgeting as she stands there in her own swimsuit, a one piece with cute little bows on the straps. "I promise. He just likes to stay close to me, and he knows he's not allowed in the dressing room."

There's some muttering from the other girls. None of them like Collette's boyfriend, Thomas, and I agree with them. He's clearly crazy jealous and possessive and a total dick, and I come close to telling her my feelings on this about ten times a day. But I haven't seen anything to indicate she's unhappy or actively being hurt, and while I try to make sure the pageant girls know they can come to me for advice or help, I'm well aware there's a fine line between being a mentor and being an overbearing mother who thinks it's any of my business who they date.

This pageant, however, *is* my business.

I walk over to Collette, and gently pull her closer to the door and away from Wendy, who, point made, stalks off to go change.

"Look, Collette," I say. "I know we agreed to let Thomas be here with you during rehearsals"—technically *I* didn't, but Carlyle did, and it's not like we've ever been particularly rigid about forbidding the occasional friend or family member from watching—"but he can't do things that make the other girls uncomfortable. Okay?" I make sure my voice is loud enough for this next part so that he can hear it through the door, if he is indeed standing there. "If he keeps making the other girls uncomfortable—like by hanging around just outside of the dressing room—then we'll have him escorted out, and he won't be able to come back for the pageant. Got it?"

Collette looks down at the floor, and I feel bad. She's a sweet girl, and I like her. And she did stop giving tarot readings like I asked, even though I've since heard some of the other girls begging her to. "Sorry," she says.

"It's okay." I give her a quick hug. "Not your fault. You know that protecting all you girls is my top priority, yeah?"

Technically, protecting the girls isn't in my job description so much as making sure they know when and where and in what order to exit the stage. But it sure as hell is part of my *personal* job description. And I hope she knows what I'm really trying to tell her here.

Collette smiles. "I know. By the way, I just saw *your* boyfriend on the phone. His aura was *very* orange."

Huh. I have no idea what that's supposed to mean, but she says it in a kind of suggestive way and seems pleased with the information.

I look up at the clock. 4:19. Shit.

And also, FINALLY. My heart starts pounding harder.

"Well, I guess I'd better go check that out for myself," I say, in my own suggestive tone—they all know now anyway—and Collette laughs.

"Allison," Carmen whines as I open the door.

But I'm off the clock now, and I'm all kinds of wound up

at the thought of whatever an orange aura might indicate. Not to mention the thought of just getting to be with Shane—my *boyfriend*—again, just the two of us.

"Just pick one, Carmen," I call without looking back and hurry out of the dressing room.

I don't see Thomas standing anywhere nearby, so hopefully he got my message. Because I definitely don't want to have to deal with him right now.

The dressing room is only a minute's walk from the green room where I'm supposed to meet Shane, but even though I start out practically jogging, my feet slow as my excitement gets taken over by the nerves.

He's going to see my scar. My lack. I know I'm going to show him. I *want* to show him, which is in and of itself a kind of miracle.

But I'm terrified. Not because he's Shane Beckstrom, hot rock star.

It's because he's Shane Beckstrom, the guy who took me to a carnival and makes me laugh with stories about his hometown. The guy who reads poetry but doesn't tell anyone. Who's smart and talented and stubborn as hell. The guy who's willing to tell me things that I know he tries to keep hidden from everyone else. Who tells me he's scared about what he feels for me. Who's worried what my parents will think of him.

The guy who's so much more than he lets people know, who's so much more than even *he* knows.

I'm terrified because, somehow, in such a short time, he's become the guy who makes me feel things I've never felt before—not for guys I've known much longer, or guys who seemed perfect for me on paper.

I close my eyes, standing outside the green room door, my pulse racing. I remember sitting with him in this room in the dark, and how he said then that he didn't have a problem with commitment, with the right girl.

I want so much to be that right girl. He must think I am, at least. I'd assumed he'd only want to date casually, but, like so many other assumptions I had of him, I was wrong. I could tell that the minute I suggested we just see where this goes.

He wants more, and so do I.

But I'm still scared of seeing the look on his face, regretting that decision.

I let out a shaky breath and remind myself that, fear aside, I'm about to go make out—and quite possibly much more—with my boyfriend, something I've been fantasizing about all day.

Even if some parts of me are afraid, there are other parts of me that are way more than ready. And those parts are not inclined to stand out in this hallway anymore.

I open the door and walk in, and there's Shane, sitting on the couch with his eyes closed and his brow furrowed. His sunglasses next to him on the armrest.

I worry that he's got a headache from the lights, but his eyes open, and he sees me. The furrow in his brow disappears.

He looks a little nervous, too. "Hey," he says, the corner of his lip turning up. His eyes flick over to the clock on the wall. "You're late."

"I guess we're even, then," I say, a smile playing at my own lips. Just seeing him, I can feel my body longing to be closer, to feel his mouth on mine.

There's a hungry look in his blue eyes that says he feels the same way.

I can't take it anymore; I lock the door behind me and stride across the room. He stands to meet me, and then I'm in his arms and we're kissing, desperately, and his hands are on my back and in my hair, and mine are on him, and the nerves melt away in how incredibly good this all feels, how strangely right.

I want more.

I push him down so that he's sitting the couch, and I'm straddling his lap with my knees to either side of him. The frantic desperation of our initial kisses slows a bit, and now our mouths are moving together softly, slowly. For all that my body yearns for more, it's also sublimely happy just like this, just drawing out this delicious tension, enjoying every second of being with him. His hands move up my legs, his fingers teasing just up under the hem of my skirt, and fire burns along my skin. He moves his hands to my sides again, slowly moving up, and—

And I flinch. I don't mean to, but I do, and there's this flicker of fear that he's going to pull away.

But he doesn't. His hands reverse directions, smoothing my skirt down over my hips. His lips kissing mine softly, his tongue tracing along mine. I relax back into him, running my hands over the hard muscles of his chest that I can feel through his cotton shirt, shivering as his lips trail slowly down my neck.

And then he's kissing the hollow of my collarbone, and his fingers lightly graze the neckline of my dress, and god, I want him to unzip me and pull it down, I want him to see, but I feel myself tense again anyway.

This time he does pull back, though he keeps his forehead pressed to mine.

"May I?" he asks, and while I assume asking if it's okay to take a girl's top off during an intense makeout session isn't something he normally does—or maybe ever does—I can also tell that he's okay if I say no. That he doesn't want to push me further than I'm ready to go.

But I want to go further and not because it's been so long since I have.

I nod, my heart racing.

It races even more as he leans forward again, as he kisses my neck and tugs my earlobe between his teeth, and I gasp with the thrill that sends through me. I can feel his fingers grasping the pull to my zipper and trailing it down my back; I feel the top of my dress roll down. Feel the heat of his fingers as he reaches around to unhook my bra.

I pull my bra forward, and it falls off onto his chest, the prosthetic falling with it.

Everything seems to go still, as I see his gaze drop to my bare chest. My breath, my heart—everything.

He stares, his lips slightly parted, but I can't read anything from his expression. His fingers slide up my stomach, then trace along the raised skin of my mastectomy scar.

My throat feels so dry suddenly it hurts. I lay my forehead on his shoulder, because I'm so afraid to see the moment that expression becomes something I can read.

"I know it's not attractive," I say, trying to keep my voice from shaking. "I get if you can't be sexually attracted to me because of it."

He wouldn't have known whether he could be or not when he said he wanted to be with me. He couldn't have. And it's not fair to hold him to that, if he can't—

"I mean, I don't have an amputee fetish, if that's what you're asking," he says. "But I am definitely sexually attracted to you." He shifts his hips as he says this, so I can feel how hard he is.

God, do I feel it.

He still wants me.

My body aches with need, and a whimper escapes my lips. We rub together, and fire races over me. He bends forward and begins to kiss the scar, and I can feel the stubble on his cheek against my intact breast, his lips and tongue moving along the skin where my left breast once was.

And it feels so, so good. So good to be wanted by him, sexually, yes, but this feels like even more than that. I can feel tears start to burn behind my eyes, and I bend to kiss his neck, to be the one getting to taste *his* skin. He whispers my name, sending chills down my body.

He pulls back, looking into my face, our eyes locking.

"You're beautiful, Ally," he says, his eyes trailing down to take in the part of my body I was most afraid of being exposed, and then back up. "So beautiful."

I can't help it—as much as I love hearing those words from him, there's still this fist that squeezes around my heart, and I close my eyes. "Not as beautiful as I was when I was whole," I say, barely above a whisper.

I hate that, deep down, I think that. But if I'm showing my scars, I might as well show the inner ones, too.

"It doesn't matter," he says. "Really, it doesn't."

I want to believe him. And yes, I can feel that he still wants me. But compared to the bodies of other girls, compared to the body I used to have, that yeah, he never saw, but can surely imagine . . .

"How can it not?" I ask.

He doesn't answer immediately. He blinks and pulls in a breath, like he himself is surprised.

"Because I'm falling for you," he says.

My breath catches. My head spins, thrilled and disbelieving.

He closes the gap between us, kissing me again. Gently at first and then faster, harder. I feel my body clamp around his, wanting him tighter against me, even closer as I'm swept over by that same feeling I've had with every kiss we've shared—this desperate longing for more, but also this feeling that somehow, inexplicably, it is already more, him and me.

I can hardly breathe, but I feel like I'm floating, like I don't need air or anything besides to be in his arms. His hands travel up and down my chest, on both sides, and I suddenly can't stand not having his skin against mine. I lift his shirt up over his head, and I press my chest to his as we devour each other. There is no velvet in the world that feels better against my fingertips than his hair, no satin or silk that feels more right against my skin than his.

When the kiss breaks, we hold each other, breathless.

"I'm okay going further," I say.

More than okay. It's all I can do to not start stripping off all the rest of our clothes right now.

Shane's expression freezes, and there's something in it like fear.

"I can't," he says, with a little shake of his head.

It's dumb, I know, but the insecurity floods back, and I find myself covering my chest with my arm.

"It's not that," he says hurriedly. "It's not about you at all."

I swallow past a lump in my throat, desperate to believe that. But what else could it—

"I can't spend the night with anyone," he says, cringing as he speaks. "Because I have nightmares."

My body relaxes, though I'm ashamed at the relief I feel, given how awful that must be for him. And if him wanting to be my boyfriend wasn't enough to convince me he's in this for more than a green-room quickie, the thought that he automatically assumes sex with me includes staying overnight would certainly clinch it. I lay my head on his shoulder and rest my hand on his chest. I can feel his heart beating fast under my palm. "From the accident," I say.

He nods. "I try to sleep as little as possible, but . . . it isn't pretty."

God, I can't imagine having to relive that accident over and over. His best friend's death. The terror, the loss. I had nightmares for a while after chemo and still very occasionally do. My doctor walking in with that look on her face. The pen tapping nervously on a clipboard. The drip of the IVs and beep of machines and smell of antiseptic.

I understand, even as I wish I could take those nightmares away from him. "And it would be too hard to have someone there," I say.

"I wouldn't want to keep you up."

I shrug; that's the last thing I'd worry about. "I sleep like the dead," I say, which is true. My family always teased me about this; once there was a fire at a house down the street from us in the middle of the night. Fire trucks came, sirens wailing, and the rest of my family was up and watching from our front porch. Not me, though. I slept right through the whole thing.

But I don't want it to seem like I'm forcing myself on him, especially given how fast this has all been moving. "I understand if you need your space, though," I say quickly. "I wouldn't have to stay over."

He hesitates. "I think it would be unbearable to be with you like that and then let you go."

Warmth fills me, and I snuggle closer. "I'd be happy to stay." I smile. "Though if you're going to wake me up with nightmares, I'm going to go home first and get a change of clothes and my retainer."

He smiles. "Your retainer?"

"Yeah. It seems like we're skipping the part where we try to impress each other and jumping straight to being real." It's funny how happy the idea makes me. Earlier today I was so panicked about him seeing the real me that I tried to set him up with *my sister*, and now I'm planning to show off my dental gear.

"I like the sound of that," he says, and the way his arms tighten around me, I think he really does. "But it also scares the hell out of me."

"I think that's something of a theme with us." God, there's an *us*. It's thrilling and terrifying all at the same time.

"You're going to see stuff nobody else sees," he says. "I want you to, but I'm afraid you won't be able to handle it."

I nuzzle my nose against the soft skin of his neck. "I'm enjoying learning all your layers." Though I say it lightly, I hope he knows how deeply I mean that. How much it means to me that he's willing to let me see.

"What happens when you reach the last ones?" He says this lightly too, but I can hear the fear in the words.

I sit up and wrap my arms around his neck, looking him directly in those gorgeous blue eyes, and I'm completely serious. "Then I think I'll probably have fallen for you."

The truth is, at the rate things are going, I'll have fallen long before then. I'm about to say that part, but he blinks and his gaze shifts to something over my shoulder, his expression turning . . . annoyed?

I stiffen, afraid for a second that someone got in the room even though I know I locked the door, but when I glance over my shoulder, there's nothing there. Now that I think about it, I've seen him do that before—look over abruptly at nothing.

"What's wrong?" I ask, looking back at Shane.

"Nothing," he says, his voice a little tight. "Just thinking."

"Oh. Okay." I don't know what to make of the lack of his reaction to my words about having fallen for him, and I know even less when he suddenly starts talking again.

"Hey, my agent Parker called earlier. He wants me to go to this benefit for refugees tomorrow night. He's kind of obsessed with the idea of me not disappearing off the public radar."

I try to swallow my disappointment at the subject change.

"I think you deserve to disappear a little, after what you went through," I say.

"Yeah, well. Tell that to Parker. He's all over me to figure out the next step in my career."

His hands are still stroking at my back, and I relax into him again. "What are you going to do?" I ask. "Are you going to go solo or try to join another band?"

"That's the million dollar question. Like, literally, I think I could make a bundle off the interview privileges." He pauses there, his lips pressed tightly together, and I can tell that's another subject that's hard for him. I don't blame him for that.

"You don't have to talk about it if you don't want to."

"The truth is, I don't know. I don't want to go solo, and the idea of joining a band without JT and Kevin . . ." There's a flicker of pain in his eyes, and he shakes his head. "I'm not exactly a team player, and I'm not sure anyone's going to want to put up with me or me with them."

"What do you want to do next?"

He doesn't pause; it's clear he doesn't need to. "I want it to be like it was. But it's not going to be, and I'm the lucky one who has all this potential that everyone's bugging me about wasting." He shrugs. "Which is fair, I guess."

I don't know that it is, not totally.

"Well, I don't think you owe any of them anything." I trace the curve of his bicep.

"Maybe not. But my agent is going to give up on me if I don't show some kind of initiative soon. I can at least show up at this benefit, preferably with a gorgeous girl on my arm." He gives me a pointed look, and I smile.

"I'm sure Shane Beckstrom has no shortage of gorgeous girls who'd love to go with him."

"Maybe," he says, running his fingers through the ends of my hair, letting them slip down my bare shoulder. "But there's only one girl I want."

The giddiness is back. The only one he wants, even now, even as I am, though he could have pretty much anyone.

"Will you go with me?" he asks.

I don't even bother pretending to consider. It's not like there's any point in hiding from the public that he's my boyfriend now, with it all over the internet—thanks, girls—and really, I don't want to. And though I'm generally not a big fan of these kinds of events, which even in the music industry are often surprisingly stodgy and, less surprisingly, full of status-obsessed sycophants, going with Shane sounds like, well . . . fun.

Besides, I have lots of non-sycophant friends in the music business who I'd like to see again.

"Sure," I say. "What's the dress code?" I'm a designer, and they all know it. If I'm going, I'm doing so in style.

"Nice," he says. "But I usually dress down. I can get away with that because I'm in punk."

I bet he can. And because a general "I'm famous enough I don't need to give a rat's ass what you think of me" attitude goes a long way at these things.

But it's not like I don't have plenty of options for him back at home. "If you want to dress up, I bet I have something you could wear."

To which he raises an eyebrow, and I laugh.

"I don't mean my clothes. Hot as *that* would be, I doubt you'd fit in them. I have plenty of costumes from bands I've worked for."

His eyes gleam. "Please tell me you have that monstrous shirt that Felix Mays wore at the VMAs. I'm pretty sure I could pull that off."

Oh my god. The thought of him wearing that shirt—especially among that group, who would recognize it very well—fills me with all kinds of delight.

"I do! And yes, you absolutely can. We'll get that while we're stopping by my place." I pause, thinking of him in my apartment. Nix caught me in the dressing room earlier to tell me that she was vacating my apartment and staying with a friend for the next few days, with a not-so-subtle implication that she's hoping I use this generous gesture of hers. Which I certainly plan on doing. Immediately.

And while I think the assumption was that I was going to his place, I'm not sure I want to wait long enough to get there.

"Or," I say slowly, "you could stay over. If you don't need to go home."

His lips pull up into that devastating smile of his. "That sounds nice, actually." His hands shift down to my ass, and he scoots me closer, and I'm finding it all kinds of hard to breathe again. "I'd like to see your apartment," he says. "Particularly the ceiling above your bed."

I laugh, but the image of us naked, of him lying back on the bed and me on top of him, blazes through my mind and from there my whole body. I feel my fingers tighten on his shoulders, my nails digging into his skin, and he lets out a shaky breath.

"Do you think we're going to make it there?" I ask.

"I think I can control myself until we get to your house," he murmurs, but his lips begin moving along my jaw, and I close my eyes.

"Mmm. Maybe I don't want you to."

He pulls back enough to look around the green room, and then his breath is warm against my ear. "Let's get out of here," he whispers. "I want to take my time with you."

A delicious shiver runs through me. I press my forehead against his. "I like the sound of that."

While I know the fear is still there—fear of too much too

soon, fear of whether this is as real to him as to me and, if it is, whether it will stay that way—the desire and this happiness of being with him are so much stronger right now.

I've lived too much of these last few years in fear; I'm not about to let it keep me from him.

TWELVE

Shane

Allison opens her apartment for me and then starts tidying up. She doesn't need to—her place is pretty clean except for fabric and costume pieces and endless sketches of all sizes strewn and hung all over various surfaces. What's supposed to be a large, formal dining room is taken over by a sewing machine and a large drafting table and cubby shelves full of various kinds of fabric. The furniture in the living room is all bold colors, funky and classy at the same time.

"This is definitely you," I say.

Allison smiles at me. "You like it?"

I nod and put my hands in my pockets. With a different girl I would have been on her the moment we walked in the door. No need for preamble. But my nerves have only gotten worse on the drive here, and Allison's grown quiet, which I think means she feels the same.

"Come on," she says. "I'll give you the tour. "

By this she means show me back to her bedroom, with a brief gesture at the kitchen. The colors at the back of the apartment are softer, and her walls are painted a sage green. A lot of the furniture is soft gray, with funky accents like an abstract painting with brilliant blues and purples and a single streak of silver. She slips into her bedroom and picks some laundry off the floor, then reaches to sweep some bras and prosthetics off the nightstand.

"You don't have to do that," I say. "I thought we were going with real."

Allison hesitates and nods. "That's right."

I walk up behind her. She has a walk-in closet with an enormous mirror on the wall right outside it. I wrap my arms around her, holding her against me, and in the mirror, I can see her expression soften.

She feels tense in my arms, and I'm not sure how much is anticipation and how much is fear. I've got a cocktail of both running through my own veins, and I realize I have no frame of reference for this. The last time I had sex with a girlfriend I was nineteen years old, and I sure as hell don't want this relationship to go the way that one did.

"You okay?" I ask.

She nods. "Nervous."

I smile. "If we're being honest about that, so am I."

"Really? I'm pretty sure you have a whole lot more experience than me."

She says that with an edge to her voice, and I close my eyes.

"I mean," she adds, "it's not that I don't have experience. I definitely do. And I've had casual sex, even. With guys I just met, occasionally. So it's not that I don't know what I'm doing."

"Noted," I say, and she wilts against me.

"I'm making this weird."

"No." I'm afraid it's me, the mess that I am, the things that I've done. But that isn't all. "Feeling about you the way I do, not wanting to mess it up—that's what's making this weird."

She turns around and looks up at me, reaches over and switches off the bedroom light and then slides my sunglasses off my face. It's still daylight outside, and soft white light filters in through the curtains. I look down at her, transfixed. My whole body feels like it's holding its breath, waiting to fall into her.

Then she rocks up on her toes and kisses me. Softly at first, then harder and harder. I lift her up into my arms, and her legs wrap around my waist, and we're floating in midair, suspended in this delirious fog of passion and desire. My body craves hers, but the longing goes deeper, right into my core, and I realize all at once that I'm not falling. I've already fallen right into the middle of this with her, and I'm not sure exactly when it happened but she's the very center of my being now, and I don't know how to separate my need for her from my need for air.

I turn and fall back on the bed, Allison still in my arms, riding up on top of me and sending tendrils of heat through my body. Her hands grip my shoulders as we grind together, the heat scorching even through our clothes.

And then her hands are reaching for my fly, and mine are sliding up her skirt and pulling down her underwear. She lies on top of me, both of us breathing heavy as our hands explore, flinching and gasping at the lightest of touches, the most sensitive places. We're gentle and careful, both holding back from escalating toward the heights our bodies desperately want to climb. I think she wants this to last as much as I do, to savor every moment of this first time together, which feels newer and more frightening than even my first time.

My heart pounds against hers, and I can't stand it any longer. I want to be inside her, but I also want the rest of our clothes out of the way. I sit up beneath her, and her legs clinch around my waist, our bodies rubbing together slowly, softly, as I unzip her dress again and take off her bra. Allison shimmies out of her dress and pulls my shirt up over my head, and there she is, naked in my lap, like one of those nude sculptures of goddesses all wracked with desire. I lean back, peeling her off me, taking her in with my eyes, and Allison whimpers softly.

I bring my eyes up to hers. "Am I making you uncomfortable?"

Her voice is as breathless as mine. "No. I was so afraid no one would ever look at me like that again."

I smile and let my eyes travel the length of her again. I run my hands up the insides of her thighs, flexing so that she rocks against me again and again. Allison's head rolls back and she moans softly, the corners of her eyes crinkling. She pulls her body close against mine again, and I'm lost in the pleasure of her skin against mine, her hands in my hair. And all at once I understand what she means about trust and vulnerability. I've had sex with a hundred groupies and as many random girls I met at clubs or shows, and none of them compared to this, to the mounting power of being with a woman I want to hold after, a woman I can't stand the thought of ever letting go.

I lie back on the bed again and pull away from her so we're lying side by side, catching our breath. "What I meant by the experience thing," she whispers, "is that you must have a pretty good idea what you like, yeah?"

I run my hands up into her hair, holding her face in my palms. "Yes. I have a *really* good idea of what I like." I kiss her deeply, hoping to drive my point home, but when we break apart, she still looks concerned.

"My past experience," I whisper, "does it bother you?"

She reaches down and pulls off my pants, which I'm pretty sure is an excuse not to answer immediately. We lie in bed, entirely exposed to each other, and I run my hand up and down the outside of her thigh, waiting.

"Yes and no," she says finally. She slides up against me so I'm hard against the soft skin of her stomach. "What's in the past doesn't bother me, but I guess it feels like a lot to measure up to."

I was afraid that's what she was thinking. I run my hand down her arm and bring her wrist to my mouth, brushing my tongue and teeth against it. "Ally," I say, "you have nothing to worry about."

"You've just been with a lot of girls with perfect bodies," she says, her voice breaking as I work on the inside of her wrist.

"Maybe," I say, "but if I could have any girl in the world here with me like this, if I could snap my fingers and make it happen, I'd choose you. Every time. *Every* time."

Allison rolls over on top of me, kissing me deeply and desperately. We're locked in this frantic embrace, and I feel beads of sweat forming on my forehead, on my arms, on my back, and our bodies slide against each other like we were made to fit. This deep-down ache spreads through me as my body demands to be inside her, encompassed by her, swallowed up entirely in my siren, my muse. Allison's legs spread, and she reaches over to her nightstand, I'm guessing for a condom.

Deep in my heart, something turns to ice. I choke on my own breath, sitting up, pulling away from her, leaning against the headboard. Allison's hand pauses, halfway out of the drawer with the square wrapper. Her eyes are wide and vulnerable.

"Shane?" she says.

I shake my head. I want her, god, I want her so bad, and JT seems to be keeping his bargain and staying where he can't see us, so I should be able to do this, but—

"I have to tell you something," I say, not even sure what it is yet, just certain that if I don't recognize my fears, I'm not going to be able to follow through.

Allison looks terrified, and I pull her into my arms again, holding her around the waist, still against my body. "I know this isn't fair, and I know you can't know what you're going to want, or what's going to happen. But I'm a mess, Ally. I'm such a mess, and I cannot handle being left by you right now. I don't have any right to demand anything of you, but after everything else—" My voice cracks and I pause until I'm sure I can speak again. "I can't do this and then lose you. Not right now. Not when everyone else has already left me."

Allison's fingers trail up my neck. "Shane. Have I given you any indication that I'm leaving?"

I bite my lip. Half the world has seen me naked, but I don't think anyone has ever seen me this exposed. "I need you," I say.

Allison smiles. "I need you, too."

Something inside of me shatters apart. No more hesitation. I pull her against my chest and roll over on top of her, kissing her desperately. In that moment, she's everything to me, and I reach up and take the condom from her and roll it on. We kiss, our tongues slipping back and forth as I slide inside her, tight enough to see stars, and we rock back and forth, our voices blending into each other like instruments in tune. Being with her is like the moment that the pieces of a song—the words and the melody and that ethereal thing I'm trying to say but can't quite pin down—all snap together, and suddenly it's good, and it works, and I can't imagine it any other way. I reach one hand under her hip, resting it on the small of her back and lifting her off the bed, joining with her in a rhythm all our own. She calls my name, and there's an urgency to it.

But I'm not ready yet for this first time to end. I drop to my elbows on the bed, supporting myself on top of her. I run one hand under her chin and kiss her gently, slowing our pace. "Trust me?" I ask her.

She nods.

I smile and pull out of her, lying next to her on the bed again and pulling her into my arms. Neither of us is finished, and she whimpers softly and reaches down, like she's checking to make sure I'm not done.

"Is this working for you?" she asks. "I mean, it's good for you, right?"

That is not even a problem. "God, yes, it's good. You can't tell?"

"Mmmm," Allison says. "I thought so, but—"

"Trust me," I say again. "Let me know when you're getting close." I climb on top of her, slipping back in where I belong. Our ardor soars to new heights, and I call out her name and she responds with mine. I was taught this method years ago by a girl who said it was the only way she'd ever been able to finish—walking right up to the edge and then backing off, rolling passion forward like waves, cresting and breaking. I liked it well enough then, but since then I'd generally regarded it as too much work for the return.

But with Allison I want to return again and again. We work up again, until we're not only floating but hovering somewhere above the clouds. Her cries grow urgent again, and her fingers dig deep into my back. "Oh, god," she says. "I'm getting close."

I kiss her deeply and pull out again, rolling onto my back and pulling her with me. She lands on top of me, her fingers digging into my hair, tugging just the right amount. I ache against her, and I'm sure this is the last time I can bear to stop.

"God, that's good," she says, her voice raw, and I murmur my agreement. I'm holding back still, holding on to everything I want to pour into her. It won't be long now.

Allison lays her head on my chest. "Tell me it means something," she whispers. "I know you said sex means something different to you than it does to me, and that's fine, but tell me it isn't just physical."

I lift her chin, drawing her back to me. "This means everything to me. I get it now, what you mean about trust. About being vulnerable. I need you, in more ways than one."

I think I see tears gleaming in the corners of her eyes, and she spreads her legs again, squeezing me between her thighs. "I don't want to be some stopgap," she says. "I don't want to be someone you need right now and then move on from when you go back to your normal life."

"You're not," I tell her. "I've needed you for years. Maybe always. I just didn't know it."

One tear slides down her cheek, and then she shifts on top of me, sliding me inside her again, and we're moving with a fever I've never felt. My vision blurs, and the fever spikes, and we both scream out together and collapse in a tangle of fears and hopes and desperation. Our mouths find each other and we kiss and kiss as our hands tremble against skin and our bodies gasp for breath.

I love her, I realize. I love her.

I'll never be the same again.

THIRTEEN

Shane

We order food in and stay in bed for hours afterward, talking and laughing and holding each other. When Allison goes to answer the door for the delivery guy, she pulls on my shirt, and I shake my head at her. "You're going to get photographed answering the door in that. The press has had enough time to figure out where you live and stake out your apartment."

Allison smiles. "Would you rather answer the door in *my* shirt?"

"I might be religiously opposed to you putting on clothes," I say. "But my shirt looks hot on you, so I say go for it. As long as you're cool with being on TMZ tomorrow standing in your doorway wearing that shirt and holding a wad of cash."

"We paid on the website," she says. "Tip included. Which you'd know, if you were paying attention. I put it on your card."

I grin at her and stretch out in bed. The truth is, I like the idea of her being in the news wearing my clothes. It probably makes me a territorial jerk, but I want everyone in the world to know she's with me. She pulls on a pair of jeans to go get the door and comes back with containers of Chinese food that didn't come from the place down the street from me, which makes it all kinds of new and interesting compared to my general diet over the last few months.

Good thing I've been spending the sizable portion of the night I'm awake working out on my gym equipment. I think I'm actually in better shape now than I was before the accident. Spending all your hours—waking or not—feeling trapped is some powerful motivation to keep your body moving.

"So," Allison says, handing me a fork and a container of mushroom chicken, "speaking of the press, have they been harassing you to talk about the accident?"

As much as I don't love talking about the accident, I'm also not ready to unpack everything that just happened between us. I'm feeling things I'm afraid to say, all of which scare me more than telling her about the way I've been avoiding the press.

Besides, she's Googled me, so she knows I haven't been talking about it. I swear reporters can write more about what I *haven't* said than would fit in any interview I could possibly give them. "Yeah. I hate it, but it's my own fault. I was always kind of a media whore before, so they feel entitled to know what's going on. And I haven't given them anything."

"Is it that you don't want to talk about what happened to JT?"

I don't want to talk about him standing next to my girlfriend's bed and sticking a finger in her honey shrimp. "Yeah. Mostly, though, they want to know what I'm going to do now. The truth is, I don't know."

Allison nods and slides off her jeans, then climbs in bed next to me still wearing my shirt. I put an arm around her and eat my chicken one-handed. "Right," Allison says. "And you don't want to go solo or join another band. Do you have any ideas what you do want to do?"

I shrug. "Music is the only thing I know."

"Have you thought about taking a less public role? Being a manager? Or an agent?"

"Yeah," I say. "But I don't really want to have to advise jerks like me, you know? I'm really bad at shutting up and doing what other people want, and I'm even worse at not telling people when they're being complete idiots."

"I don't know," Allison says. "A lot of the managers I've worked with are happy to tell people when they're being complete idiots."

"Yeah, well, I think it would drive me nuts."

Allison nods. "So you don't have any ideas?"

"I don't know. I've mostly been sitting at home, so busy *not* writing that album my agent thinks I'm working on that I haven't had a lot of time to put thought into it."

That makes no damn sense, but it's true all the same, and Allison doesn't call me on it. "Do you feel like maybe you don't want to move on? Like if you decide what you're going to do next, it's a betrayal of JT?"

JT licks his fingers. "Dude, I don't care if you move on."

"I think it's even dumber than that," I say. "I think it feels like giving up. Like if I don't admit that my life is over, maybe it won't be."

"That part of your life, anyway," Allison says, and I run my fingers up under the hem of her shirt.

"Yeah, okay," I say. "That part of my life."

She snuggles up against me, and JT wanders off down the hall.

"I used to think it would be cool to own a nightclub," I say. "To be in charge of the atmosphere and the community and the curation of shows, you know? I wouldn't really want to do it, because the idea of dealing with staffing and zoning and liquor licensing is kind of a nightmare, plus I don't like the idea of being trapped in one place all the time." I roll my eyes. "I know. I sound like a total asshole, right? Most people are stuck in one place dealing with all kinds of crap for their jobs. But I'm spoiled."

"I don't know. I'm just as spoiled as you are."

"So you get it?"

"I do," she says. "I just wonder if there isn't something that would involve the parts of owning a club that sound good to you, but not the bad parts. Like, event management for a venue?

With your connections you could probably start somewhere pretty big."

I chew a bite of chicken, considering. "I'd be stuck in one place, still. And I'd probably end up dealing with a lot of details I don't want to be in charge of." I pause. "But there was this thing I used to talk about doing with Kevin and JT. We wanted to sponsor a music festival."

Allison looks up at me. "Yeah?"

"Yeah," I say. "I had this idea for a whole series of festivals, actually, but we figured we'd never have time for it. I thought it would be awesome to pull in a bunch of headliners, with the requirement that they have to do something novel, something people can't see anywhere else. It could be a new song that's not on any of their albums, or a cover that their fans have been dying for, or swap out with the singer or guitarist from another band. So the big draw for the festival is you have all these bands doing stuff you can't see otherwise, and then you also get a bunch of new bands who haven't gotten the attention they deserve yet, you know? We'd be sort of paying it forward to the people who haven't made it yet, and we'd get to direct people's attention to bands we think they should know about, people who ought to be getting more press than they are."

"Clearly that is what you should be doing."

"Eh," I say, spearing a mushroom with my fork. "I don't know."

"You should. Because that's the most excited I've seen you about anything. You barely even stopped talking about it to breathe."

I smile, running my hand under her ass. "The most excited you've seen me, huh?"

She swats at me. "About your *career*."

"It would be a hell of a lot of work. There's a lot of stuff I wouldn't want to deal with. Like finding a venue and getting permits and all of that. I'd want to do the part where I pull strings and use my connections and get bands to play, and the legwork finding new bands to showcase, but a lot of the rest of it—"

"You'd hire someone for the rest," Allison says.

"Okaaaaay," I say. "But that's going to be a huge undertaking. It would cost a shit-ton of money upfront, and then it might fail. So yeah, I could probably bankroll it, or take out loans, but if people don't come or if something goes wrong, I could lose everything."

"That's why you get investors," Allison says. "With your name alone you could get people to invest, even more so if you made some phone calls and got people you know to agree to attach their names to it too."

That's something I've never thought of. "Investors, huh?"

"Yeah. There are people who pretty much just do that. They have a lot of money, and they're always looking for endeavors to invest in. If it pans out, you have to pay them a cut, but there's less risk up front. That's what I did with my fashion line."

I look at her. "You know how to do this."

"Yep," she says. "I can help you with that. I know how to put together a kick-ass professional presentation that got even my most skittish investors on board. You could totally do this."

I'm quiet for a moment, thinking about whether or not that's something I'd want to do, if it were possible. It was always a thing Kevin and JT and I had talked about doing someday, when we weren't touring or writing the next album. We might have put together one of these events, or headlined it and used our name and had someone else put it together for us.

"I always thought it would be cool to have a whole series," I say. "Different festivals around the nation. That would be a full-time gig."

"It would," Allison says. "It'd involve a lot of travel."

"Yeah, it would. Not just going to the events, but going to see bands, networking, finding new music and bringing big names on board." I look at her. "Would you be cool with that?"

Allison looks startled. "With you traveling?"

Oh, god. I shouldn't have said that. I've suggested that she needs to be okay with what I'm doing in the future, which is suggesting that we're going to have a future, which, yeah, I want, and she did offer to help me with the project, but—

"I'd be fine with that," she says. "I have to work a lot, but the fashion design work I can do from anywhere, so sometimes I could come with you." She squirms slightly. "If you wanted."

"That would be awesome." A part of it still sounds lonely to me, the hazard of having worked my entire adult life alongside my two best friends in the world. "I don't love the idea of being in charge of something like that all by myself, though. I'd rather have someone work with me. Share the decision making, you know?"

"I'd help you," Allison says.

"Which I appreciate," I tell her. "But you've got your own fashion line to work on, plus the pageant stuff, plus costuming, so . . ."

"Fair point. But I do have a lot of connections to bands."

"Which I will exploit, trust me," I say.

"And I'm always happy to offer an opinion."

I laugh. "Yeah, that's the truth."

She elbows me and I bend down and kiss her shoulder. "I wonder if Kevin would be interested in something like that."

"You should ask him," Allison says.

I shrug. "I don't know. I've badgered him so much about coming back to the band that I think he's kind of done with me. He's moving to Denver, and he's got his own thing going on."

"Does he have a job?" Allison asks. "Because he could probably work with you from Denver."

I hate this idea. I know it's an asshole thing to feel, but I don't want Kevin to move away. I don't want him to move on and leave me behind, but it's already happened. It's already done. "I don't think I could ask him. I don't think I could stand it if he said no."

Allison is quiet, and I know she thinks that's the wrong call, but I can't imagine saying those words to him, not right now. If he told me he wanted nothing to do with it . . . I can't take any more rejection.

"You can think about it," Allison says.

"I will. You really think I could do something like that?"

"I think you'd be great at it."

I set the empty carton of chicken on the nightstand and burrow down under the covers, my arms sliding up Allison's body under the shirt. She murmurs softly and sets her food aside too, slipping down into my arms.

"You don't sleep," she says, "so what do you do? Watch TV? Play video games?"

"Yeah," I say. "Exercise. Listen to music, sometimes. Lie in bed and try not to sleep. Probably tonight mostly that one."

"Mmm," she says. "I'm definitely going to sleep. But if that doesn't bother you, I'd love for you to stay here."

I pull her closer. "I'd love that. Are you a cuddly sleeper?"

"I might be. Is that okay?"

Nothing sounds better. "Definitely. But I can't promise I won't grope you a little."

Allison laughs. "Go right ahead. I give you pre-consent to grope me. I will probably not wake up, and I can fall asleep in minutes, so . . . sorry about that."

I rub my face against her cheek. "It's okay. I'm just happy to be here. I'm probably going to wake you up with my nightmares, so I'm the one who should be sorry."

"Maybe having someone to cuddle with will help."

I truly hope she's right.

FOURTEEN

Shane

It's bright where I am, so much so that my eyes can't adjust to the light. I squint against it, trying and trying to see, but the more I look, the more stars scatter across my vision. I'm cramped in a tight space, and my legs are aching, and my head feels thick, like I'm starting to get high.

Someone is screaming, outside in the light, and her shadow passes between me and its source so that the light blinks and then intensifies. My hands are slick with something hot and sticky, and I know what it is and where it came from. I can smell blood and burned rubber, and if I crane my head right, I can almost see Kevin pinned by the metal of the roof. He's not moving. No one is moving. Time seems to have stopped, except for the screaming.

"Shane!" the woman's voice screams. "Shane!"

I blink against the light. There's a thick, pink fluid splattered over the upside-down dash, but I don't turn. I can't turn. I know if I do, he'll be there, his head bashed in by the roof of the car when it rolled.

"It's over," I hear JT saying. "It's over, it's over, it's all over."

The woman's voice is wailing now. It's Allison, and she's crying, and I'm sure that she's stuck somewhere, too, she's pinned and scared and bleeding. I find the door handle with my sticky fingers and yank on it, but the light is bright, and I can't see, and the door won't open.

"Shane!"

I jolt up in bed, my whole body drenched in sweat. I'm shaking, and for a moment I don't know where I am.

"Shane." It's Allison's voice again, but she's not screaming now. She's next to me, and her arms encircle my waist. She holds on to me as I struggle to breathe. "Shane. It's okay."

It's not okay. It's not even close to okay. "I'm sorry," I say. "I woke you. I told you that you didn't want me to sleep over."

"Um, no," she says. "I'm glad you're here. You've been doing this alone every night?"

"Pretty much." I shake my head, and a tremor runs through me. My body feels cold.

"Is my being here better or worse?"

I want to say neither, but my heart is slowing now, and I'm catching my breath. I run a hand through my hair, pushing back beads of sweat. "Better. I mean, the dream was bad, but right now, this is better."

Allison pulls me down next to her and wraps her whole body around me. She's still wearing my shirt, and I bury my face in her shoulder, holding her tight.

"I'm sorry this is happening," she says. "Do you want to talk about it?"

My chest tightens. "No."

"Did you get even a little sleep?"

I look over at the clock. "Yeah. A couple hours, I think."

"Did you get some groping in?"

I laugh. "Yes, I did. You didn't notice?"

"Mmmm," Allison says. "I had really good dreams."

"I bet."

"I'd share mine with you if I could. Dream Shane is really good in bed."

Ha. "Better than real Shane?"

"Nah," Allison says. "No one has anything on real Shane."

As I come down from the nightmare, I'm becoming more aware of her, of the way she's wrapped around me. My body is responding to her touch, and I bring my face up to hers and kiss her desperately.

She moans against my lips, and moments later she's reaching for another condom. Her touch awakens every sensitive nerve in my body, and then we're moving together and I'm lost inside her, burrowing into the shelter of her arms. Holding her after, I feel safe and calm for the first time in as long as I can remember. I love her and this and us so deeply and desperately that I don't know what to do with myself.

Allison stretches and wraps her arm around my shoulders, resting her head on my chest. "Yeah," she says. "*Really* glad you spent the night."

"Me, too. Thanks for putting up with me."

"Ha. Is that what you think I'm doing?"

I kiss her gently on the mouth. "Okay, maybe you seem like you're enjoying yourself a little."

"A *little*." She pokes me in the side. "Seriously, though, are the dreams about the accident?"

"Yeah," I say. "Being trapped in the car. We were in there for almost an hour."

"Are you serious?"

"They had to pry the car apart to get us out."

"And you thought both your friends were dead the whole time?"

"Yeah." I hesitate. I've never told anyone this part. "I thought I might be dead, too. I thought maybe that's what happens when you die. You feel like you're locked inside your body, and you're trying to move, and you can't."

"You couldn't move at all?"

"Not much. I thought for sure I was dead or paralyzed, but it was just the shock. I heard later that I kept kicking the dash, like I was trying to get out, but at the time it felt like everything was still. Weirdly quiet. Except when people outside started yelling. And the one guy who was like, 'Oh my god, that's Shane Beckstrom.'"

Allison grimaces. "And Kevin was unconscious?"

"Yeah. He started groaning when they moved him, and that's how I knew he was alive."

"But JT died on impact?"

I nod. "I saw what happened to his body. Trust me. No one could survive that."

Allison holds me tighter, and she doesn't ask for details, which I appreciate. What she says next surprises me.

"Where do you think JT is now?"

I almost tell her I'm pretty sure he's kicking it on her couch complaining about how he can't hold a controller and I'm too busy getting laid to play video games to entertain him.

But I catch myself in time. That's not what she means.

"You mean, like, do I believe in God?"

"Sure," she says. "Life after death in general."

"I used to believe in God," I say. "Not in any particular religion, but in God and an afterlife."

"But not anymore?"

"No. Not since Kevin killed him."

Allison looks incredulous. "Kevin killed God?"

"Yeah. I wrote this song once about my relationship with him. God, I mean, not Kevin. About feeling like I could never measure up, never please this disapproving absent father figure. When I played it for the band, Kevin was all, 'That's not about God. It's about your dad.'"

"You think he was right?"

"Hell yes, he was. So I tore up the lyrics and decided that nothing about my belief in God had anything to do with actual spirituality. It was just me projecting deity onto my father's shit, and that wasn't helping anybody. So that's when Kevin killed God."

"I believe in God," Allison says. "I may not be the best Catholic around, and I don't go to church as often as my parents would like, but I find God there."

"At church?" I wouldn't have expected that about her; she seems too practical to bother with religion. But then, she's also clearly got layers.

"Yeah. Have you ever been?"

"Not to a Catholic church. Kevin's mom dragged me to her Baptist church a couple times. The only part I liked was the band."

"The music is different at mass, but I like it. My family is pretty hardcore about it, actually. One of my brothers is thinking about becoming a priest."

"Wow," I say. "That's intense."

"Yeah. I'm less intense about it, but I like the ritual of the service. I prefer it in Latin, actually, because then it's just the ritual. It's one of the places I feel like I find God."

I shake my head. "I'd like to believe again. It would be nice to think that JT won't just disappear. That his spirit will be up there hitting on angels and trying to look up the Virgin Mary's skirt."

Allison laughs. "Yes. I'm sure that's exactly where he is."

I'm not, but it doesn't bother me like it probably should. It doesn't make a difference if I believe or not. Either an afterlife exists, or it doesn't. Wishing won't make it so, and refusing to hope in it won't make it disappear.

I can't bring myself to believe that I have that kind of power.

FIFTEEN

Allison

I should be exhausted, sitting here in the auditorium, watching the choreographer work with the girls on one of the dance numbers. Not just because of waking up to Shane's nightmare—which I can tell he's still self-conscious about, even though I was happy I was able to be there for him. But also with how late we stayed up before that, talking and laughing and holding each other. How early we were both up this morning, like we instinctively wanted as few hours away from each other, even just in sleep, as possible.

And don't even get me started on the sheer breathtaking physicality of making love with him, over and over and over. Sex that is more all-consuming, more emotionally fulfilling, than it's ever been before. Not to mention earth-shattering—no wonder I could barely keep my hands off him.

After all that, I should be exhausted, but I'm not. I'm wide awake, smiling, riding this giddy high.

The doors to the auditorium open, and Shane walks in wearing his sunglasses and holding two to-go cups of coffee. He grins over at me, and now I want to be riding something else this morning.

Again.

"Hey," he says, taking a seat next to me.

I make a big show of looking at the time on my phone. "Did this thing break? Because I swear it's telling me that you're only fifteen minutes late."

He hands me one of the coffees. "Might have actually been on time if I didn't stop for these."

I breathe it in; I might not need the caffeine as much as I'd have thought this morning, but it smells heavenly. "Totally worth it."

We catch each other's eyes—or as much as I can see through his sunglasses—and I think he might be having as much trouble holding back a dopey smile today as I am.

"And it's all good," I continue, "because their dance practice is running a little long."

"That's not keeping Carlyle from looking like he wants to kill me." Shane tips his head toward where Carlyle is, in fact, glaring over here.

"Well, if *he* was the one you were bringing post-sex coffee to, he might not be so mad," I say, nudging him.

"I'll keep that in mind for tomorrow."

I stifle a laugh, and Carlyle glares harder at us, even though I'm sure he can't hear us over the girl-power pop song and the barked orders of the choreographer.

We drink our coffees and hold hands, and it feels so simple and right just sitting like this with him, so purely happy. It feels like . . .

I stop myself before I can put any more words to it. There's no need to examine this too thoroughly, not so soon. I told him I'm not going anywhere, and I mean it. But there's a twinge of fear, quiet this morning but still there, that this is too good, too right.

And Shane and I both know how quickly things can change, how life is never entirely in our control.

I grip Shane's hand tighter, and as if he can read my mind, he grips mine back.

We sit and watch the girls move in tandem—or try to do

so, anyway—around the stage. They're in yoga pants and sports bras rather than their dresses right now, but they are in the heels they'll be wearing the night of the pageant. They're also wearing these big flower headdresses with large wire-enforced orange poppy petals, which on pageant night they will pair with glittering green high-slitted gowns, like they're part of an adult-themed Anne Geddes calendar.

I've worked with the Miss California Poppy pageant for years now, and participated in it for just as many, but this is easily the most literal the theme has ever been taken.

"So," Shane says after a moment. "Sexy flowers? Is that what this is supposed to be?"

"Apparently." I take a drink of my coffee.

"What would the internet call those? FILFs?"

I nearly choke on my coffee with a sudden laugh, and Shane grins at me, clearly very pleased with himself.

"Well, the joke's on you," I say. "Because the script requires you to call them a 'Bouquet of Beauty.'"

"Good god," Shane says with a groan. "*That's* what that line was referring to?"

Now I'm the one grinning, even knowing there's a more than decent chance this line will never actually be spoken. Perhaps *because* of that.

The girls seem to be doing pretty well at picking up the admittedly-uncomplicated moves, but then Becky cuts Gwen off mid-sashay, which causes Gwen to stop and Yvonne—who is beaming out at the audience—to plow right into her, nearly toppling them both over.

I cringe.

Gwen rounds on Becky. "You did that on purpose, you—"

"Time to move on!" Carlyle wisely announces. Perhaps he's also decided that if Shane is actually here, he's going to get some real practice out of him. "Contestant intros in five!"

There's a scramble from the stage as girls flock to the dressing room, and a lesser scramble from the audience seats as the coaches join them—there tend to be more of those that show up the closer we get to the pageant. Carlyle doesn't technically require the contestants to be in their outfits at this point, but we've only got a few more days of practice, and coaches like to make sure their girls can get in and out of their dresses quickly and with as minimal destruction to hair and makeup as possible.

I watch Becky's smug look as she all but skips off the stage, and Gwen's death-glare after her. I should definitely keep an eye on that situation, lest some camellias end up trampled by a marimba.

I reach in my bag and pull out a few pages of script. "Here you go," I say to Shane. "The intros. In case you somehow lost your copy in the green room garbage."

Shane gives me a mock-insulted look. "If I was going to 'lose' the script, it would be in someplace much more deserving. Like one of those industrial shredders." But he takes the pages from me, anyway. My guess is the script is actually still sitting on the green room table, but I'm not taking the chance.

We get up, but we're barely out of our seats when Collette jogs over to us—as much as she can jog in three-inch heels. She's got her flower headdress clutched in her hand, and a nervous expression. I notice Thomas hovering back by the stage, frowning at us. I'm kind of hoping whatever this is gives me an excuse to bar him from future practices.

"Hey, Collette," I say when she reaches us. "What's going on?"

She looks around furtively, as if making sure no one is in hearing distance. Other than Shane, of course, but she doesn't seem to mind him being here, and I can already tell he's too curious to leave unless he's directly told to. Now I'm worried that Thomas actually hurt her, and I might have to kill him rather than just kicking him out of the building.

"I had a vision," Collette says, her blue eyes wide. "Of some bad things that will happen very soon."

Well, I wasn't expecting that. Though with Collette, maybe I should have.

"A vision," I say, trying not to let my skepticism be quite so obvious.

"And I thought you needed to know." She lets out a shaky breath, closing her eyes like she's steadying herself. "One of those bitches is going to get sick before the pageant. And someone else is going to break their nose. Like, in front of everyone. On TV!" She sounds more horrified by that last part than the actual nose-breaking.

I suck my lips inward. "Okay, first of all, calling your fellow contestants 'bitches' isn't something—"

"It wasn't me who said that!" Collette says. "It was Cher!"

I blink. "Cher? Like the singer?"

Collette nods. "She's the one who always appears in my visions."

Next to me, I hear Shane make a little snorting sound like he's trying to stifle a snicker. I very deliberately don't look at him, lest I have to do the same thing.

Collette doesn't seem to notice, her expression so earnestly serious. "I think it's because I was her in a past life."

There's another pause.

"Cher's not dead," Shane points out.

Collette gives him a long-suffering look. "I mean *young* Cher."

"Right," I say, figuring that battle isn't one worth fighting at this moment. "Well, I appreciate you telling me, but I've done a ton of pageants over the years, and I've never seen anyone break their nose—or any of their body parts." A girl did get her hair caught in the trap door of her magic-show wardrobe a couple years ago, and I had to give her a very impromptu onstage haircut, but I decide not to mention that. "But I'll make sure to keep an extra close eye on everything, okay?"

Collette's brow furrows. It's clear that's not what she wants to hear, but she nods again. "Okay. Thanks."

Then something far more worrisome than visions from not-dead singers occurs to me. "You haven't told any of the other girls about this, have you?" Pre-pageant superstition is already a thing, and if they get wind of *this*—

Collette's lips twist and she nervously tucks a strand of her pale blond hair behind her ear.

Shit.

"I didn't mean to," she says. "But I was telling Thomas about it before dance practice, and Simone overheard."

Double shit. If there's one girl in this pageant who is most likely to make sure this particular piece of paranoia reaches every ear, it's Simone.

"Okay," I say, and hope Collette isn't reading my internal cursing on my face. "It's all right. Just—try not to tell anyone else, okay?" The last thing I need is a bunch of beauty contestants terrified of an onstage facial injury.

Though I have a feeling it's too late for that.

Collette nods quickly and jogs back off toward the dressing room. I let out a long sigh.

"Oh my god," I say, rubbing at my forehead.

"On the plus side, Cher didn't say anything about some asshole shredding his emcee script," Shane says dryly, and I give him a look, though I can't help but laugh. Which is always a rare thing this close to the pageant.

I never thought Shane Beckstrom might be the very person who might get me through this with my sanity intact, but I'm finding I don't mind that at all.

SIXTEEN

Shane

Before the benefit gala, Allison actually does dig up the shirt Felix Mays wore to the VMAs. It's bright and sparkly and much more flashy than the stuff I usually wear, but I'm also a rock star with a reputation for not giving a shit what other people think, so I generally assume that I can get away with anything, fashion or otherwise.

At least in this case, Allison agrees with me. I pair it with strategically torn jeans and a pair of beat up black boots. The shirt hung loose on Felix Mays, but it fits me pretty tight. Allison examines all the seams before we leave her place to head to the benefit, making sure that she doesn't need to take a minute to let any of them out.

"All I'm missing is that god-awful cross he wore," I say.

Allison smiles. "Felix kept that, so I don't have it for you." She does, however, produce a loop of thick chain from a box filled with different laces and trims. "But you could try this."

In the end, I decide the chain is too much, and I go without. Allison disappears into her room and comes out wearing a black cocktail dress with layers and layers of sheer black fabric falling from the waist, so it's at once a little black dress and a floor-length one, showing off her legs through the chiffon, but giving her the silhouette of a more traditional gown.

"*Nice*," I say, and Allison smiles at me.

"Yeah?"

"Definitely. I love it." I wrap my arms around her waist and pull her close to me. Her arms brush my bare skin under the open shirt, and I smile. "Is that a surprise? I think you'd look hot in just about anything. And mostly nothing at all."

"We'd get a lot of publicity if I went to the benefit in *that*."

My throat closes up, and I remember why I haven't been going to these things. "There is going to be a lot of press there," I say. "Outside and inside."

"We're Facebook official. Plus, I probably got photographed in your shirt last night. So I think we're past worrying about that."

That's not what worries me. Allison seems to catch on, and her smile fades. "Are you up to this?" she asks.

"Ha," JT says from behind her. "Definitely not."

The truth is, he's probably right. I've had a hard time with the lights and crowd at the pageant rehearsals, and there are so few people involved in that compared to this.

But in three days, I have to be ready to get up on a stage and emcee. It'll help that there's this separation between us and the audience, so I won't have to interact with people off script except when I choose to, but still.

I don't want to make a fool of myself in front of Allison. I want to be able to function like a normal person. I need to try.

"Yeah," I say. "But I don't know how long I'll want to stay."

"We can leave whenever you need to," Allison says. "And if we get there and you don't want to go in at all—"

I hate that I'm fragile enough that she has to say this. "It'll be fine. It's just a bunch of industry people. It's not like I care what they think of me."

JT snorts, and I fight the urge to roll my eyes. All right. That's never been true. But it used to be that I only cared what people thought inasmuch as they kept thinking they wanted to put out our albums and send us on tour and book us for gigs.

The haters could keep on hating, for all I cared.

It's not like I want sympathy from anyone now. In fact, it's the opposite. I don't want anyone to know what a wreck I am.

Anyone but Allison, apparently, and I haven't even been completely honest with her.

She runs a hand up my arm. "It'll be okay."

I hope she's right.

We take Allison's car to the benefit—I'll do basically anything not to drive, because I don't want her to see me have one of my behind-the-wheel freak outs, or worse yet, get her hurt. Just the thought of that brings back the memories of my dream, Allison's voice screaming my name, calling out in pain.

I tighten my fists, slip on my sunglasses, and try to push her voice out of my mind. It almost works.

We arrive at the hotel where the benefit is being held. I don't have an invitation or anything, but Parker's got my name on a list, and the bouncer at the door clearly recognizes me. He waves us on through ahead of the line.

The benefit consumes most of the bottom floor of the hotel. There's a ballroom all decorated in roses and ivy, with an open bar and dozens of waiters wandering around with platters of food. I recognize several faces in there, and I notice a lot of people recognizing mine, even with the glasses. Hell, I've been wearing them so much since the accident that I'm probably more recognizable in them than without them.

The party sprawls out into the step-down back foyer of the hotel, and the large back doors are open, inviting people to wander into the well-lit gardens. By the end of the night there's going to be a lot of well-lit people hiding in the recesses of those gardens, hooking up or getting high or both.

In another life, I would have been one of them, and while I could really go for a joint right now, the last thing that's on my mind in the middle of this many people right now is sex. Even with Allison. I feel too raw, too exposed, like everyone in this hotel can see right through me, like they all know what a fraud

I am, how damaged and broken. I never used to feel that way. Kevin used to say I was a chameleon, able to slip into virtually any social situation and get along just fine.

I guess that's just one more part of me that died along with JT.

JT, on the other hand, doesn't seem to have gotten the memo about that. I spot him on the far side of the room, dunking his head under the champagne fountain.

I hope he's going to go party and leave me alone. "Come on," Allison says, taking my hand. "Why don't we get a drink?"

"Good idea," I say. I realize I've just been standing there, staring into the ballroom like I'm afraid it's a trap. I squeeze her hand and stride over to the bar, where we both order drinks. It's dark enough in here that I can't see much with the sunglasses, but I'm afraid to push them up.

I don't want anyone to see me. I don't want anyone to know. I already feel like the whole room is staring at me, and I'm probably ten seconds away from some people I used to work with—or some music fans who've paid way too much money to rub elbows with the people in this room—coming up to bombard me with questions. I scan the room, trying to figure out who that's going to be so I can surreptitiously avoid them.

That's when I see Felix Mays staring at me from across the room. Probably for an entirely different reason. He turns to Jenna, who's hanging on his arm next to him, and says something to her. She looks over at us and her eyes widen.

"Don't look now," I tell Allison, "but I think your friends are wondering what you're doing with me."

She looks up, and I gesture to the other side of the room, where I now notice that Alec Andreas is standing with them. He's the only one of them I've actually met in person, and he's only ever spoken to me to tell me to get out of his way.

"Oh," Allison says. She doesn't seem embarrassed to be with me, even though she probably should be. "I love Jillian's dress. I wish I could pull that off."

I'm assuming Jillian is the girl on Alec's arm. She's wearing this strappy thing that crisscrosses over her chest, barely concealing her nipples. "You could," I tell her. "Why not?"

Allison hesitates. "Without the prosthetic, you mean?"

"Yeah," I say. "I mean, if you were to buy something like that you'd have to shorten one of the straps, right? But you would look amazing." Something occurs to me. "Hey, have you ever thought about doing a line like that? Like, for women who've had mastectomies? It would probably have to be online, because it's a niche thing, but you could design dresses that are meant to be worn without prosthetics, like, for women who want to go to formal things, but don't want to have to hide their bodies." As the words come out of my mouth, I wonder if I'm really stepping in it. I mean, it's not like I think Allison wearing a prosthetic means she's hiding. I get that it's none of anyone else's business what she looks like, and she just wants to blend in and remain conventionally attractive—which is not something she needs to worry about any day of the week. I'm about to open my mouth to tell her so, but she beats me to it.

"You really think I should do that."

I shrug. "If you want to. It just seems like something there would be a market for. Body empowerment and all that? But maybe I'm wrong."

Allison shakes her head. "I love that about you."

I look at her skeptically. "My crazy-improbable business ideas?"

"That too," she says. "But no, I mean the way you actually think that I should be proud of my body. And that other people who've had the same surgery should show off their bodies, just the way they are."

"There probably wouldn't be a lot of money in it," I say. "But it would be good publicity, and I bet you'd make a lot of women feel really good about themselves."

Allison looks up at me. "You're incredible."

I shake my head. I don't think I should be getting credit just for appreciating a clearly beautiful woman whose scars are as sexy as the rest of her, but I'll take it.

"I should go say hi to them," Allison says. "You don't have to come with me."

"Want to hide me from your friends?"

"No. But I don't want to rope you into a conversation with them if you're already feeling overwhelmed."

God. She's treating me like an invalid, and it's not undeserved. "Nah," I say. "I'll be fine." We wander over, but as we get closer, I notice Jenna trying to get someone's attention, and Felix still looking at me like I don't belong here.

So they don't approve of me dating Allison. That's not unexpected, but it makes me feel even more out of place.

God, is this how Kevin used to feel at events like this? He got used to them eventually, and he always made a show of being fine, but especially in the beginning, he was always itching to get out as quickly as he could.

I'm not going to let myself bail for at least an hour. That's the minimum amount of time I need to be able to deal with the crowd of people staring at me to maintain at least a portion of my self-respect.

"Dude," JT says from behind me. "You lost that a long time ago." I flinch, and have to fight not to turn around and look at him. Allison notices, and her grip on my arm tightens.

"I'm fine," I say.

We reach Felix and Alec and Jillian, and Alec raises his glass at us. "Allison!" he says. "Good to see you."

Allison lets go of my hand to hug Alec and then Felix, who makes some comment about the memories he has tied to my shirt. But I don't really hear it, because I've just located Jenna again.

She's standing behind Alec, right next to two people who've just emerged from the crowd to join the group.

Josh Rios and Anna-Marie.

Anna stares at me, clearly surprised to see me. I'm equally surprised to see her—yeah, we both live in LA, but our paths haven't crossed since the last time I saw her back in Wyoming, when she told me what a dick I was and stormed out of my apartment. I think a lot of that has been by design—she didn't even come to JT's funeral, though she did send flowers. Neither she nor Josh are in the music industry, but they're clearly here with their friends. Allison's friends. People who, I remember now, all hate me because of what I did to Anna-Marie.

Anna-Marie is wearing a black dress with streaks of gold woven into the fabric, and she's also largely and unmistakably pregnant.

"Hey, Anna," I say, trying to sound relaxed. "Congratulations."

Anna-Marie looks up at Josh, and he puts a hand on her back protectively, like somehow I'm a threat to their relationship, just standing here at a party with my girlfriend.

I never liked Josh much, and he most definitely never liked me. Though I suppose that last bit was mostly my fault.

"Thanks," Anna-Marie says.

All eight of us stand there looking at each other, like we don't know what to say.

Which pisses me off. Anna-Marie was one of the most important people in my life, once upon a time. The only people who really cared about me before Allison were Anna-Marie and the guys in my band. Now JT's dead, and Mikey left us a long time ago, and Kevin's out.

And she couldn't even be bothered to call after she heard what happened to me. The only reason I wrote that fucking song about her in the first place was to get back at her for ditching me. She left town and never called, didn't even give me her new number so I *could* call, even though she knew that's what everyone did to me, even my own mother. She fucking *knew* that I didn't have anyone else, but she didn't care. Didn't even have the time of day for me when she came back into town, at least not after she decided she didn't want to use me to hook up.

"I didn't know you guys were dating," Jenna says, and I get the feeling it's mostly to break the silence.

"Yeah," Allison says. "It's kind of new." She glances up at me like she's worried about me, and I hate that she has to be. I hate that I'm the idiot who still cares about what Anna-Marie thinks, when she made it clear a long time ago she wanted nothing to do with me—and that was before I wrote those songs about her in retribution.

"You're Shane, right?" Alec says, like he's confused as to why we haven't been introduced. Not that he cared who I was until I came and crashed his conversation with my new insanity and old baggage. "What are you doing these days?"

Allison looks like she wants to murder Alec for asking me that. "I'm between gigs," I say, hoping that comes out as breezy as I want it to.

"I get it," Alec says. "I'm kind of looking at the next phase, myself."

Like hell he is. He went through a rough patch professionally after the VMAs incident years ago—so bad he even ended up on a reality show, if I remember right. But over the last year or two, he's put out some successful albums and is climbing his way back up to the top, with some music that's a hell of a lot more interesting than anything AJ used to play.

Or Accidental Erotica, for that matter.

"If you're interested in collaborating," Alec says, "I'd be happy to discuss it sometime."

Everyone looks confused except for Jillian, who shoots an apologetic glance at Anna-Marie. Anna-Marie is examining her fingernails and probably wishing to be anywhere but here, since apparently being in my presence is the worst thing in the world and has been since before we broke up.

I struggle to keep my attention on Alec. "Are you looking to get into punk?"

"I've been doing some experimenting," Alec says. "I'm pretty firmly pop music, but I like playing with other influences. I've been working with some rappers, but I'd love to get together and jam sometime, see what we can come up with."

I stare at Alec through my sunglasses. The old me would have been thrilled at this offer, not because I have any desire to work in pop, but because the old Shane Beckstrom saw potential in every opportunity. The old me would have gotten together to jam with Alec and pushed every possible angle to milk as much benefit out of that connection as he could. It was smart, and it's what got my band to the level of success that we had.

"Sure," I say. "Maybe sometime."

It'll never happen. I already know it. Because I can't pick up a guitar, not even at home by myself. Every time I do I think of Kevin, his arm so messed up he can't play the chords, or JT, blood and brains running down his face, his head bashed in.

I'm no good to anyone now.

Because I'm dead. I died in that accident.

"Don't be so dramatic," JT says from behind Allison.

My eyes start to burn behind my sunglasses, and the room suddenly seems much smaller. It's spinning, like the van did after that truck plowed into it, turning and twisting with a crash and a bang and then suddenly standing still. Perfectly still.

"Shane?" Allison says. I lose my balance and stumble backward, right into a table where some people are sitting. I can't tell who they are or if I recognize them, because my vision is tunneling, and there's a roaring in my ears, and I'm fighting to breathe. There's a crash of shattering glass as I knock something off the table, and I feel the windshield glass against my skin, bursting into a thousand puzzle-shaped pieces, leaving behind sharp bits of grit which I'll find later in my teeth.

I push the sunglasses up off my eyes, but it doesn't help. I can't see. I can't breathe. I can't be here, not for one more second. I turn and tear off across the ballroom, stumbling over someone who doesn't get out of my way fast enough.

"Shane!" I hear Allison say. And then I'm out of the ballroom and stalking through the garden, looking for one of those remote corners, not to get high or hook up, but just to get away.

SEVENTEEN

Allison

I follow Shane as he all but runs from the ballroom and out into the gardens. People turn to look, but it's not as dramatic out here, more curiosity than shock. Unlike in the ballroom, where they saw his expression as he knocked into the table. As the glass shattered and he jumped like a gun-shot had gone off, sweat shining on his face, his blue eyes wild. Terrified.

Or maybe they didn't notice all that like I did, and just saw a rock star having a meltdown or some drug-induced fit. It doesn't matter. I don't care what they think they saw. I only care about him.

I don't call his name anymore, though, not wanting to draw further attention, for his sake. My heels catch in the grass of the garden—Shane isn't keeping to the curated pathways—and my heart hammers in my chest.

I started to worry as soon as we got here tonight. He was so nervous, but not in the fidgety, anxious way I get right before the pageant starts or before a big meeting with my investors. He was nervous in this too-still, frozen kind of way, like if he doesn't move, no one can see him.

I wondered if this was all a bad idea. Especially when I saw my friends, and he got even more nervous about what they'd think of us together. For my part, I wasn't worried about that. If my family doesn't get a say in who I date—which they don't—then my friends and work colleagues definitely don't. Also, I knew that Jenna and Felix weren't the type to make a big deal of it, even if they think Shane's a dick, and Alec, well . . . Alec doesn't tend to care about things that don't directly affect him. I thought it would be fine. Awkward for a minute or so and then fine.

I hadn't, however, counted on Anna-Marie being there. And it's pretty clear Shane didn't either.

"Shane," I finally say, and he stops, though probably more from the fact that he would have needed to hurdle a large decorative hedge if he wanted to keep moving in that direction. I catch up to him and touch his elbow, and he turns. It's dark out, but the hotel has these glowing lamps around, so I can see him well enough. My heart breaks at the pain on his face. Pain and fear and, I think, shame.

"Hey," I start, stepping forward. I want to wrap my arms around him and hold him like I did after his nightmare, but something about the way he's standing, the walled-off energy exuding from him . . . I'm not sure he wants that. Maybe he didn't even want me to follow him out here.

"Sorry," he mutters, scrubbing a hand through his hair. "God, that was . . . I'm sorry."

"It's okay," I say, and then I do put my arms around him and press my face into his neck, which is too warm and yet clammy, like he's running a fever. "It's okay."

"It's not," he says, but his body relaxes a little into mine.

Then he tenses again, pulling back. "What do you want?" he asks, his voice harsh.

I blink, confused, but then see he's glaring at someone over my shoulder. My chest squeezes too tight, already knowing who.

Anna-Marie.

She's standing there, just at the edge of the path, her eyes wide. *She's* clearly nervous in the fidgety way, her fingers toying with the fabric of the gown around her largely pregnant belly. Josh is there, too, but a few feet behind her, like he's trying to stay out of their way, but is ready to jump in if necessary.

I understand the impulse. The thick tension between them is back, and I step away, like there's no room for me in it. There's a pit in my stomach that started when he saw her again, and it only grows now.

"I just—" she starts, then blinks too rapidly. "Are you okay?"

"Why the fuck are you asking now?" Shane snaps. "You never cared before."

She looks like she's been slapped, then her expression hardens. "What the hell is that supposed to mean?"

They aren't being quiet, but thankfully there doesn't seem to be anyone hanging around this part of the garden, and we're mostly blocked off by tall hedges.

Shane's eyes narrow. "It means don't pretend you give the tiniest shit about me, Anna. You don't get to act like you fucking care all of a sudden." His anger is a palpable thing, rolling off like waves, his hands clenched into tight fists.

Anna-Marie gapes. "Are you kidding me? You're accusing *me* of being the one who doesn't care—after all the shit you—" The words are getting caught up in her flustered rage, and Josh takes another step forward.

"Right," Shane says. "Just keep playing the fucking martyr. It plays well for sympathy, I'm sure."

"Oh, *I'm* the one who uses people now? You are so—" She snaps her lips shut, shaking her head. "Never mind. Why do I bother?"

"You *don't*," Shane says, and I can see his hands trembling. "That's the point. So just get. The fuck. Away from me."

There's this frozen moment of them glaring at each other, and I can't breathe around all the tension, around all this raw emotion, and the pit in my stomach is gaping.

I've fought with people, and I've had awkward, even pissy, run-ins with exes, but never like *this*.

I almost wish Josh would look at me, that there might be this moment of mutual fear of what the hell this is between them, or, even better, some assurance that he understands it on some level that I don't. But he's just glaring at Shane and hovering at Anna-Marie's side.

Then Anna-Marie, her lips pressed into this tight, thin line, spins on her heel and walks away, and the moment is broken. She makes a motion like she's brushing away tears, and Josh puts his arm around her shoulders, and then they're gone, out of sight around the pathway bend.

I look at Shane, and I think I see tears gleaming in his eyes before he turns his glare to the ground. My throat is so dry I'm not sure I can speak.

He said he was long over her, but that . . . I don't know exactly what that was, but it didn't feel like being over someone. The pit in my stomach feels icy around the edges.

"What?" Shane says, and he's looking at me with that hardness in his eyes. "You're clearly thinking something. You might as well say it."

"Of course I'm thinking something, after that," I say, snapping back more than I mean to, and he blinks rapidly, looking away. I swallow, not wanting to say it, but feeling like I need to. "Are you still in love with her?" I try to keep my tone as non-accusatory as possible, as calm, but I feel the words waver at the end.

His head jerks back to me. "In love with her?" The incredulous, pissed-off look he gives me is worse than when I tried to set him up with Nix. "*No.*"

My arms fold across myself, and probably now I'm being the one who's too still, fear pulsing in me with every heartbeat. "I know you don't think so, but it's been years since you've even seen her last, right? And that was so emotionally charged—"

"Yeah, it's charged as hell, and I'm pissed, but it's definitely not romantic." He runs a hand through his hair, and I can see that his hand is still shaking. "She was this big part of my life, and she just walked out, you know? Like it was nothing." Every word drips with bitterness.

"When she left Wyoming," I say. "After you guys broke up." I'm trying to keep my voice even. Trying to understand. Wanting to believe him.

"Yeah. I mean, she was still in Wyoming for like a year after we broke up, and we didn't see each other or anything, but that was cool. I wanted space, too, after all that shit, so fine. But then she just left the fucking state, not a single word or text or anything. And then shows up four years later, doesn't even bother to tell me she's coming back to town, doesn't give a shit about me, even after everything." He shakes his head, glaring up at the dark sky. "She didn't care then, and she doesn't now, and it fucking pisses me off for her to pretend she does."

I look back along the pathway, even though Anna-Marie and Josh have long since disappeared from sight. But I can still remember the look on her face throughout all that—the worry, then the hurt and anger. She clearly does care, in one way or another. Sure, she's an actress, but there's no need to act here, in some secluded part of a hotel garden where no one can see her but her ex, his new girlfriend, and her husband.

But I don't think telling him that will help anything right now. And it doesn't help me feel any less afraid that the unresolved issues between them are something more than Shane is willing to admit.

We're not standing all that far apart, but the distance between us feels like miles. I know part of that is my fault, but I can't seem to step across it. Not without knowing.

Is it just his issues with being abandoned? Clearly he has those, from what he's told me of his past and his fear that I'd just walk away from him after we slept together.

Is that it? Or is it more?

"Okay," I say, trying to curb my growing panic, that I'm in this so deep so quickly with a man who may never be over another woman. "But you don't get like that about Kevin, or even when you're talking about your parents, and it's just—" I squeeze my own arms tight enough I can feel my nails digging into my skin. "It's like she has this hold on you that—"

"I'm not in love with her, Ally," he says. His eyes bore into me, all of his intense emotion zeroing in like a laser beam, and it's at once exhilarating and intimidating. "I'm in love with *you*."

I gape, not able to even breathe; even he seems taken aback by blurting that at me, and his blue eyes blink.

"God, I'm sorry, I shouldn't have—not like that." He presses a trembling palm to his face.

My eyes are burning, and I take a step forward. "Are you really?"

He looks at me, and I can see the truth on his face, even before he speaks again. "Yeah. I am. More than I ever was with her, even back when we were together. I love you, Ally." He swallows, his voice thick. "Only you."

The icy fingers of my fear melt away, and those words light up every part of me. And while before now I haven't let myself go there in my own mind, I know by the way those words make me feel, by the way *he* makes me feel . . .

"I love you, too, Shane," I say, a small smile tugging at my lips as I look up at him. "I love you, and I believe you." I wrap my arms around him, and it's like I can feel his entire body exhale against me, even as he pulls me in tighter, pressing his face to the top of my head. I can feel the wetness of tears against my hair, and my heart, so warm with happiness at knowing he loves me, also squeezes in sadness for his pain.

I do believe him. I may not understand it all, but those words, the look on his face when he said them . . . He may have emotion in regards to Anna-Marie, but it's not *that* emotion.

He loves me. I close my eyes, breathing that thought in for a moment.

"Hey," I say, pulling back just enough to see his face. "Let's sit down, okay?"

He wipes at his eyes and looks around for a bench or something, but there isn't one here. I tug him down to the grass, which is cool against my legs but thankfully not damp, and he sits next to me, with me burrowed up under his arm.

There's silence for a bit, but it doesn't feel scary like it would have just moments before. It does, however, still feel heavy, weighed down, and I wish I could help him shoulder some of that.

Then he speaks again, staring down at our linked fingers. "You're right, about Kevin and my parents, but it's not . . ." He shakes his head, and the tears spill down his cheeks. "Like, yeah, I hate that Kevin's leaving me. But I can't be mad at him, not like that, because he was there in that van. He lost everything too."

I run my thumb over his knuckles and nod against his shoulder.

"I mean, he has Maya, so I guess not everything," Shane says with a tinge of bitterness, scrubbing at the tears.

"What about your parents?" I ask quietly.

He shrugs, and there's a whole world of feeling in that small gesture. "My mom . . . I mean, she walks away. It's what she does. It's what she's always done, from before I can remember. If I were to yell at her like that . . ." He closes his eyes. "She might never come back. Not even for tickets or whatever she can get from me. And my dad . . . god, no."

The stark pain in his voice brings the tears back to my eyes. "You'd be too afraid to confront him like that." I remember the way he talked about what a jerk his dad was—"an alcoholic and a first-class asshole," I'm pretty sure he said—and I have a feeling there's lots more there that he hasn't shared.

Fear and hurt and anger that he probably tries not to let himself feel at all, let alone yell at his dad.

I think maybe I get it now, why he can freak out like that at Anna-Marie. Because it's safe; he has nothing else to lose there, in a relationship that ended years ago. Even if it clearly still hurts him that it did—the friendship part, at least.

Shane lets out a shuddering breath. "It's just that everyone leaves me," he says, his voice breaking, and my heart along with it, "and I have—"

"Me," I say, looking up at him. Hoping he can feel how

deeply true it is.

He gives me a sad smile and kisses the top of my head again, leaving his lips pressed there for a long moment. Then he pulls back. "I have something I need to tell you. And I get if it freaks you out, if it means I'm too fucked up to—"

"Shane," I say, squeezing his hand. "Just tell me."

I think maybe he's going to tell me something about his dad, about things I'm beginning to suspect may have happened to him in his childhood.

Instead he says, quietly, "I see JT. Like, a lot. Hanging around and talking to me and generally being an ass, but like . . . he's here."

I'm not super great at hiding how stunned I am, or the reflexive looking around I do, but Shane lets out a small, nervous chuckle. "I mean, he's not here right now. But lots of times he is."

"Like . . . a ghost?" I don't totally disbelieve the possibility that ghosts exist—I do believe in an afterlife, and that people's spirits continue on after death—but I have a hard time imagining they don't have better things to do than hang around earth generally being an ass.

Shane presses his lips together briefly. "No. It's not that. He doesn't see anything I don't see, and he doesn't know anything I don't know. It's some product of my messed-up brain, like the headaches and the nightmares." He hangs his head, and his blond hair flops forward, covering his face.

I brush the hair back, tuck it behind his ear, and he looks at me out of the side of his eye.

"Is it scary?" I ask.

He pauses, like this wasn't what he expected me to say. "JT? No. It's kind of nice to still get to see him, you know? Despite that part about him being an ass." A little smile forms, then drops away just as suddenly. "But the fact that I'm one big mental shit-storm who hallucinates his dead best friend on the regular? Yeah, that's less great."

"It makes sense to me, though," I say. "Wanting to see him again. Your brain trying to give you that."

His brow furrows as he turns to face me. "I just told you I'm hallucinating JT, and you think it *makes sense*? Like, this doesn't freak you out?"

I shrug. Maybe with some other guy it would have seemed too much to deal with, but not with him. Not with what we have. I give him a sly smile. "I mean, compared to the idea of Ghost JT hanging around and watching us have sex, I'd say the idea of you hallucinating him is preferable."

Shane groans. "Yeah, well, you should know I've told Hallucination JT he's not allowed to watch. And so far he's kept up his end of that." He pauses, and when he speaks again his voice is strained. "But really, though. I'd get it if you couldn't handle this, and if—"

"*Really*," I say, squeezing his hand. "This isn't scaring me away, Shane. I love you. And yeah, I'm worried about you. But I'm not going anywhere."

His mouth drops open and closes again. He blinks quickly, and I wonder if, after everything that's happened in his life, he's afraid to trust that.

I don't blame him, but I do hope he lets me prove to him that I mean it.

"Okay." He lets out a little breath of what sounds like relief. "Okay."

"What does your doctor say about all this?"

Shane tenses up in my arms. "Um," he says, grimacing.

My eyes widen. "You've been having hallucinations and *you haven't told your doctor?*"

His expression is all the answer I need, and I give him a little smack on his chest. "Shane! You can't keep stuff like that from your doctor!"

"I couldn't—I just . . ." He sighs. "I couldn't tell anyone."

"Not even Kevin?"

"Not even Kevin. You're the first person I've told."

My heart warms, knowing the level of trust that must have taken. Honored that I'm the person he trusts that much. But . . .

I open my mouth, but he beats me to speaking.

"I know, I know. You think I should talk to an actual medical professional."

"I do."

He nods against my hair. "You're probably right," he says, though it's clearly reluctant.

"Get used to saying that, dating me," I murmur, and he laughs.

"Nope. Enjoy it now. The next one may be a long ways out."

I pinch him, and he squeezes me back.

"But," he says, his body relaxed into me again. "Since I'm being so generous in my acknowledgment of your rightness at the moment, is there anything else you think I should do?"

His tone is light as he says this, but it's forced; I think he actually wants my opinion on steps he should take.

And I do have one other idea.

"I think you should talk to Kevin about it," I say. "When you're ready. Like, really talk to him. Maybe even bring up the music festival idea."

He lets out a shaky breath. "God, you don't mess around."

I feel a twinge of fear. I know I can be intense, and I've even been accused of being bossy—particularly by my siblings. But I don't exactly want "naggy" to be the defining characteristic of myself as a girlfriend. Especially because what he really needs is support and love, both of which I want desperately to give him, even if my version of support and love has occasionally leaned towards the "swift kick in the ass" variety.

"If you're not ready, that's okay," I say quickly. "I don't want to force anything on you—"

"No, I asked, and I meant it. I just—I'll try, okay?"

I smile. "I have another suggestion."

He gives me a baleful look. "I'm going to seriously regret letting you start this mental health honey-do list, aren't I?"

"It depends on what you think about the idea of getting out of here right now and going home. And being less clothed."

His smile widens. "I think I could handle that."

EIGHTEEN

Allison

I wake up the next morning, my body pressed tight up against Shane's side, feeling warm and safe. My body slides a bit on his satin sheets—which, he told me last night, happen to have a bunny on the tag. I don't love that my boyfriend has Playboy bedding, even if he did seem abashed about it and offered to change the sheets.

But there's something else bothering me this morning, some unsettled twinge I can't quite identify.

I stretch out, and he shifts slightly, but his breathing is still deep. I'm glad he's getting some sleep, at least. He woke from the nightmares again last night, yelling and sweating. But like before, we held each other, and I felt his racing heartbeat slow against me, his body relaxing. I hate that he has to deal with this, but I'm grateful I can be there for him, to be able to comfort him even a little. To be the person he trusts.

He's in love with me, and I'm in love with him, and it's crazy and incredible all at once. But even though it does scare me, being in this so deep, so soon, I don't think that's what's giving me this unsettled feeling.

I want to burrow deeper into him, chase away that feeling with the comfort of just being in his arms, but a glance at the alarm clock on his nightstand shows that it's only about ten minutes before I'd need to wake up anyway. We're only days away from the pageant, so these last practices are especially important. I wonder if that's the real cause of this prickly anxiousness. I always get extra stressed right before the pageant, and this year I feel less prepared for the show than usual. I've been . . . distracted. My mind more on Shane than on my job.

I can't bring myself to regret that—I can't regret anything between us—but it does mean I've got to bring my A-game to the pageant over the next couple days. The girls deserve that; they're going to be extra stressed too.

I peel myself gently and reluctantly away from him, and he makes a quiet little murmuring sound but still doesn't wake. I turn off my phone alarm and head for the shower, hoping the warm water will relax me, but it doesn't. I try mentally running through the tasks of today, which are many, but my brain can't seem to focus on any of it. Instead it keeps tugging back to the benefit last night.

For some reason, despite all the revelations of last night—not just the being in love part, but the hallucinations of JT, and the deep pain over his parents—my mind keeps tripping over that fight with Anna-Marie, putting me more on edge.

Which is ridiculous. I know he loves me, not her. I meant it when I told him I believed him, and that hasn't suddenly changed overnight—especially after making love like we did, knowing how deep he's in this right along with me. So why can't I let that go?

We had planned on spending the night at his place, even before we went to the benefit, so thankfully I have a change of clothes for today and my makeup. I get ready, waiting until the last possible moment to use the hair dryer, to give him a bit more sleep. But, really, he needs to be getting up soon, too. Maybe I can actually get him to work on time for once.

That teasing thought brings a little smile to my lips, but it's not long before that unsettled feeling steals it away again, especially as this time it comes with a thought attached.

He's Shane Beckstrom. You think you're going to change him?

I blink at myself in the mirror, stunned, pausing in my hair-styling efforts. I click off the dryer so it's not blaring in my ear.

I love him for who he is. I don't want to change him—at least not any more than just being part of a good relationship should change someone, making them grow for the better. Like I can already feel myself doing when I'm with him.

But that's not the same as changing who he is. Right?

And what does that have to do with him and Anna-Marie?

I run a comb through the waves of my hair, the churning anxiety growing stronger, as the connections start to form in my mind. I straighten all my things on the side of the sink so I'm not taking up too much of his space and then head back into the bedroom.

Shane's awake, sitting at the edge of the bed, the covers thrown back. He's still naked, which is always an amazing sight, but he's sitting in this hunched-over way, with his head in his hands. It's still a bit dark in here—he's got blackout curtains, and there's only the wan light of the alarm and the light I left on in the bathroom—but I wonder if he's got a headache. Or maybe having the hallucinations and trying to get rid of them.

Sadness squeezes at my chest.

"Everything okay?" I ask.

Shane looks up at me. "Yeah, of course." He smiles, but there's something guarded about it. Wary.

Is he regretting how open he was with me last night? The thought hurts more than it has any right to, especially given that it may not be true.

"Good," I say, smiling back, but I'm not sure my smile is any more convincing than his. I sit down next to him, also on the edge of the bed. It feels a little stilted, so I lean into him—which is instantly much better.

His body relaxes a bit. "You smell fantastic," he says, pressing his lips to the top of my head.

"You better believe I do. I used your shampoo and conditioner." I grin over at him. "Though I had no idea that what you really wanted was for me to smell like you."

He laughs, and it cuts through that unsettled feeling like a ray of sunshine. "You definitely do *not* smell like me. It's all Allison."

I lean over to kiss him, his lips warm and soft and gentle against mine. "Well, okay, I did use my own body wash. You got me." I put emphasis on that last part, because the truth is, he does have me—all that he wants of me, which I think is every bit as much as I want of him.

His lips twitch up, but he doesn't say anything back. His gaze cuts away.

Maybe now's not the best time to bring up the thoughts taking shape in my unsettled mind, but I know it'll drive me crazy all day if I don't. It'll keep me from being able to focus on the girls and the pageant, like I need to.

"Hey, can I ask you something?" I say.

His blue eyes narrow, but not in an angry way. More like guarded again. "Usually you just ask."

That's probably true. I've never been big on preamble.

I hold his gaze. "Do you really not feel bad about what you did to Anna-Marie?"

Now he looks a little angry. "No. Why?"

I feel my hackles rise, but force my voice to stay level. "I mean, I get that you were hurt by her leaving and not staying in touch, and I get that you were pissed. But—"

"You say you get it," he cuts me off. "But clearly you have a problem with it."

I do have a problem with it. Because even though he was hurt, even though he was mad, he still used someone he cared about, still told lies about them in the press and let those lies continue for years, and that's something a person should feel something about. Especially when it's so obvious, no matter how much denial he's in, that what he did hurt her, and continues to hurt her.

Someone who could use another person like that, without any remorse . . . A person like that won't have a problem doing that again in the future.

I don't believe that's who Shane really is. But I can't be the idiot who overlooks something like that. I can't ignore the possibility he might do that to me someday, or ask me to be complicit in doing it to others—which is not who *I* am.

But maybe now really isn't the best time to talk about this. I sigh, frustrated—mostly with myself for not heeding my initial instinct to wait. "Never mind."

Shane eyes me. "Really? Or are you expecting me to pry it out of you?"

I don't appreciate the implication that I'm playing stupid mind games, so my reply is sharper than I intend. "You don't want to talk about it, so I'm not talking about it. Why don't you just go take a shower so we can get to work on time?"

He rolls his eyes. "Your car is here. You can leave whenever you want."

Okay, now my frustration is less with myself. "Or you could get ready and get there when you're supposed to for once."

"Sure. Fine." His tone is every bit as pissy as mine, and it's hard to believe we went from the raw openness of last night to sniping at each other like this. I know it's at least half my fault, but dammit, I'm still peeved. He pulls on his boxers and starts to head to the bathroom, and I can tell how tense he is, even just from the set of his shoulders. Then he turns, running a hand through his hair. "No, you know what? You want to talk about Anna-Marie? Let's talk."

"You think you're in a good place for that?" I fold my arms. "Because it doesn't really sound like it."

Maybe he's not the only one.

"What the hell do you want from me? To say that I feel bad about what I did? That I'm all wracked with guilt?" His face is flushed, and I can tell mine is too.

"I want you to be honest with me and with yourself," I say tightly. "I want to know how you really feel about it."

"Do you? Because I already told you how I feel about it and you keep bringing it back up."

"I told you we shouldn't talk about this now," I snap. "I need to get to work, and—"

"Yeah, now we shouldn't talk about it, because you don't want to hear what I'm going to say, right?" His hands are balled into fists again, like when he was yelling at Anna-Marie last night. He's not yelling now, though his voice is strained. "Because I already told you I'm a dick. I told you that from the beginning, and it's not my fault if you didn't believe me."

I feel cold all over. He did tell me that, but the truth is, I still don't believe him. I believe he can be a dick, that's for sure—right now is proof—but I don't believe that's who he is, not really. It's like how I can love him, even if I don't love this fight.

But I hate the doubt. The possibility that maybe I'm being a naive idiot, after all.

"Fine, Shane." I can't think of anything else to say.

"What the hell does that mean?"

"It means you made your point. And I just want to get to work, okay?" I can feel a headache forming, and maybe it's because I'm about to cry, but I don't want to do that right now.

We glare at each other a moment longer, then he stomps into the bathroom. A few seconds later, I hear the water running. I sink back onto the bed. Probably I should leave now and see him at rehearsal, when we've both had a chance to cool off. I know how difficult it must have been for him, sharing all that last night. The last thing I should be doing is pushing him this morning.

But I can't pretend that I'm not scared, too. I feel the black satin sheets, cold under my palms. He said he has cotton sheets around somewhere, but he never did get around to changing the bedding. It isn't really a big deal—I don't love the sexual Slip

'N Slide feeling of them, but it's not like satin sheets themselves actually bother me all that much.

Except for this creeping doubt it instills in me. I know Shane has layers, deep ones, and that so much of the image he projected was a protective mask, keeping people out. Keeping himself from being hurt.

I know that, but it doesn't mean he won't someday decide he wants all that back. That the mask—and the life that came with it—is preferable to being with me.

I force myself to take deep breaths. Even if I know we'll talk later, and it'll hopefully go better, I don't want to leave without saying goodbye—as much for me as for him. As I wait for him, I dig my phone out of my purse, sifting through the deluge of messages from pageant coaches, and a particularly frantic string of texts from Heather—whose talent is elaborate face painting and who regularly runs marathons for multiple sclerosis—about how she sneezed four times this morning and believes she is the bitch who is going to get sick. I make a note to myself to bring her some tea, which I will tell her is a Mendez family secret to preventing colds, and hope the placebo effect works on her. She must be prone to suggestion, given that she's decided she's sick based on not-dead Cher's beyond-the-grave appearance.

I hear the water shut off just as I finish taking the note. I draw another deep breath and am about to shove my phone back in my purse when a text dings. It's Nix.

Did this really happen?

I frown, especially as another one comes through right after.

Are you guys okay?

I open the message and see the link she's posted, and my heart skips a few beats at seeing the article title:

Beckstrom's Dramatic Breakdown at Benefit

Oh no.

My palms feel sweaty on the phone as I read through the article, my heart sinking deeper with each word.

I figured the scene in the hotel would be reported somewhere,

Shane's panic attack attributed to being high or just the behavior of a "bad boy rock star," but this is much worse. Because this article doesn't just talk about the glasses breaking or Shane fleeing the hotel ballroom

No, this article talks about *everything*.

A "source" goes into great detail about the confrontation with Anna-Marie in the gardens and about how "Beckstrom's new girlfriend" (the article, of course, makes sure to include my name and, weirdly, age) was upset, demanding to know if he was still in love with his "equally emotional" ex. This source continues to lay out our conversation, about how Shane "claimed" to be in love with me and yet still felt betrayed by Anna-Marie.

And then, the source—who I want to punch in the face—goes on to tell about Shane's hallucinations. All the details he told me in confidence, all the things he was so afraid of even me knowing, let alone the rest of the world . . .

"Clearly," the article's skeezy source opines, "Beckstrom has a lot of problems, both in his health and personal life, and they're causing all his recent erratic behavior. I hope for his sake, and for his fans', that he can pull himself together."

I want to throw the phone against the wall, but I manage not to. Barely.

How could this have happened?

Even as I ask the question, I know the answer. It happened because we were at a public event, and hedges aren't exactly sound-proof, and any passing waiter or attendee toking up on the other side could easily have heard all of it. It happened because people are assholes who can't mind their own business. I feel weirdly violated, knowing that this intensely personal conversation we had—this conversation where Shane and I first told each other we loved each other—is splashed all over the internet. Even more, I'm furious on Shane's behalf and heartbroken for him.

He was so open and vulnerable, letting me in on things he's been so desperate to hide, and now . . .

The tears are stinging my eyes by the time Shane opens the door from the bathroom, but I blink them away. The steam from the bathroom trails out, and he eyes me warily as he pulls on a pair of jeans.

"I thought you didn't want to be late," he says in a flat voice.

I swallow, my throat painfully tight. "I got a message from Nix," I say. I hold out my phone, and he takes it.

I watch his face carefully as he reads it, but his expression doesn't change. It stays flat and stony, which is worse.

He hands the phone back to me. "Yeah, okay."

"*Yeah, okay?*" I can't believe he's not reacting at all, and it cuts me in a way I'm not anticipating. "Some asshole just put all that out there, and that's all you have to say?"

"What do you want me to say?" There's not even anger in his voice anymore. It's just cold, and it hurts.

Tears burn behind my eyes. "I don't know. Something. Aren't you upset about this? I am. All this personal stuff about you and me, and the stuff about JT—"

"Whatever." He pulls a shirt over his head. "It was going to get out eventually anyway."

"Yeah, but—"

"Look, Allison," his blue eyes hard as flint. "This is just how it is. You want to be with me? You're going to have to deal with shit like this. If you can't handle it, you might as well leave now."

The lack of emotion in his voice is like a slap. It's not like I haven't been around rock stars for the last several years. I know about things leaking to the press, and true privacy being a laughable concept.

I know this, and yet I'm upset anyway, and I think I have a fucking right to be. And, more to the point, I think he does too.

"I told you I'm not leaving," I say, trying to keep my voice as even as his.

He shrugs. "I've heard that before."

"Oh my god. You are not seriously deciding that I'm leaving you over this. Just because I wanted to talk about your obvious issues with Anna-Marie? Do you not see how irrational that is?"

His eyes are ice. "Who do you think leaked all that to the press?"

My mouth falls open. Anna-Marie knew a lot of this, but I highly doubt that after storming off, she came back around to eavesdrop on us and then call TMZ. I'm not even sure Shane believes this, or if he's just trying to pile on more justifications so he doesn't have to feel bad about what he did to her.

"Some reporter who saw you leave the party," I say. "Honestly, that's who I think did this."

"Whatever," he says again and starts rifling around his drawers for clean clothes.

I stare at his back, wanting to shake him. It hurts that this, too, is apparently something we can't talk about. Something he wants to shut me out of.

I can't do this right now.

"I'm going to rehearsal," I say, my voice now matching his, flat and toneless. "Are you coming with me?"

He doesn't turn around. "I've got stuff to do. I'm going to be late."

My chest aches, even as I feel my own hands balling into frustrated fists. "Fine. I'll see you there."

I take my purse and leave his apartment. I doubt having to deal with a pageant full of hypochondriacs—and especially with Carlyle, now that Shane's going to show up late again—is going to improve my mood any, but at least it can't make it any worse.

NINETEEN

Shane

I know I should go to pageant practice, but all I'm doing there is reading that awful script and pissing Allison off by not following it exactly, and I can't stand the idea of having another fight with her today. That one was bad enough that she's probably already rethinking the wisdom of dating an asshole like me. I don't want to look her in the eye right now and watch her recalibrate, watch her realize she's too good for me, that she has been all along.

Everyone will have read that article by now, and despite what I said to Allison, that obviously bothers me. I've spent the last few months holed up so no one will know how crazy I am, then I go out for one night, and it's all over.

Everyone knows.

I lie on my bed with my hand dug into my hair, gripping the roots, not sure how I'm ever going to be able to bring myself to make a public appearance again.

"Dude," JT says. "When did you become such a whiny ass?"

"I've always been a whiny ass," I tell him. "Remember?"

"Yeah. But you used to be *fun*."

My phone rings, so I'm spared responding to JT. Talking to him used to be something of a comfort when I was alone, but now all I can think about is what Allison says.

I should talk to the doctor. I should tell them what's happening. It's probably treatable if I would just face the reality that I'm never going to see my best friend again and get help.

"Don't do it," JT says. "You don't want those people messing with your head."

I look at my phone. I'm hoping it's Allison, calling to tell me she's sorry, and then I can say I'm sorry, and that I didn't really mean it, and that of course I'm upset about all that shit in the press and of course I'm sorry about what I did to Anna-Marie and I just don't want to admit it because then I'll have to recognize how pissed and sad and remorseful I am about all the things, and it feels like black clouds about to burst and drown me.

It's not Allison, though. It's Kevin.

"He's worried about you," JT says. I'm not sure if he's saying this because he means it or because he wants me to do anything besides call my girlfriend and tell her the truth.

I can't blame him. If I get help, that's probably the end of him.

The phone stops ringing, and it goes to voice mail. A few seconds later, a text comes through, also from Kevin. *Saw the press. You okay?*

My eyes burn, and I wipe them. It shouldn't mean anything to me, Kevin asking if I'm all right. I want to believe that he doesn't care about me anymore, but I know this, too, is just a means of holding back the storm, of trying to not feel any of the things, all the things.

If I let myself care about any of it, I'm not sure how I'm going to survive.

JT is right. Kevin is worried about me. Kevin's been worried about me for a long time, but I drove him away by being relentless about the band getting back together, when I knew Kevin was going to be leaving anyway, even before the accident. He and Maya weren't going to stay with the band forever.

And while I'm pissed as hell with him for leaving me

now—why *now*, when I've lost everything?—I also understand.

Kevin couldn't help it. He lost everything, too. Everything but Maya.

The burning returns to my eyes. I was jealous of that, I realize now. Jealous that Kevin had Maya, and I had no one. Jealous that Maya had a hold on Kevin that trumped more than two decades of friendship and over ten years of working and traveling and doing everything together. I wanted to believe the band wasn't over because then I wouldn't have to feel all the pain and anger and despair behind that jealousy.

It feels different now, and that's because of Allison. I understand more now, because I feel the same way about her that Kevin feels about Maya.

And I yelled at her, and I drove her away, like I did with Kevin. Like I did with Anna-Marie. Like I do with everyone.

The clouds burst open, and I'm crying. I can't call Kevin and bawl at him. I know I need to, but I'm not ready. But I have to do something. If I just let the rain fall and fall then I'm going to drown. I think briefly about calling Allison and crying to her, because it's not like it's anything she hasn't seen, but I'm not sure how she'd take it. It might be the last straw, the last sign to her that I'm not worth all this trouble, that I'm too broken to be worthy of her.

There's only one phone call left, because I'm sure as hell not going to call Anna-Marie. So instead I pick up the phone, and I look for the number of the doctor, the one who saw me for my concussion.

"Don't do it," JT says.

But I turn my back on him, just like I have everyone else, and I make the damn call.

One of the benefits of being a celebrity who's just been in a high profile accident is that it takes all of four calls for me to get an appointment with an actual psychiatrist who will see me same day. I'm paying through the nose and agreeing not to bill it through my insurance, but I don't care.

I need to do this now, before I lose the conviction.

JT follows me out to my car, but he sits in the back seat and sulks. He sulks all the way out to the doctor's office, and he slumps in the corner while I tell the doctor what's happening, that I'm seeing my dead best friend following me around. I fill out twenty pages of questionnaires rating everything from my stress level to my desire to die to my sex drive, and when I'm done, I expect to hear the word schizophrenia come out of the doctor's mouth. Instead I'm given a diagnosis of post-traumatic psychosis, a prescription to fill, and a return appointment in two weeks.

When I'm done at the doctor, JT still won't look at me. I fill the prescription, but I don't take the pills. I set them on my dresser and hole up in my bedroom again, not sleeping, not eating, not taking the damn medicine. But I do read through the entire information brochure that came with them. The drugs are supposed to help with everything from severe psychological distress to delusions and hallucinations.

"Why don't you just take them already," JT says. "That's what you got them for, isn't it?"

He's still sulking, though, slumped on the corner of my couch with his arms hugged around himself. It's clear from his tone that he wants me to do anything but.

I imagine this is what I sound like, a lot of the time, which makes sense, I suppose. He's not JT at all. He's just a hallucination.

He's me.

My phone beeps again. I have three texts from Allison.

Where are you?

Are you even coming to rehearsal?

And finally: *Are you okay?*

Rehearsal is going to go for several more hours yet, and I should get off my ass and go in. I should also take these damn pills, instead of just reading about them, even though apparently they may cause headaches, which I already have, and erectile dysfunction, which I don't.

I also have another text from Kevin: *Dude, don't ignore me.*

Because I feel better about talking to Kevin right now than about getting simultaneously fired and dumped, I text him back and ask if he wants to meet me for a late lunch, to which he immediately agrees.

I take deep breaths, grab my sunglasses, and head out again. Look at me, accomplishing so many of the things Allison put on that list.

Too bad it's almost certainly too little, too late.

Kevin is already at the restaurant when I arrive. I see his car in the front, and when I mention him to the waitress, she takes me around to the back, where Kevin is sitting wearing a pair of sunglasses inside, even though there's no one seated around him. Good to know I'm not the only one tired of getting recognized in public and asked about the accident, even if I am the only one of the two of us with a serious concussion.

I'm glad to be in the back of the restaurant, because today the questions would be about more than the accident.

"Hey," Kevin says. He takes off his sunglasses and looks at me with concern. I slide into the booth across from him and leave mine on.

"Hey," I say back. "I'm really sorry to drag you into all this. Is the press bugging you?"

"I don't care about that," Kevin says, which confirms that yes, they are. "Dude. Is it true what they said? About JT?"

I'm glad he's just coming out and asking me. I don't know that I have the will to explain it all for a third time. "Yeah, it's true. I saw a doctor about it this morning. Post-traumatic psychosis, apparently."

Kevin lets out a breath. "That's rough. You're really seeing him?"

"Yeah," I say. "Although, oddly, not right now."

"I keep having dreams about him," Kevin says. "Like, where we're kids, and he's telling me all about this accident we're going to be in when we grow up."

"Yeah," I say. "I have nightmares. I can't sleep." The drugs are supposed to help with that, too, and if they don't, there are other things the doctor can prescribe. "I have a prescription. Drug me up and then my problems are supposed to go away."

"Do you think that'll work?"

I'm at once afraid it won't and afraid it will. "I don't know. I haven't taken them yet."

Kevin nods. He doesn't tell me that I should. Kevin rarely tells me what to do, because he knows from copious experience that I don't listen.

"I wish you'd told me," Kevin says. "That sucks that you've been going through that alone."

And while I know this isn't true, I have to say it anyway, just to hear him deny it. "I wasn't sure you wanted to hear about it."

Kevin shakes his head at me. "I wanted you to shut up about keeping the band going. We can't, and we both know it, and you couldn't admit it. But I never wanted you to stop being my friend." Kevin plays with his sunglasses and looks like he might be thinking about putting them back on.

I take mine off. The light is dim enough in here I should be okay for a little while.

And I need to stop hiding from Kevin. He's obviously hurting too. I knew that he was, I just couldn't get past my own hurt to admit it.

"I'm sorry," I say. "I shouldn't have harassed you about that so much. I think I was just trying to hold on to something—anything—when everything was slipping away."

Kevin looks surprised that I'm willing to admit that, which

I guess is fair.

"I didn't want you to go away," Kevin says. "You're my best friend, you know? I was always closer to you than JT. And I miss him, too."

"I know you do," I say. "Maybe that's part of why I shut you out. Because I didn't want to deal with it."

"Not dealing with it seems to be going great for you."

I glare at him across the table, and he smirks at me. Stupid Kevin. He has a really nasty habit of being right, and I don't like it any better now than I used to.

"So tell me about this girl," Kevin says. "Allison?"

I roll my eyes. "We had a fight this morning. It's probably over."

Kevin looks skeptical. "Because you had one fight? Dude, it sounded from that article like you guys were pretty serious."

The article said I was in love with her, but I'm guessing Kevin has taken that with a grain of salt, as we've both been accused in the press of being in love with various people over the years, and it's only been true for each of us once.

"It was pretty serious," I say. "For me, anyway."

"Did you break up?"

"Not yet."

Kevin raises an eyebrow. "Did you think you were going to get serious with someone and not fight with them? Shane, it's *you*."

"I know, okay?" I'm sounding more defensive than I want to, but this is Kevin. He's used to it. "I know I'm not capable of long-term relationships. Trust me. I haven't forgotten how bad things were with Anna-Marie."

I remember what I said to Allison this morning—that Anna-Marie was probably the one who talked to the press. Another thing to feel fucking guilty about. I know it wasn't her. She ran off before I said most of those things, and even if she hadn't, she's not the type to call up the press and spill it all, even if it would make for the perfect revenge.

"That's not what I meant," Kevin says. "Dude, we were in *high school*. Everyone sucks at relationships in high school."

Kevin didn't. But he also didn't date, or speak to girls. "Is that the voice of experience?"

"Fuck you," Kevin says, but he's grinning.

"Look," I say. "Even if it isn't over yet, it's not like it's going to last much longer. It's *me*, right? No woman is going to put up with me for long, and Allison's too self-respecting and mature to get caught up in this shit storm."

The waitress brings us drinks and asks us if we're ready to order, even though neither of us has looked at the menu. Kevin orders a burger, and I order the same, mostly so I don't have to make any more decisions. All the while, Kevin is looking at me like he wants to say something. When the waitress leaves and he still doesn't spill it, I imagine it's because he's worried about how I'll react.

Probably wisely.

"You might as well just say it," I say.

Kevin presses his lips together. "You're really that into this girl?"

He doesn't relax, so I know this isn't the actual question.

"Yeah," I say. "She's kind of amazing. And she's put up with my sorry ass so far, even if it isn't going to last."

Kevin sighs. "Shane," he says finally. "She's not your mom."

"Fuck you," I say, less good-naturedly than he did. "I'm aware of that, thanks."

"Are you?" Kevin says. "Because you seem pretty fixated on this idea that one fight means she's going to leave you."

"What is that, some Freudian shit? I didn't fight with my mom before she left. I was four fucking years old."

"I *know*. And you've been terrified ever since that everyone is going to walk out on you."

"To be fair," I say, "everyone has."

"Not me. And not JT. He had no fucking choice in that, so it's not fair for you to blame it on him."

That's true. I know it is. "The end result is the same. Maybe it doesn't matter what the cause is. Everyone disappears eventually."

"Not me," Kevin says again.

I meet his eyes, and I know he's doing this on purpose. He wants me to go ahead and say that he chose Maya over me, that this constitutes leaving me, so that he can go ahead and deny it, and tell me that's not fair.

But deep down, probably thanks to Allison, I already know.

"You're right," I say. "Not you."

Shock registers on Kevin's face, and it takes him a moment to recover. "Really? You actually feel that way?"

"I was pissed, okay? I was terrified when you met Maya that she was going to take you away from the band, but she didn't. And after the accident, I was pissed that you had her, and I didn't have anyone. But yeah, I get that you need to put her first, because she's your girlfriend, and you love her. I get it."

"You get it," Kevin says slowly. "Because you feel the same way about Allison?"

That leap takes me by surprise, true though it is. "Why would you think that? I haven't been dating her long."

"Because you haven't been dating *anyone* in fucking years," Kevin says. "Because I haven't heard you worry about any girl leaving you like this since Anna-Marie, and maybe not even then."

"Because I was too much of a snot to admit it back then."

"Probably. But seriously, if you're that into this girl, I need to meet her."

I smile. "I want you to. If we're still together."

Kevin shakes his head. "That's what I need to see. What kind of woman can put up with your sorry ass."

I kick at him under the table, and Kevin grins again, then grows serious. "I've thought about that a lot, since the accident," Kevin says. "About how when I met Maya, I kind of grew out of the lifestyle, you know?"

I know. It terrified me at the time, like Kevin was leaving me behind.

"It would have happened for all of us, eventually," Kevin continues. "You met Allison, and it changed things. And that would have happened to JT, too. He would have grown up. But now he never will."

I nod. I still haven't seen a sign of JT since I got here, and I wonder if he's left me, since he knows I have those pills. Since I betrayed him by telling people about him.

"The guy I see," I say. "It's not really JT. It's like this twisted version in my head, but it's not really him."

"It's probably good that you know that," Kevin says. "And I know that it's a sickness, and I shouldn't be jealous, but damn, some days, I'd take it just to see him again, you know?"

"I know," I tell him. "That's why it's taken me so long to talk about it. Because I knew once I did, it was the beginning of the end." I sigh. "I'm sorry I haven't been a better friend through this. How are you and Maya doing?"

"Good, actually," Kevin says. "I mean, my arm is still messed up, and she's still got some anxiety stuff about how she could have lost me, and I'm still messed up about losing JT, obviously. But—" he half-smiles, "—I may have bought a ring."

I smile. "You going to finally ask her? You know she's been wanting to marry you for a while."

"I know," Kevin says. "And yeah, I'm going to ask. Just waiting for the right moment."

Knowing Kevin, that could be a while, but I'll razz him about that some other time. "That's awesome," I say.

"Yeah?" he asks. "You think so?"

I know what he's really asking, and I nod. "Yeah. It's not like I *want* you to be alone and miserable, just because I am."

"Were," Kevin says. "Because you were. And if you're done obsessing about me coming back to the band, I'd like to see more of you. I just couldn't take that anymore. I couldn't live in this fantasy world where our lives hadn't fallen apart. Man, it just hurt too bad."

"I know. I'm sorry I couldn't admit that at the time."

"Did you really get into a screaming match with Anna-Marie?"

Oh, god. I'd forgotten that was in the article too. "Yeah. She happened to be at the benefit last night. That's what started the whole thing between me and Allison." I pause. "Do you feel bad about what we did to her?"

"To Anna-Marie? Yeah. I've always felt bad about it. I felt bad at the time, and I think I told you that."

"I remember you asking if I really wanted to do it," I say. "But I'd already posted the video on the internet and talked to TMZ."

"And I didn't push it. I just went along with it, even though she was my friend too, and I should have said something." He shakes his head. "Everyone back in Everett always thought I was the ringleader, you know? The one Black boy in town getting the white boys into trouble. When really, I was always the ultimate follower."

That's true. And it reminds me of something I've been aware of for a while. "I've been meaning to tell you this," I say, "but with all the news lately about police shootings and stuff—it got me thinking about how much more danger you were in than the rest of us when we used to do stupid shit."

"Ah, yeah," Kevin says. "My mom was always telling me, 'Kevin, you can't do the things those white boys can do.' Never stopped me, though."

"I should have looked out for you better," I tell him. "Not that I think I wouldn't have still done all that crap and dragged you along, but I should have been more aware that you were in danger."

"Not that we ever did anything that crazy," Kevin says.

"I don't know. I think if we threw one more set of piss balloons at the school windows, the vice principal was going to burn the place down just to get rid of the smell."

Kevin laughs. "And the eggs."

I laugh along with him. The one grocery store in town locked up all the eggs in the refrigerator section, just to keep us from going in and buying them up—or stealing them, when we were refused service—just to throw at every car in town.

"The locks didn't do them any good," I say. "We just started raiding chicken coops and bothering the chickens."

"We were a bunch of punks, that's for sure."

Our burgers come, and we eat for a minute, probably because neither of us knows what to say. Finally, Kevin breaks the silence. "I'm sorry that I couldn't keep the band going for you," he says.

"I know," I say. "Are you really moving to Denver?"

"Probably. We haven't completely decided, but there's nothing keeping me here now. Not work-wise, anyway. And Maya would like to be closer to her family." He eyes me as he says this, like he's judging if I'm going to freak out about it. I hate that this is the reality of it, but I don't blame him.

Not at this moment, anyway.

"What are you going to do?" Kevin asks. I know he's asking because he's worried about me, and I wish I had some kind of reassuring answer, but I don't.

"I have some ideas," I say. "I talked to Allison about them, and she thinks I should go for it, but I don't know."

"Why not?"

I shrug. "The only real career I've had was being in the band with you guys. The idea of going it alone isn't appealing." When it comes down to it, despite my behavior these last few months, I'm not a loner. I need people around to survive.

"What's the idea?" Kevin asks.

I close my eyes. "I can't tell you."

"Seriously?"

"Yes, seriously. Because I'd just want to talk you into staying and working with me, and you'd say no, and I really can't take that right now."

"Maybe I wouldn't," Kevin says. "Say no, I mean."

I stare at him. "You're moving away."

"To Denver," he says. "Not Russia. And like I said, nothing's set in stone."

If I tell him, I know I'm going to try to talk him into staying.

The truth is, I want to do this music festival thing, but I don't want to do it alone, and the idea of working with Kevin again, even if it's not making music—

I'm desperate to hold on to any part of my former life, and my friendship with him tops that list.

"It's up to you," Kevin says, swirling a french fry around in some ketchup. "But I think you should try me."

I'm going to tell him eventually. If I'm going to be awful and needy about it, we might as well get it out of the way. "Do you remember when we used to talk about hosting a music festival?"

Kevin's been trying to pretend he's okay with me keeping this from him, but now I have his total attention. "Yeah," he says.

"We were talking just a one-time thing, but I was thinking it might be fun to run a series of festivals, like in different parts of the country. And we—*I*—could still be involved in music. Use my contacts, you know? Get our friends to play, and reach out to bigger bands who might headline, and find new bands and get them exposure, pay it forward a little. And have everyone perform something at the festival you can't see anywhere else, so there's that novelty. Maybe get the recording rights for it all, and put out albums of stuff that's one-of-a-kind, if we could get the contracts worked out."

Kevin is nodding along through all of this, and when I finish, I hold my breath, waiting for him to tell me that I'd be good at that, I should do it, but he's done with music. He's out.

"That sounds awesome," Kevin says. "I'd need to talk to Maya about it, obviously, but I'd really like to be a part of it."

It terrifies me how badly I need to hear this. "But you're leaving."

"Most likely. But it might not hurt you to have someone out in Denver working with you. Covering that scene. We've still got a lot of contacts out there. And I could fly back a lot."

"But it won't be the same," I say.

I hate myself for saying that, even though it's what I'm thinking. Even though it's true.

"No," Kevin says. "It won't be the same."

"I absolutely think you could work from Denver," I say, hating myself even more for what I have to follow this with. "But I'm not sure if I can handle working with you after you've moved away." I want to say that I could, but I know myself. If I feel like he's left me, I'm going to be a brat about it. I'm going to whine and sulk and pitch fits. Kevin deserves better than that. I don't want to drive him even further away.

"If I stay, though," Kevin says, "are you for real about this?"

"If you were in, I'd definitely want to do it. So talk to Maya, and let me know, okay?"

"Yeah," Kevin says. "Yeah, okay."

I know I'm being a dick about this, but Kevin doesn't say anything about it. He's known me longer than anyone—he and I were friends way before me and JT, all the way back in kindergarten. No one gets what a jerk I can be quite the way Kevin does.

But he still wants to work with me. And even if it's not possible, even if I can't handle it, it's not nothing.

TWENTY

Shane

I'm back home, lying on my bed, which is now covered in cotton sheets, though I can't do anything about the satin bedspread until I buy another one. I'm staring at the ceiling when my front door opens. I don't get up. I know who it is, and I left the door open for her on purpose.

Allison stands in the doorway, and the minute I look up at her, I know that she's pissed. I knew even before that, I realize. There was anger in her footsteps, coming up the hall. Anger in the unanswered texts. Anger in every interaction we've had today.

"Hey," I say.

"Hey," she says. "What the hell is wrong with you, not showing up to work? You can't just do that. Where have you been?"

It's the kind of thing Anna-Marie would have said to me, back when we were dating. She would have demanded to know where I was, accusing me of cheating on her with angry hysterics.

This is different. Calmer, more controlled.

Which scares me even more.

I don't know how to tell Allison where I've been, so I pick up the bottle of pills on my nightstand and toss it to her. Allison catches it and then looks at the label. Her face softens.

"You saw a doctor?"

"Yeah," I say. "I told her about the hallucinations. Apparently it's post-traumatic psychosis. Which is a thing, I guess."

The anger melts out of Allison, which is undeserved. She comes over and sits down on the bed next to me.

"You should still be pissed at me," I tell her.

"Oh, I am," she says. "You could have called me or texted. You could have answered any of my messages and not left me to make excuses for you. Carlyle was furious."

"I'm sorry," I say.

She deflates a little, letting out the rage she was working back up to. "I'm sorry, too. About this morning."

"That wasn't your fault," I tell her. "I'm sorry for what I said about the press. Of course you're allowed to be upset about it. *I'm* upset about it. I just wanted to pretend like I wasn't so that I wouldn't have to deal with it."

Allison nods. "How'd that work out for you?"

"Not great."

She lies down next to me and puts a hand on my arm. Part of the comforter slips back, and she smiles. "You changed the sheets." She snickers. "They're still black, though."

"Of course. To match the room."

Allison makes a show of looking around skeptically at my dark wood headboard, the black nightstand, the black leather couch and black dresser. "Are they trying to match, or blend in?"

"You don't like black?"

"Black is fine, but other colors do *exist*."

"Eh," I say. "I have white accent pillows."

"Yes, very creative."

"Look," I say. "I kept it this way on purpose. It was a signal to the girls I brought home that I wasn't emotionally available." I'm not sure that I consciously realized that's what I was doing when I bought these sheets and set up my room this way, but it definitely was. I never wanted any woman to feel invited to stay. That's a hell of a lot deeper of a reason than I would have admitted to at the time. "Shit. That's a layer, isn't it?"

"Yes, Shane. This is definitely a lair."

I pinch her side, and she squeals. "A *lay-er*," I say. "I do not have a *lair*."

"Oh, yes, you do," Allison says, gesturing around.

Shit. She's probably right. My room does have a lair-type quality to it. Dead Shane might have had more social skills, but he was also an asshole.

"So did your doctor's appointment really take so long you couldn't possibly show up to practice?" she asks.

I knew I hadn't heard the end of that, but she doesn't sound like she's about to break up with me. I'm not entirely sure how I dodged that bullet. "I talked to Kevin."

"Yeah?"

"Yeah. He texted me because he read the article, and we went to lunch."

"So you could text *him*—"

I wrap an arm around her waist. "I know. I'm sorry. But I thought if I talked to you, maybe it would be over."

Allison looks stunned, but I keep going, because if I don't, I'm afraid I'll lose my nerve. "And I realized some stuff about Anna-Marie. I do feel bad about how I hurt her, not because I'm still in love with her, but because she was my friend, and I know I shouldn't have done that to her. But I don't want to feel bad about it, because that means I have to feel bad about everything, you know? I have to think about how much that whole relationship sucked, and how I still care about her as a person, and how bad I feel about how everything fell apart. It's easier to be angry."

"That makes sense," she says. I wait for her to go on, and when she doesn't, my whole body tenses up. I try to find the words for what I'm waiting for, to put thoughts to the answers I need from her.

"Is that good enough?" I ask finally.

Allison looks confused. "Good enough for what?"

I'm not sure how to answer that. "For you."

Allison's mouth falls open. "Shane," she says. "You're more than good enough."

My eyes are burning again, and I swipe them with the back of my hand. "That's not true."

Allison's hand slides up under the hem of my shirt, wrapping around the bare skin of my back. "That's not what this is about," she says. "I don't think it's okay, what you did to Anna-Marie. And I feel like you need to recognize that it was wrong, or I worry that you're still that same person. That you'll do it again. But it's not about you not being good enough."

"Isn't it? You're trying to figure out if I'm a good enough person for you to be with."

"I'm trying to figure out if I'm setting myself up to get hurt," Allison says. "Because I'm dating a guy who has done some really douchey things, and I don't want to be the idiot who thinks her love would change him."

"I was changing anyway, before I met you. Being with you, it's more like shelter from the storm."

Allison leans closer against me. "Really, though, I don't want to change you. But I also don't want to overlook it when you're out of line, you know? And I'm not exactly sure how to make that distinction."

"Yeah, okay," I say. "And I appreciate that you'll tell me when I'm being a dick. I need that."

"Okay, maybe. But so do I. You don't need that because you're somehow unworthy."

I look up at the ceiling. "That's hard for me to believe."

Allison hesitates for a moment. "Why?"

Answering that requires a deeper admission of my own issues than I like. "Probably because of my dad," I say. "He's been telling me my whole life how worthless I am. How I'll never amount to anything or do anything right."

"He must be proud of you. After all the success you've had."

"Ha," I say. "Tell that to him. He sure doesn't think so."

Allison runs her nails along the small of my back, and I pull her closer. "I don't think your dad and I are going to get along."

"Bet on it. He's a bitter old alcoholic who doesn't get along with anyone. But having a shitty relationship with my dad isn't an excuse for the stupid shit I've done. It doesn't justify what I did to Anna-Marie."

Allison nods. "I was thinking about that today—when I wasn't busy being pissed at you—that it was a weird situation, yeah? It's not like you're going to have a high school girlfriend again. And I sure as hell hope that you wouldn't do something like that to me."

"God, no," I say. "This is different. We actually talk about stuff, you know? Instead of just screaming at each other." Anna-Marie and I talked about issues too, though even she didn't know about the things my dad did to me when I was younger. Only Kevin knows that stuff, because he was there.

Anna-Marie and I were really good at talking about our issues with other people. Just not so much our issues with each other.

"Do you really think she was the one who talked to the press?"

"No," I say. "I want to blame her, because it's easier. But no, she wouldn't have done that." I don't think even *I* would have done that. It's one thing to spread lies and another to reveal someone's personal crises to the world.

"That's what I thought," Allison says. "But you know her better."

"I did once," I say. But if she changed that much, I'd be surprised. "But I'm not going to do the same things to you that I did to her. I might still make shitty decisions, but not the same ones. I'm different now, and I have you, and you'd tell me if I'm doing something awful. We might get in a fight about it, but ultimately I'd listen to you, and I'd stop."

"Okay," Allison says. "You want my advice on the Anna-Marie situation?"

I groan. "I don't know. Do I?"

"I think you need to talk to her," she says.

"No way. You saw how well that went."

"Okay, sure," she says. "When you were yelling at her. But I think you need to apologize."

She's right about that, but I don't think an actual conversation would do anyone any good. "I don't want to start another fight, but I could probably send an email."

Allison looks doubtful.

"What, you think I can't write an email?"

"I think you clearly still want her in your life," Allison says. "Which will probably require more than that."

"You saw what happened!" I say. "We clearly shouldn't be in each other's lives. Besides, are you even okay with that? Last night you thought I was *in love* with her. Why would you want her in our lives?"

"I feel threatened by how charged all this is," Allison says, "by how much emotion you have wrapped up in it. But if you guys could just be friends and not be so worked up over it, I'd be fine with it. I *like* Anna-Marie. I'd like to be friends with her."

So would I, but I don't think it's possible. "I wouldn't get your hopes up. We haven't been friends in almost a decade, and I don't think one apology is going to change that."

"Maybe not," Allison says. "But you can try."

She's right, and I just said I would listen to her, and I already regret it. But it's the kind of regret that I don't really mean, because I know she's right.

I just don't want to do it.

"I'll think about it," I say. "Is that good enough?"

Allison sighs against my shoulder. "It's not about being good enough." She moves closer, so our faces are close and our noses are touching. "I was angry with you, and I was pissed you didn't show up for work. But I didn't think for a minute that we were going to break up." She's quiet. "Did you want to?"

"No," I say. "Of course not. But I thought maybe you would. I know it's a lot to deal with. My baggage and my psychosis and my history with Anna-Marie."

Allison shakes her head and rests her forehead against mine. "I don't think I was even worried about Anna-Marie, so much. But I think sometimes I worry about you wanting to go back to your old life. What happens when you're sick of being with the girl who's good for you, and you want to be a rock star again?"

"Allison," I say, "you're not like a vitamin. You're not some chore that I'm with because you're good for me. I *want* this. And that part of my life is over. That person I was—he's dead."

"You keep saying that," Allison says. "But what if you find out he's still in there after all?"

I press my lips to her forehead. "Even that person would have wanted you. I was running away from something I was afraid I'd never find. Avoiding commitment because I was sure no one would ever really want to be with me, that I was incapable of meeting someone's needs, of making them happy. I would have jumped at the chance to have this, if I could have stopped being an idiot long enough to admit that I wanted it."

Allison kisses me, and it's deep and beautiful and everything I need. "I'm in this," she says. "I'm scared, but I'm not going to let fear drive me away."

"Me neither," I say, and we dissolve, tugging desperately at each other's clothes, falling into the frenzied dance of her and me and our passion for each other. It's raw and dizzying, and though I feel completely defenseless, more tender than anything I've ever known.

Afterward, I admire her lying in my bed, fully naked, looking like the goddess she is, and I hold her between the layers of cotton until she falls asleep in my arms.

And as I lie there listening to her breathe, I can't help but think that if someone as amazing as her can love me back, then I must not be as much of a mess as I think I am.

TWENTY-ONE

Allison

The pageant rehearsal is chaos the next day, as everyone grows increasingly stressed. This is normal for the day before the pageant, even on years when the emcee doesn't decide to skip a whole day of practice, so I can't blame Shane for this. Honestly, even though I was worried about him and pissed at him for not responding to my texts, I'm so glad he went to see a doctor and talked to Kevin that I don't even mind so much that he missed rehearsal for it. And though Carlyle asked if I thought he should show up early today to make up for yesterday, I said I didn't think it was necessary.

Now I'm starting to regret that choice, but not because I don't believe that Shane will be able to memorize the script in time or because I think the girls need the official host reading the script instead of Trevor the sound assistant, who's been filling in. Really, I feel like having him here with me right now would help me feel more centered, more comfortable, in that strange but incredible way he has.

How far we've come since the beginning of the week, I think with a smile. I definitely wouldn't have thought then I'd feel anything but stress and annoyance (and, admittedly, sexual frustration) at being around him.

I definitely wouldn't have imagined how deeply in love with him I'd fall and how happy about that I'd be.

Shane hasn't gotten here yet, but Nix has, and that helps. It's not her job, but she usually pitches in; right now she's working with Deena on the scarf dance routine. I don't think Deena needs the help—she's an excellent dancer, and while Nix is, too, scarves aren't Nix's usual form of expression—but what it's really doing is calming the girl down from an emotional meltdown she had earlier when her coach told her she was one breakfast muffin away from planning a funeral for her thigh gap.

God, I hate some of these coaches. Deena's not only a great dancer, she's a brilliant girl with a master's degree in chemistry, and her damn coach has her worrying about her *thigh gap*.

At least, though, she's not worrying about getting sick, like half the girls are. My "Mendez family secret" tea (which is really the cheapest brand I could find at the grocery store) seems to be working, and many of the psychosomatic sniffles have disappeared. I'm hoping this also has the effect of tamping down the fears that one of them will break their nose on stage, which the *other* half of the girls won't stop talking about.

I'm stitching some of the feathers back on Yvonne's costume (*again*, because no matter what I do, this thing inevitably starts molting) while Becky-of-the-camellias practices answering interview questions five feet away and begs for my input on each one, even though her coach is right there with her. We're barely an hour into today's practice, and I already feel like I'm losing my mind.

" . . . And I think that as a free society, we should be free to embrace, um, diversity," Becky says, waving her hands around as she talks. "Like with flowers. I love my prize-winning camellias, but that doesn't mean daisies and tulips aren't also beautiful and valuable." She beams. "America is a big, lovely garden, and that's what makes it so great."

Her coach frowns. "Say it again, but stop moving your hands," the older woman says. "You're not directing a symphony."

"Allison?" Becky says. "What do you think about my stance on diversity?"

I think it's cloying and dismissive of real racial issues, but the truth is, it'll play well with the largely white and old-fashioned judges.

And I love Becky, but I don't have time the day before the pageant to be the voice of racial education. I open my mouth to tell her that the judges will love it, when a guy's angry voice cuts through the din.

"I just don't think it's appropriate, is all," the voice says, and my hackles start to rise. Collette's boyfriend, Thomas. Of course.

"But it's for our group dance number," Collette says, her voice sounding more tired than usual. I turn to see them arguing by the rack of glittering green "poppy stem" dresses for the big floral dance. "And all the other girls have the same slits on their dress."

"Just because they all want to dress like—" He cuts off when he sees several of the girls—and myself, I admit—shooting him death glares and daring him to finish that sentence. His brow furrows and he lowers his voice. "I just don't like you showing the world your whole leg like that."

Her "whole leg"? What the hell? Is he not aware of the swimsuit competition? Her suit is more modest than most, but she's not exactly wearing a burlap sack.

"But—" she starts, clearly flustered and not nearly as pissed as she should be at him.

He leans in, stroking her arm. "You know I don't like other guys seeing those parts of you. I like keeping you all to myself."

My stomach turns, and my hackles are higher than Lord Shelldon's when he sees a squirrel outside the window. It's a leg slit in a dress on a locally televised pageant, for god's sake, not like she's dancing topless at a strip club. And even if she *was*, he has no right to—

I force myself to calm down, because feathers are getting smashed in my tightening grip.

Collette worries at her lower lip. "I know, but I'd have to talk to my coach, and I don't know if I could dance in it right if I stitched it up, and . . ." She sighs. "I'll think about it, okay?"

He looks like he's going to argue more but sees me watching them. He nods, and looks away. "Good, babe. That's good. I just want what's best for you."

Yeah right, you do, jackass, I think.

Collette gives him a wan smile, and he takes off to "hit the vending machine," and I hear a few of the other girls muttering under their breath. I'm debating whether I've finally reached the point where I can't keep my opinion of him to myself any longer and am officially making this my business, when my phone rings from the purse slung over the back of my chair.

I hope it's Shane, because I could definitely stand to hear his voice right now, but there's not really any reason he'd be calling me rather than texting. I fish my phone out and blink at the name.

Jaspar Meagle.

Now my stomach is unsettled for other reasons. Mr. Meagle is one of the top investors in my fashion line, but he's also the most skittish of them, the one it took the longest to convince.

And while I get regular emails from him requesting detailed updates and more-than-occasional assurances, he's never called me before.

I doubt this means anything good.

"But if I don't gesture with my hands," Becky's saying, "I don't think the judges will understand how important my garden metaphor is. Right, Allison?"

I make a motion for "I'll be back" and drop Yvonne's costume into a feather-laden pile on my chair, then hurry out of the noisy room as I take the call.

"Mr. Meagle," I say, hoping I don't sound too breathless as I jog into the foyer. "So good to hear from you."

"Ms. Mendez," he says coolly. I try not to read anything into his tone. He sounded just as underwhelmed with life when he finally agreed to invest—and nearly made me shit myself when he announced the amount he was putting in.

"I hope you received the latest projections I sent over," I say. "I updated the fabric pricing, and while the base price increased, I hope you saw that once I negotiated down the shipping—"

"Yes, I saw all that, of course. But that's not what I'm calling about. It's another thing I saw that has me far more concerned."

My palms feel sweaty. "And what is that? You know I'm always happy to address any concerns."

"There was an article in the entertainment news recently that featured you and Mr. Beckstrom, who I am to understand is your . . . ?" He trails off.

"My boyfriend, yes," I say, uncertain as to where exactly this is going. My romantic life isn't his business, but I'm also not ashamed of it.

"Right. Well. I'm not the most current with the pop culture scene, but after the . . . allegations in the article, I did some digging to find out more about this Mr. Beckstrom, and I must say, I wasn't thrilled with the things I found."

My throat feels tight, and my hackles are rising again. "I see," I say, fighting to keep my voice even. "Of course you understand that much of what gets reported about celebrities is rumor or outright lies." I feel the need to say this, even though probably most of what he's referring to about Shane—the whole sex, drugs, and rock 'n roll lifestyle—is more or less true. "And I don't see how that would affect our business relationship, regardless."

Mr. Meagle lets out one of his dissatisfied sighs, this kind of drawn-out hmmmmph. "Normally it would not, but I've taken quite a financial risk with you, Ms. Mendez. Much of that has been based on how impressed I've been with your responsible nature."

"Which I appreciate, but I don't see how my personal life changes—"

"A responsible nature that I can't help but doubt, when I see this kind of thing," he continues smoothly over me. "And more than that, I worry about my name and business being associated with such public dramatics."

The rising fury I feel over his snap-judgment of Shane mingles with the rising panic of what this might mean.

Panic, for now, wins out. I *need* this guy's money.

"Mr. Meagle, I can assure you that my relationship with Sha—Mr. Beckstrom will not in any way affect my responsibility to my line or my professionalism in moving forward with it. And as for your reputation, I am confident that nothing from that article will reflect negatively on you or on the line. The celebrity news cycle moves quickly, and by the time the line is launched, the public will have long forgotten any—"

"Ms. Mendez," he says, and there's a note of wearied finality that makes my heart sink. "I'm afraid my decision is already made. I've contacted my lawyers and have proceeded with a contract cancellation, which, as you recall per the terms . . ."

He drones on for bit of legalese, but I can barely hear him over my own crushing dismay. My knees feel weak, and I lean against a wall for support.

My biggest investor is pulling out. Mr. Meagle's investment share of my line is how I was going to be able to pay for all the fabric that is due to start shipping in the next few weeks. It's how I was going to cover the warehouse and more. I've gotten a portion of it, which he won't be able to get back, but it's only a small portion of the full amount he was going to fund. And I've already contracted with my suppliers overseas . . .

Shit, what am I going to do?

" . . . And of course, I've notified a few of the other investors, the ones I personally recommended this project to, of my intentions," Mr. Meagle continues, and *now* I'm back to paying attention again, my heart pounding even harder. "They are free to do as they will, but I felt they should be aware of the situation."

"Mr. Meagle," I say, and I hate how I sound like I'm about to cry, because dammit, I *am* about to cry. "Please, let's not be rash. I can assure you—"

"I don't think I am the one who has been rash in this situation, Ms. Mendez," he says. "And I don't feel that any assurances you could make would change the nature of my problem here. The damage has already been done, as far as I am concerned. But I wanted to tell you myself before my lawyers contacted you, out of respect."

If he wants praise for that fine and honorable decision, he's not going to get it from me.

"I understand," I manage, and he says a curt good-bye and hangs up.

I stare at my phone for a long moment and sink to the ground. I can't believe this just happened. And if he talks to the others, and if they pull out too . . .

My dream, the one I've had for years and years, the one I've worked my ass off for, will be dead in the water.

My whole body feels numb, and yet I can feel the tears burning in my eyes, ready to spill out.

More than anything, I want Shane to be here right now. I want to cry to him and call Mr. Meagle every mix of obscenities I can think of and have him hold me and agree with me that Mr. Meagle deserves every one of those names and probably several others that Shane would think of.

I'm just about to press the button to call him, but stop.

I can't tell him this, can I? He'd only blame himself. And yeah, Mr. Meagle is bailing because of that article, but that's not Shane's fault. Honestly, it says way more about Mr. Meagle than it does about Shane, that the asshole is disregarding the many, many hours of our professional working relationship based on his interpretation of my dating life.

Shane already feels like shit about what happened at the benefit. He already feels like he's somehow unworthy of me and can't believe me when I tell him otherwise.

He wants this dream for me almost as much as I do. If he thinks he took it from me . . .

The door flings open, and Nix comes out. "Allison," she says with a grimace, "Carlyle is freaking out about whether the girls are prepared for the—" She stops, seeing the look on my face. "What happened? Are you okay?"

I shake my head, though the answer is already obvious. "No."

Nix crouches next to me, her brown eyes questioning.

"Mr. Meagle is withdrawing his investment," I say, my voice wooden. "He saw the article about Shane and me, and he's out."

Nix gapes. "What?"

"He thinks my dating Shane shows some fundamental lack of responsibility on my part, which will somehow affect my business. And he doesn't want his business involved." Now I can feel the edge in my voice coming back, the outrage.

"That's—That's—" Nix sputters, her own anger tripping her up. Nix tends to get really flustered when she's pissed, something our brothers take full mocking advantage of.

"Super shitty? Seriously, phenomenally messed up?" I offer.

"Yes! Phenomenally." Nix chews her lip. "Have you told Shane yet?"

I give her a baleful look, and her eyes widen.

"You're not going to tell him?" she asks. It's pretty obvious what a bad idea she thinks this is. And maybe it is. But she hasn't seen how down he gets on himself. She hasn't heard the stark sincerity with which he's told me he's not good enough for me, that I would be better off without him.

She hasn't, but I have. And it terrifies me.

The thought of losing my investors is terrible. But the thought of losing him is worse.

"I'm going to tell him," I hedge, picking a stray piece of feather off my skirt. "But not now. I've got to figure out what I'm going to do about the situation first."

"Allison—"

"I *will* figure it out," I say tightly. "I've gotten the money before. I can do it again." This has to be true; it has to.

She gives me a look, and I know that's not what she's trying to say. But I don't want to hear that, not now. Not when so much of me wants to call Shane, wants to hear from him that everything's going to be okay.

I can't handle that risk, not right now.

"Mr. Meagle said he's talked to the other investors, the ones he brought on board," I say, diverting the conversation back to the immediate problem.

Nix's jaw drops even more. "That ass-face! That huge—That big, giant—"

"Definitely an ass-face," I agree, cutting off her next bout of sputtering. I look back to the practice room, where costumes need to be fixed and talents need to be rehearsed and girls need to be kept from tearing their hair out from pre-pageant jitters. "Look," I say. "I need to focus on the pageant right now, and I don't have time to talk to the investors until later this afternoon. I imagine I'll be getting calls, though, and soon. Could you handle those for me? Just tell them I'm aware of their concerns and will be contacting them later today to address those."

Nix's brow furrows. "Sure," she says, though she looks worried.

"You can do this." I press my phone into her hand. "Just be brief and succinct, and don't let yourself get mad at them."

Her lips quirk up a little. "I'll do my best." Then she gives me a hug, which I let myself melt into. She's a great sister, and I love her to death.

But I still wish it was Shane's arms around me right now.

It will be, I tell myself, as I thank her and head back into the pageant fray, my gut twisting. I'll figure this out, and we'll talk through it all when it's not so immediate and fresh.

Then everything will be fine.

TWENTY-TWO

Shane

Allison left early for the pageant this morning. She's got so much to do, she says, and they're not really things I can help with. I take a shower and check my phone a dozen times and realize the best thing I can do for her today is to get off my ass and actually show up on time.

Late last night—when I wasn't sleeping, which was most of it—I composed this email in my head to Anna-Marie. I'm slowly working my way through that list of things Allison says I should do, not because I feel obligated, but because I know she wants me to do this stuff because it's good for me, and I trust her judgment. The words were so clear last night that I grabbed my phone off the nightstand and found Anna-Marie's email address—or at least her old one—and sent her the damn email around four in the morning.

I apologized for what I did to her—both for yelling at her at the benefit and for telling those lies about our relationship. I said I was sorry for the songs I wrote that implied that she was cheating on me when she and Josh got together, and I told her I was sorry for what a shitty boyfriend I was and an even more shitty friend. I want to say it felt good to say it, but it didn't. It felt awful to admit that I did those things, that they mattered, that I shouldn't have done them. It always feels awful to own up to what an asshole I am, not in some off-handed, defensive way, but for real.

Which is probably why I do so little of it.

Anna-Marie hasn't responded, which is reasonable since it's been like three hours and it was an old email address and she might not even get it at all. And if she did, why would she respond? She doesn't owe me anything, and she hasn't cared about me in years.

Except she did follow me out of that benefit, and she seemed genuinely concerned. At the time that pissed me off, but now I'm wondering if Allison's right, if she does care and I did hurt her.

I want to say I didn't mean to, but I did. Everything I did—the song and the albums and the interviews, hell, even the slide show I gave her new boyfriend of the naked pictures she'd sent me when we were together—I did it to hurt her the way she hurt me. That was a dick thing to do, and Ally is right. The right thing to do is apologize.

Even if it turns me into a psycho who has to keep checking his phone, waiting for her terse response about how much she hates me.

It's what I want to hear, I realize. Because I deserve it.

I worry, though, that I was right about her to begin with. She doesn't care, and she's not going to respond at all.

I manage not to get in an accident on the way to practice, even though I check my email an unhealthy number of times for someone behind the wheel. I get the irony there—usually I'm paranoid about driving, but today I'm paranoid about my empty inbox, and I guess one edges out the other.

I show up on time to pageant practice for once, with coffee for both me and Allison. I know she's stressed—we're getting down to the actual pageant tomorrow afternoon, with the last-minute practice in the morning. I've been distracting her from what's usually the busiest week of her year, and I feel bad about that. I want to make it up to her, and the least I can do is show up and actually do my job for once.

When I get to practice, things are worse than I thought. Allison is helping one of the girls adjust the straps on her gown to fit with her enormous breast enhancements in place. Carlyle is yelling about how all the wardrobe issues should have been worked out before practice began, and Allison looks like she's about to cry.

She glances my way, but I don't even get a chance to say hi before a girl with long black hair and wide brown eyes runs over to her, almost tripping over the hem of her long glittery gown and carrying one of those damn poodles.

"Allison," she squeals, looking stricken. "It's happened! The vision came true! Catherine Zeta-Bones got into my pageant coach's curly fries and she just threw up!"

"Catherine Zeta—" Allison starts, confused, and then her gaze drops down to the dog.

Of course, I can almost hear her thinking. Or maybe that's just what *I'm* thinking.

"And female dogs are called 'bitches'!" the girl continues, which makes several of the girls gasp. The one Allison is helping with her straps puts a hand over her nose like she's trying to prematurely prevent onstage breakage.

Allison lets out a long-suffering sigh. "Just because your dog horked up some curly fries, it doesn't mean—"

"Oh my god," another girl cries. She hikes up her long evening gown to run back to toward the dressing room. "Maxwell!" she screams to someone I assume is her pageant coach, and who I also assume is in the dressing room. "You need to get me a plastic surgeon on stand-by for right after the pageant! That way if I'm the one who breaks her nose—" Her words are muted as the door closes behind her.

The other girls look at each other, as if sussing out the odds the nose-break will be them, and then they scatter, calling out for their pageant coaches, too.

Allison rubs at her forehead wearily.

I come up behind her and wrap an arm around her waist, handing her the coffee with my other hand. She takes it and leans into me like she's going to collapse. "Hey," she says. "You're on time."

"So I am," I say. "I kind of feel like I already know the answer, but how are you doing?"

"I've had better days."

"Just the pageant?"

Allison twists out of my arms and takes a long drag of her coffee. "Yes."

As if there needed to be anything else. "How can I help?"

"Learn your lines," Allison says. "And actually say them right today."

I smile and kiss her cheek. "For you, even that." I grab my script and head back toward the green room. At the end of the hall, the door to the outside has been left ajar, and I see Nix pace by, cell phone in hand.

I didn't realize she was going to be here today. I only mean to catch her eye and wave hello as she paces by again, but I hear the words she's saying, and I freeze.

"No," Nix says. "Ms. Mendez wants to assure you that her relationship with Mr. Beckstrom will have no effect on the line moving forward. I know Mr. Meagle had concerns—yes, I know he was the one who recommended the project to you, but—yes, of course. Yes, Ms. Mendez will call you this afternoon. Of course. I appreciate you taking the time. Of course. Thank you. Bye."

Nix hangs up the phone just out of sight of the door and stomps her foot, letting out a frustrated yell. I want to do the same, but I'm too stunned to move.

Her relationship with Mr. Beckstrom won't have an effect on her line moving forward? Why the hell would it?

Nix steps into the doorway to come in and spots me standing in the hall. Her eyes widen, and she looks caught. "Oh hey, Shane!" she says. She's not a great actress, and she's clearly not happy to see me. It's obvious why.

"What the hell was that?" I ask.

Nix shrinks back a little. "What was what?"

"Who the fuck is Mr. Meagle? And what do I have to do with Allison's line?"

Nix looks up at the ceiling, squirming like she did when Allison tried to set her up with me. "Maybe you should ask Allison."

"I just talked to her. She didn't say anything about her line."

Nix cringes. "Look, Shane, I think you should talk to her about it, because—"

"Nix," I say. "Just tell me what's going on."

She bounces her toe on the ground behind her. "One of Allison's investors pulled out because of that article about the two of you. And now he's got the others all riled up, and Allison has to do the pageant, so I offered to field the phone calls for her so she doesn't lose any more."

My mouth falls open. "She lost an investor because of me?"

"Because of the press," Nix says. "Which is stupid, because she's worked her ass off and made all her deadlines—"

"But being with me makes her look irresponsible." I should have thought of that. I should have thought that the article might have an impact on her life, but instead all I thought about was myself. "Was she—was she not going to tell me?"

Nix looks up at the ceiling again. I ball my fists, wanting to punch one right through the wall.

Allison's line is in jeopardy because of me, and she didn't think that was something I needed to know. Worse, she didn't want to talk to me about it.

"How long has she known?" I ask.

"Just since this morning," Nix says.

"Is she going to be able to move forward with her line? Without that investor, I mean?"

"She will," Nix says. "She's going to have to find more money somewhere, but it's Allison. She'll find a way." She hesitates.

"I'm sure she was going to tell you."

She's a terrible liar. "Sure she was," I say. And I turn around and stalk back to the green room before Nix sees how upset I am.

I feel responsible for Allison losing her investor. Of course I do. But what hurts is that she didn't tell me about it. Yeah, I just got here, but she could have called when she heard. She's been fielding enough of my crap, listening to me whine about the accident and Anna-Marie and my dad and all sorts of shit. But when something happens to her that has to hurt and panic her and cause all kinds of stress, she calls Nix.

Not that I think I should be the one fielding phone calls. I'd tell them they're assholes for doubting Allison, and that wouldn't help any. But if I was hit with news like this, I'd want to talk to her. I'd want her to be there for me, to tell me it's going to be okay.

Except that yesterday, when that article broke, I pretended I didn't care instead. Is that why she openly lied to me when I asked if it was just the pageant that was bothering her? Does she think I wouldn't be there for her, or just that I'm not strong enough?

Fuck. I lean back on the couch, the same place Allison and I made out just days ago, before going back to her place for the first time. I want to be there for her now, but I'm pissed as all hell that she doesn't want me to be. I imagine Nix is off telling Allison right now that I heard her talking. And then Allison is going to be the one insisting she intended to tell me.

I wish I believed that was true, but I see it now. I'm the weak one in the relationship, the needy one. She's with me because she feels bad for me, and maybe she gets something out of being the one who has it all together.

But a one-sided thing like that—it can't last. Sooner or later, she'll get sick of me, and that will be that.

"Shane," Allison calls from the auditorium.

I set down my script and stand up. I know I'm not handling this well. I know being an ass about it is just going to reinforce that I'm not good enough to handle her problems, that I need to be handled with kid gloves. But damn it, I'm pissed, and I'm hurt, and I've never been one to handle that well.

I step out into the hall. The door to the outside is closed now, but I see Nix pacing again through the smoked glass windows.

"We need you on stage," Allison says.

I stare at her. Nix hasn't talked to her. She has no idea that I know. "Are you sure you're all right?"

She pulls her lower lip between her teeth, and for a moment I think she's going to tell me. "I'm fine," she says. "But if you don't get up on stage, Carlyle is going to lose it."

"Okay, then," I say, and I follow her into the auditorium and take the stage doors up to my microphone.

I left my script in the green room, I realize. And I didn't even read it. I remember some of the basics, but I definitely haven't memorized it. I could go get it, but as the girls start lining up for their evening wear runway walk, I feel my nerves hardening.

Fuck this. They should have fired me yesterday for not showing up. Carlyle probably would have, but Allison talked him out of it. Wouldn't want to upset me, given how fragile I am.

I know it wouldn't hurt so bad if it wasn't true, but it still makes me want to burn the place to the ground.

The first girl—Simone, I think—comes gliding across the stage and walks up to the front. Allison gives me a look, like I'm forgetting something.

Talking. Right. About the girl in the dress. I pick up the microphone and take a look at Simone, who's wearing a striped wrap-around dress. "First up, ladies and gentlemen," I say, "please welcome Simone, Princess of Zebras."

Simone gives me a horrified look over her shoulder, and I can see Carlyle saying something to Allison. "Very funny, Shane," Allison calls. "Can we get back on script, please?"

But I'm just getting started. Next up is Carmen, who's wearing a dress that I remember from the script that I'm supposed to say she designed herself. I don't know if that gets her extra points, or if she's relying on the strange seaweed-looking streamer things that hang from her belt for that, but either way— "And here is Carmen, Queen of the Lagoon—" I look at the girl who's just stepped onto the stage. She's a redhead in a shimmery gold dress with honest-to-god gold coins glittering from her neckline. I can't remember her name. Is it Chloe? Regardless— "And next we have Absylonia, mistress of the dragon's hoard—"

"Shane!" Allison shouts. The other girls giggle, then fall silent. At the front of the stage, Carmen looks down at her dress.

"Do I look like a lagoon?" she says. Absylonia stomps her foot and shuffles backstage.

"What?" I say to Allison.

She's shaking her head at me, like I know exactly what, and I do. I'm just not sure that she does.

"Take five, everyone," she says. Then she stalks through the stage door and up the stage-left stairs. I meet her in the wings. No need to have this conversation in front of everyone. I'm pissed as hell that she didn't tell me about the investors, but by now I'm more pissed at myself for being an asshole instead of just calling her on it. I'm proving her point about me. I'm useless, and I'll never be able to have an actual, healthy relationship. I'm incapable of it.

"Shane," Allison says when she reaches me. "What the hell is the matter with you?"

"What?" As if I don't know exactly what.

"Carmen is in tears, that's what," she snaps. "And Amanda's going to want to change her dress."

Ah. That's right. Amanda. Not Chloe. God, which one is Chloe?

"I asked you for *one* thing today," she continues with a glare, "and you can't even stay on script."

I shrug. "Guess I'm not good for anything, am I? Don't say I didn't warn you."

Allison shakes her head at me. "What the hell, Shane? What's wrong with you?"

"I'd tell you," I say, "but I guess we don't *talk* about these things, do we?"

In the dim back-stage light, Allison looks like she wants to strangle me, which I deserve. But I also see the exact moment when she realizes that I know. Her shoulders slump, and she looks down at her shoes. "You talked to Nix."

I turn, partially obscuring my face in the black fabric stage wing. "Don't be mad at her. I spotted her outside and I was going to say hi. She was talking one of your other investors into staying. She didn't know I was standing there. It's not her fault."

"I was going to tell you," Allison says. She sounds almost as defensive as I do, which is a feat.

"Right," I say. "Sure."

"I was. I just wanted to get it under control first."

Of course she did. Because she doesn't trust me. And I'm fucking proving her right, and I can't stop.

"Sure. Wouldn't want to let me know about anything that isn't under control."

Allison's voice is low. "What is that supposed to mean?"

I shrug. "Nothing."

"Shane," Allison says. "Don't do that to me."

"It means you don't need me," I say. "Not the way I need you. And that fucking hurts, Ally. What do you want me to say?"

Her mouth opens and closes again.

"Allison!" Carlyle shouts from the auditorium.

Allison's whole body looks tense enough to snap. "We can talk about this later." She looks up at me, and I think maybe she's about to cry. She's begging me, I realize, to tell her that's okay. That we can talk about it later. That there will be a later.

"Yeah," I say. "Yeah, of course."

She sniffs and nods and practically runs down the stage-left stairs. I follow her at a slower pace, off to the green room to grab my script.

TWENTY-THREE

Shane

Allison dismisses me for a couple of hours around lunchtime. Carlyle has a meeting with some of the judges for this weekend, and they're done doing stage work until later this afternoon. Mostly, though, I think Allison just doesn't want to have to deal with me.

I collapse in the green room and throw on my sunglasses. There's a headache building somewhere behind my eyes, and I pop a couple of pain killers with one of the complimentary bottles of water. JT is standing in the corner, leaning against the wall. He's been sullen and mostly silent since I got the medication, even though I haven't so much as opened the bottle. I pull out my phone and ignore him.

I have an email from Anna-Marie.

Thanks, Shane, it says. *Would you want to do lunch and talk?*

I stare at it. No, I don't want to do lunch and talk. I want her to tell me she hates me over email so that I can know that the bridge is forever burned. I'm over Anna, have been for years, but I've never been able to get over her leaving. I'm not in love with her, but I considered her family, one of my people. The fact that I meant nothing to her after we broke up—

I take a deep breath, running a hand through my hair.

It hurt, but it wasn't an excuse for the way I responded. I want to go find Allison, to ask her what she thinks I should do, to talk it through and get her advice. But I'm still mad at her for not needing the same from me. I get that my advice is probably worth less than nothing, but that she didn't even want my shoulder to cry on—

I'm pretty sure I'm being unreasonable, but I can't sort out why, which is exactly the reason I shouldn't talk to anyone in person, much less Anna-Marie.

I squeeze my eyes shut.

And try to ignore the part of me that wants to say yes, just to know that there's one more person in the universe who cares about me enough to have a conversation.

Even if it is about what a dick I've been.

Sure, I respond. *I'm free for the next few hours.*

I turn on the lock screen on my phone and stretch out on the green room couch. Anna-Marie probably won't answer for hours, and she almost certainly didn't mean today. She'll get back to me after a while and clarify that maybe we could get together next week, which will be better anyway—

My phone dings. There's a response, in which she names a place twenty minutes away and asks what time.

Shit.

Am I really going to do this?

I don't think Allison would be mad at me for seeing her. She wanted me to talk to Anna, to work things out, so there isn't always this baggage from the past hanging over me. And there's zero chance of me rekindling anything with Anna-Marie, not only because she's married and pregnant, but also because I have no desire to be with anyone who isn't Allison.

Who may not want to talk to me right now, and she doesn't have to get involved. But I'm still going to do her the courtesy of letting her know.

I respond that I can be there in twenty and go back to the auditorium, where Allison stands in a cluster of girls. Amanda and Carmen both glare at me, and all of them fall silent. Allison turns around, and her expression is a mix of weariness and guilt. I wonder if she was talking about me with the girls or if this is just how she feels about me now in general.

"Hey," I say. "I'm going to head out for an hour or so."

"I told you that's fine," Allison says. Her voice is tense, and I hope it's because she doesn't want to get into it here, in front of the girls, and not because she's done with me in general. Maybe she's thinking through what I said, about how she doesn't need me the way I need her, and realizing both how true and how messed up that is.

"Can I talk to you for a second before I go?" I ask.

That actually seems to make her relax. She nods and walks out of the auditorium. I follow as the girls whisper behind us.

When we get out into the hall, Allison turns around to face me. "I'm sorry I didn't tell you about the investors."

"I'm sorry for being such a dick about it. But I just wanted to let you know, I emailed Anna-Marie to apologize."

Her eyes widen. "You didn't have to—"

"Yeah, I did," I say. "Because you were right. It's something I should have done a long time ago."

Allison gives me a weak smile, and I'm not sure if she's proud of me, or regretting having ever suggested that I contact my ex-girlfriend, who just days ago she'd decided I was still in love with.

If it's the latter, she's not going to like this next part. "Anna-Marie asked me to meet her for lunch, and I told her I would."

"Really?" Ally looks as surprised as I am about that.

"I know. I think I owe her an apology in person, if she wants it, so I'm going to go. But I'll be back in time for practice this afternoon. I promise."

Allison opens her mouth and then closes it again, like she can't decide what she wants to say, and I realize that even though I want to pull back in my shell and pretend I don't care, I do care. I hate this tension between us. I hate that she doesn't feel like she can talk to me.

I hate that I'm not a better boyfriend, and I'm so damn scared I never will be.

"I love you," I say.

Allison looks at me in surprise, and I think maybe she's about to cry. "I love you, too."

I hold out an arm, and she wraps hers around my waist, and we hold each other, just for a second. It doesn't solve anything that's messed up with us, but it's something. An intention to try, a promise that we both still want this.

That alone is almost enough to make me break down and beg her not to give up on me.

Instead, I kiss the top of her head. "I'll be back soon," I say.

I turn and walk out to my car, not letting myself look back. She already thinks I'm fragile.

I don't want her to see how right she is.

Anna-Marie is waiting in the restaurant when I arrive. I can see her from the reception stand. I wave to the hostess as I head back, keeping my sunglasses on.

If I'm honest, I'm not worried about the lights making my head hurt. I just want to hide.

Anna-Marie smiles tentatively as I approach. Her long, reddish-brown hair is clipped back, and she's wearing a dark blue tunic-style shirt over leggings. Her hands rest on her pregnant belly, which rises above the table top.

"Hey," I say.

"Hey. Thanks for the email."

"Yeah," I say. "No problem." We look at each other awkwardly, and I sigh and take off my sunglasses. Much as I don't want to, wearing them is probably rude, and I don't want to do any more damage to Anna than I've already done.

"How are you doing?" I ask.

"Good," Anna-Marie says. "Busy. My new show started airing.

It's only a half season to start, but it seems to be doing well, which is a huge relief."

That's right. She's graduated from soaps to a sitcom, which I've heard is hilarious. I haven't watched it, but I've read about it. She's the star, and the reviews of her performance are enthusiastic. I'm guessing it'll get picked up for more soon. "That's great," I say. "How's Josh?"

"Good," she says. "He's keeping busy, too. There's a lot we need to get done before the baby comes."

"And that's good? I mean, your baby's healthy?"

"Yeah," Anna-Marie says with a small smile. "As far as we can tell."

She pulls her napkin onto her lap and fiddles with it. The restaurant is a soup and sandwich place, but the ritzy kind with thin bread and overpriced desserts. Neither of us has even looked at the menu.

God, this is awkward as hell.

"How are things with Allison?" she asks. "Is that new?"

"Yeah," I say. "Really new, actually. And it's good, I guess." I try not to wince at how doubtful I sound. I don't mean to make her think I'm not into the relationship. The opposite is true, which is why the question of how it's going is hard to answer. Somehow, being here with Anna-Marie reminds me even more of how bad I am at relationships. How I promised myself I'd never try again, because of how much it hurts when I screw it up.

"I'm sorry, too," Anna-Marie says.

I look up at her. "What?"

"That's why I wanted to meet you," she says, looking apologetic. "To say that I'm sorry about the way things ended with us, and me leaving like that. You were right that I just disappeared. I think I needed to. It wasn't just you I was ghosting; it was all of Wyoming. My family. Everything. I had to leave it all behind to survive."

I nod. That makes sense. I think I always knew that was why she left. She had a fair share of her own problems there, even beyond me. "I get it," I say. "I just—when we broke up, I thought we'd always be friends, you know? We both needed some space, so that first year, I didn't try to get in touch. We were caught in that sick loop where we'd get back together and then hurt each other and break up again, and I didn't want to start it back up. I was just about to reach out and see if you wanted to get together as friends when I heard that you'd moved out to LA."

"You still could have called," she says. "I had the same number for years."

I shrug. "I could have. But I think I was too busy being hurt that you didn't care enough to give me a heads up that you were leaving."

"It wasn't personal," she says. She opens the menu, but she doesn't look at it. "It didn't occur to me that you would even want to keep in touch, after everything." She blinks down at the table, tugging her lower lip between her teeth. "Honestly, I didn't really think about how you would feel."

Something inside me breaks, and my eyes start to water. Shit. I'm going to cry right in front of her. I should have left my glasses on. Instead I scratch at the bottom of my eye, like maybe I've got something stuck in it, but I know it's bullshit and not even convincing.

That's the crux of it, I guess. She didn't even think about me. That's what hurt so bad—not that she left, but that I had already fallen so far off her radar that it didn't even occur to her to send a text.

After everything we'd been through, after five years of being the center of each other's worlds, she just didn't think about me. And it made me angry to be forgotten, but now I realize that all that anger, all that asshole stuff that I did, was just covering up for this deep well of hurt.

She didn't think about me, because she has a family, even if she was running away from them. She came out here and made friends and has people in her life who love her, who are important to her. And the only people I've ever been important to are the guys from my band, so I did everything I could to keep us all together.

And now it's gone. It's not so much that Anna-Marie forgot about me, as that everybody does.

She's not your mom, I hear Kevin say.

Anna-Marie is staring at me with pity, and I resist the urge to tell her to go to hell, just to get her to stop.

"I'm making this worse," she says. "I'm sorry."

"No, it's fine." But the tears are welling up now.

Shit. This was a mistake. But I'm here now, and I owe her. I can't run away.

"It just sucks to hear that you didn't matter, you know?" I say.

She shakes her head. "It's not that. I didn't *let* myself think about you, or my family, or any of it. I just couldn't—" She draws in a deep breath. "I'm sorry about all of that. I really was happy to see you, when I finally got back to Wyoming."

"No you weren't," I say. "You were already hung up on Josh."

"I was. I was falling in love with him. But I would have loved if, after all those years, you and I could be friends again."

"That's what I wanted, too," I say.

She gives me a look. "Right. That's what you were after when you showed up that night at my dad's. Friendship."

I roll my eyes. "Yeah, okay, so I wanted to sleep with you. I think it was habit, you know? I didn't know how else to get your attention. I think that's all I really wanted. For you to pay attention to me. Even when Josh showed up, I was mostly pissed that you didn't have time for me. It's not like I wanted to get back together. If you had called me up when he got into town and talked to me about what was going on, I think I would have been cool with that." I shrug. "It's not an excuse. But I was an afterthought. A convenience. I thought we were important to each other, and you showing up and not caring—it was evidence that I was right all along. That you didn't give a shit about me. And that's why I did what I did. Because that hurt so bad, I just wanted to get back at you and make the pain go away." I wipe my eyes with the back of my hand. "But it doesn't make it okay. I'm really sorry about what I did—the songs, the lies, everything. I shouldn't have done that. You didn't deserve it."

Anna-Marie gives me a sad smile. "It's okay," she says. "I forgive you."

My resolve shatters. Suddenly I'm crying—not just a few tears, but full on crying, sitting at this damn table in the middle of this stupid restaurant. I've told myself a thousand times I don't care about Anna-Marie. I thought I'd burned that bridge. I lit a damn bonfire trying. I couldn't stand wishing that we could be friends, that I could matter to her even a little, and so I burned the whole thing to the ground. But I didn't know how badly I needed to hear that she forgives me until she said it.

"Really?" I say.

"Yeah," Anna-Marie says. "Don't get me wrong, what you did was not okay, and I was angry with you for a long time. But I've been going to therapy for a few years now, and one of the things my therapist helped me to realize is that I'm sad you're not in my life anymore. I'm sad that we aren't friends. And that week in Wyoming—I never meant to hurt you, and I'm so sorry that I did. I think I was just so caught up in my own issues, you know? I was so caught up in what was happening with me and Josh. I was scared to death of a relationship, and I didn't know how to talk about that with anyone. And what I wanted with you, it just got caught up in that. I fell back into old patterns, too, because the past was so much less scary than the future."

I nod. "That makes sense." And it does. I think of something else Kevin says to me with some frequency.

Shane, not everything is about you.

I'm not great at remembering that. I'm not sure how much I even try. But factually, I get that it's true.

"Should I not have said any of that?" Anna-Marie asks. "Have I made it worse?"

"No," I say. "Thank you. I really needed to hear that. I thought I'd messed up so bad there was no way you'd ever forgive me." I wipe my face with my napkin, on the verge of getting myself together again. I'm aware that our waitress is hovering, watching me, trying to decide whether or not she should interrupt.

Anna-Marie shrugs. "You were a dick," she says. "But I wasn't great to you either. Not just when I came back to Wyoming, but before, when we were together." She takes a deep breath. "That's another thing I've realized in therapy. All these years, I blamed you for being a shitty boyfriend, but I was a really shitty girlfriend, you know? I was always accusing you of cheating on me, when really those insecurities had way more to do with my issues than your flirting."

I shrug. "I was a flirt. And I could have curbed it better than I did. But I didn't cheat on you."

"I believe you," she says. "Tell me if this sounds wrong, but what I've come to believe is that I picked a lot of those fights with you. I'd be sure you were going to cheat on me, which was more about my issues with my dad than about you. And then you'd be hurt that I didn't trust you, and you'd lash out at me—"

"Oh god," I say. I've never thought of it that way, but— "Yeah, that's exactly what would happen. Like, you were saying I wasn't good enough, which had more to do with *my* issues with *my* dad—"

"Exactly," Anna-Marie says. "Then we'd scream at each other and break up and sleep with other people just to hurt each other."

"God, yes," I say. "And then we'd feel awful and come crawling back to each other and get back together and then do it all over again."

Anna-Marie sighs. "We were both dicks," she says. "And I'm sorry for my part in it and for being a shitty friend, too. But obviously you matter to me. If you didn't, what you did wouldn't have hurt so bad."

"I'm sorry, too," I say. "For everything."

"It's okay," Anna-Marie says. "I think part of what made me sad over the last few years is that I had all these realizations about what happened, but I couldn't call you to talk about it. I wasn't sure how you would react."

"Probably like I did the other night," I say. "So you made

the right call."

"I was so worried about you after the accident," she says. "You said I didn't care, but I cried for days about what happened to JT. I thought for a long time about whether I should come to the funeral, but I just didn't think seeing you would be good for either of us." She frowns down at the table. "Now I think probably that was a mistake."

"I don't know," I say. "I've been really messed up."

"Yeah," Anna-Marie says. "I read the article. And since they got everything else right . . ."

She's quiet, waiting for me to confirm that it's true what they said about me hallucinating JT.

"Yeah," I say. "That was all true."

"I'm so sorry, Shane," Anna-Marie says. "I'm sorry about JT, and about Kevin, and the band."

"Yeah," I say. "Me, too." I don't know what else to say about that, so I'm quiet for a moment, and Anna-Marie swears under her breath.

"Who do I have to kill to get a sandwich around here?" she asks. "Can't they see how pregnant I am?"

I laugh, and the waitress must decide that it's okay for her to come over at that moment, because she joins us and takes our orders. She doesn't quite look at me, and I'm not sure if it's because she recognizes me, or because I'm a maniac crying in her restaurant. Either way, I'm no more keen for eye contact than she is.

When the waitress leaves again with our orders, Anna-Marie takes a sip of her water. "Josh has a best friend named Ben. They've been friends—more like brothers—since they were kids, and it's like they have this bond that's irreplaceable because they have all this history. And I don't know that you and I could ever be that close, but I think you're that person for me, you know?" She considers. "Only with way more baggage."

I laugh, despite myself. "Yeah, that about sums it up."

She hesitates. "So do you think we could be friends? Like, we don't have to hang out all the time. But we could get together for lunch every once in a while, to chat and catch up. I'd like to meet Allison, more officially, if you want, and I think you and Josh would actually get along now that neither of you has a reason to feel threatened."

I think about what she's asking. I want to say yes, because being friends like that sounds nice. But it also sounds superficial. It seems like something I might have been capable of before, if I could have gotten past my anger, and something I might someday be capable of again.

But now, with everything so raw, with my life so thoroughly demolished—

"Would Josh be okay with that?" I ask. I'm looking for the easy out, and I know it. I want to deem it impossible so I don't have to say no. I can't have a surface friendship right now. Holding my life together is taking everything I can muster, and I don't know how to be okay, to chat lightly over lunch. I think I have two modes right now, open and closed, and I'm sure she doesn't want to deal with the things I'll say if I'm open, and she knows what an asshole I am when I'm closed off.

I don't want to do that to her anymore. I don't want to do it to Allison, either, and I have been anyway.

"Josh is still pissed at you," Anna-Marie says. "But really, he just doesn't want me to get hurt anymore. If we can be friends, he'll be fine with it. As long as you don't write any more songs about me."

So it's just me, then, who can't do this. "I'd like to be friends," I say, "but I can't right now."

She looks a little sad, but she nods. "Is it Allison? Because I understand if she doesn't feel secure about it. We've got a lot of history that's hard for people to understand."

I want to blame Allison, because that would be easier, but this is my fault, not hers. "It's not that. It's just—I don't think I'm capable of that kind of friendship."

Anna-Marie looks confused. "What kind of friendship do you want?"

"I want to be able to do what you're saying," I say. "To get together and chat and catch up. But right now . . . my life is a mess, and I don't know how to be normal. I'm a little short on people to talk to about how messed up I am. Not that I can't talk to Allison, but it's a lot to put on her, and—"

I need support, is what I'm saying, but I feel stupid putting it that way.

"I can call you when I'm stable again," I say. "When I'm ready for surface friendships. When I can get through a fucking conversation without bursting into tears."

"It doesn't have to be just surface stuff," she says cautiously. Maybe even hopefully. "If you wanted, I'd really like to hear about what's going on in your life. If you trust me with that."

"Yeah?" I ask.

"Yeah, of course. I thought that was probably too much to ask for, but if you want, I'd like to know how you really are."

I feel like I'm going to start crying again, but instead I start talking. I tell her about JT, about seeing him following me around, only it's not JT, really, more like my own id. And about getting the medication and being afraid to take it and never see him again. Anna-Marie tells me about the things she's learned in therapy and how she's gotten closer to her dad and stopped talking to her mom altogether. She tells me about the work she and Josh have done as a couple, and I break down and tell her all about my fight with Allison and about how deeply in love I am, and how scared.

"I get it," Anna-Marie says with a sigh. "I don't think I can adequately express how much I understand the feeling of being scared to get hurt like that."

I believe her. She and I hurt each other that way, over and over again.

"Does it ever get better?" I ask. "The fear, I mean."

"Yes," she says. "It doesn't totally go away, but the fear does get quieter. And being in this stable, healthy relationship—I was able to start feeling safe and secure, more and more as time goes on. It helps a ton that Josh is so patient with me, and he never gives me a reason to doubt his love for me or his commitment." She smiles. "Do you think Allison could be that person for you?"

"I don't know," I say. "I want her to be. And I want to be that person back for her, but I'm such a fucking mess."

"If there's one thing I've learned from my marriage," Anna-Marie says, "it's that being a mess doesn't make you unable to love someone. In some ways, it makes it more deep and real."

"I want that to be true," I say. "More than anything."

Anna-Marie smiles, and our sandwiches come, and she practically inhales hers. But my mind echoes with the last thing she says before we start to eat.

"Good news, Shane," she says. "It is."

On the way back to the pageant, I call Kevin. He doesn't answer, but I leave him a long message about how it doesn't matter if he moves to Denver, I'll do whatever I can to make this festival thing work. I want Kevin to work with me, and if I can't handle it, I'll get help, I'll go to therapy, I'll do whatever I have to do so that we can build a new partnership. A healthy one.

It's a big promise, but it's one I hope to keep.

When I hang up, JT glares at me from the passenger seat. I'm on time, as promised, and all I want is to see Allison and hug her and tell her how much I love her. I know I said it before I left, but talking to Anna-Marie about all that stuff—

It's cemented in my mind how much I want this. How much I want to try, even if I suck at it.

JT just keeps glaring.

"What?" I say.

JT shakes his head. "Nothing."

"Talk to me," I tell him. "God, it sucks not talking to you. I miss you."

"Yeah, maybe. But you're still going to take those pills."

I grip the steering wheel. "I haven't yet."

"I know. But you just promised Kevin you'd get *help*. And even if you didn't, she's going to talk you into it."

I don't have to ask to know he's talking about Allison.

"I want to tell you to break up with her," JT says. "If you do that, maybe you won't take them."

"I'm not breaking up with her," I tell him. "But you could ask me not to take the pills."

"Fine. Don't take them. I don't want to go away."

"Okay. I won't." I'm not sure that I mean it, but I feel like I need to say it. It still feels like a betrayal of JT, even inside my own head.

"But you will," JT says. "Because you're not healthy, and this isn't good for you, and in the end that'll be more important to you than I am."

"Do you care if it's unhealthy for me?"

"No." He frowns at the dashboard, then adds, reluctantly, "But JT did. If he was really here, if I was really him, he'd tell you to take the pills. He'd want you to be happy."

"I'm not happy," I say. "I'm pissed. I'm mad as hell at you for leaving me. I know you couldn't help it, but I'm pissed at you anyway. Everyone leaves me. I'm always alone. Everyone has someone and I don't. You're supposed to have a family, you know? Everyone is supposed to have a family, people you can go to when everyone else leaves. Kevin has one, and JT, and Anna-Marie has her dad, and Josh. Allison's really close to her family, and when it ends, they'll be there for her. And I'll have no one."

"Yeah. When it comes to families, you really got screwed."

"I need her." The pitch of my voice is climbing and I think I might cry again. "I need her, but she doesn't need me."

"Yeah, well," JT says. "She wants you, and I'd say that's pretty damn good."

It is. I know it is.

I just wish I could believe it was enough to make it last.

TWENTY-FOUR

Allison

It's about an hour before the pageant begins, and it feels a little bit like being in the eye of the storm: preternaturally quiet. The frantic energy of yesterday's practice has died down to a murmur now as the girls practice various calming and breathing exercises or quietly recite interview answers to themselves as their coaches or wardrobe specialists finish last-minute adjustments to hair and makeup. As usual, the main round of interviews was actually conducted earlier this morning, in an offstage portion for the judges to get to know the girls better. And though that earlier interview accounts for a significant amount of their overall score, there will still be another question portion on stage—and I can tell several of the girls are hoping to redeem themselves from their earlier answers.

Right now, the house is open and the voices of the earliest-arriving audience members hum in the auditorium. All the girls are wearing the floor-length, figure-hugging red, white, and blue sequined gowns that they'll dance in for the opening group number—which Nix claims shouldn't be called a "dance," but rather "walking in various configurations to music like a marching band who forgot their instruments."

She's pretty much right, but I'm not about to say that to the girls. Or Carlyle, who out of all of them looks the most likely to hyperventilate. This isn't abnormal for him right before a pageant, but even he seems to have let the dog-vomit fulfillment of Collette's prophecy make him extra anxious.

"I can't have one of these girls get their nose broken in my pageant," he said to me earlier, while the girls were in their interviews.

"It's not going to happen, Carlyle," I said back with a sigh. The same words—with name interchanged—that I'd said to pretty much every pageant contestant and coach for the last twenty-four hours. "Collette had a dream, and a dog threw up curly fries and then was fine. These two things are not connected."

He kept wringing his hands anyway. "Well, I suppose Cher is probably too busy to give much thought to our little pageant, let alone give dream predictions about it." He gave me a hopeful look, like I might contradict him on this, and assure him that Cher is undoubtedly a fan and might even be in the audience tonight.

I didn't.

Now, though, he's back to full-fledged anxiety, flitting from station to station, checking on sound and props and the girls and back again. Even though he's not going to be on stage, he's wearing his "lucky" purple velvet suit, and the wave in his hair is extra tall. Shane told me about how he envisioned a little surfer riding that wave the first time he saw Carlyle, and now I can't picture anything else when I see him.

I catch myself snickering, and Shane's voice calls from behind me. "And you haven't even seen me in *this* yet."

I turn around, smiling, and my eyes widen when I see him. Not because he's wearing some crazy-ass rainbow shirt, but because he's wearing a dark blue, slim-fitted suit, with a royal blue shirt underneath. It's not his usual rock star style, which I love, but *damn*.

It's pretty much the same suit that Carlyle has insisted every host wear at this pageant for the last ten years—with slight variations in color and fit—but none of them has ever looked so gorgeous.

He wrinkles his nose, but he's clearly hiding a smile at my reaction. "I know, right? I look . . . respectable or something."

"You look hot." I lean up for a kiss, which he returns. "And also like you're about to run a Fortune 500 business meeting."

"So *that*'s what does it for you . . ." he says with a smile, his arms still around me.

"I'm pretty sure you wearing anything does it for me," I return. "And maybe especially nothing."

"Yeah, well, I pitched that idea to Carlyle, but apparently the naked emcee thing is a no-go. Even though I made a compelling argument for increased ratings."

I laugh, and he grins, and it feels so good. Things have still been a little tense between us since yesterday. He slept over at my place last night, and we made love and held each other, and he told me about his lunch with Anna-Marie, which sounds like it went even better than either of us—and probably also she—could have expected. But we were both still skirting the real issues between us. I know we still need to talk, really talk, about what happened with the investors and me not telling him. But honestly, the whole situation is so stressful I can barely bring myself to think about it, at least while I'm still dealing with the pageant.

What the hell am I going to do?

"Hey," Shane says, his eyes lowering, his voice cautious. And I'm suddenly pretty sure the same thing's on his mind as is on mine. "Did any of the other investors end up pulling out?"

My nerves heighten, along with my guilt for not talking about this openly with him in the first place. For still having trouble doing so, somehow, even though I desperately want to. "No, thank god." A scared part of me wants to leave it there, but I force myself to continue. "But I still have to replace that money. Once this pageant is over, I'll start networking again, update my pitch presentations, all that."

He nods. "You need it soon, though, yeah? Like, you're already on the hook for money you don't have."

I haven't told him this, and I doubt Nix went into that much detail—especially considering Nix doesn't usually know that many details about the day-to-day aspect of my business—but he's been essentially living with me much of the last week, and he's a smart guy. He's heard me on the phone with manufacturers, and he's figured out that I owe a lot of people for work they've already done.

"Yeah," I say quietly. "Not all of Mr. Meagle's investment was already spent, but—"

"How much money was it?" He asks. "Not just the amount spent, but the amount he pulled?"

There's something about the way he asks this, and I suddenly have a feeling where he's going with this, and it's not just so he can know the details of my business transactions. My heart pounds.

This is a big deal, and I don't want him to feel obligated in that way, to feel like I expect this just because we're together or—

"Allison," he says, squeezing my hands.

"It's a lot," I say. And, god, it really is. That panicky feeling is building again.

"Yeah, okay." He gives me a knowing look, a little half-smile. "How much is a lot? In actual numbers."

I swallow past a lump in my throat. "One hundred thousand dollars."

He nods again, like that's not so unexpected. Or not *one hundred thousand dollars.*

"Can I invest?" he asks, and even though I was guessing this is where he was going, my heart stutters.

I'm overwhelmed by emotions I'm not sure I can sort out, but love for this man is definitely at the top. "Shane, you don't have to—"

"I know I don't have to. And, yeah, you're my girlfriend and I want to support your dream, but honestly, I know what a damn good investment this is." His blue eyes are bright, even more so than usual in that royal blue shirt. "Your line is going to be amazing, and I want in. If you'll let me."

He wants to invest in me. In my talent. My business, my dream, which has teetered on the edge of a cliff since yesterday.

I can feel tears starting, sheer relief and gratitude and so much love. But also fear and guilt over how I handled all of this. And over how much I don't want to take away from *his* new dreams.

"What about your festival?" I ask. "Would you still be able to afford to do that? I mean, I know we'd get investors on board, but you'd need capital to start with for something like that."

"I'll be fine. I'm actually really good with money." He gets a sad kind of smirk on his face. "My dad used to say I'd never amount to anything, and one of the many reasons he'd give is that I wouldn't ever be smart with my money, get a 401(k) or anything like that."

I'm pretty sure I start glowering at even the mention of his dad, let alone hearing again the kinds of things his own father would say to him. But Shane strokes my knuckles with his thumb. "So I made sure everyone in the band had retirement accounts, insurance, savings, all that stuff. I know how to handle these things. Despite that irresponsible bad-boy reputation."

I can't help but smile, and shake my head. "Layers."

He reaches up and pushes some of my hair behind my ear, then trails his fingers down the side of my face. "Also, our sales went through the roof after the accident. I have the money, if I move some things around. So, can I invest?"

The tears are building, and I blink them back. "Yes," I say, and hug him tight—though I'm careful not to press my face against his suit and leave any makeup stains that Carlyle will have a stroke over. "Thank you."

It's at that moment I realize another reason why I had so much trouble coming to him with this. I was terrified to lose him, yes. But I've been independent for so long, especially since the cancer. They say things like that make people realize how much they need to be able to lean on others—and I certainly did so with my family at the time—but afterward it had the opposite effect. I couldn't stand being an emotional drain on those I loved, and I pulled away from them, away from relationships in general, focusing on my work to the exclusion of anything else. Scared of the cancer coming back and having yet another person to hurt. And—irrationally, I know—scared of it coming back and having no one there for me this time.

I've worked and pushed myself like I'm on my own, and I've done that for long enough that it's hard to trust that I can truly lean on someone else.

But I don't want to do that anymore, and with Shane, I don't have to. More than that, being with Shane makes me see that maybe I never did.

I want to tell him all of this, want to really apologize for pushing him away like that, for making him not feel needed, but he starts speaking, once again in that cautious tone.

"You know," he says. "We talked about you redecorating my place. But if you actually wanted to live there—or maybe if I lived at your place—I'd be fine paying the full rent, if you needed to save some for your line. I mean, I'm paying it anyway, and—"

"You want to move in together?" My eyes are wide, and my heart is skipping like crazy.

Shane shifts uncertainly. "Yeah. I mean, if you—"

He cuts off when Carlyle appears beside us.

"Allison, I need you to get the girls ready. Shane, you need to get your mic from Henry." He turns to the practice room in general. "Places, everyone!" he announces, and just like that, the eye of the storm has passed. We're back to loud exclamations and nervous laughter and the beginning of last-second wardrobe freak-outs—no small number of which are girls checking their heels to make sure they're still structurally sound.

Then Carlyle grabs Shane by the arm and practically hauls

him toward the stage, like he's not sure Shane will be able to find it on his own, and Shane gives me a last, beleaguered look before he disappears out the door, and I smile back at him.

Moving in together. Crazy, but, like everything else crazy this week, it feels right.

I allow myself one last deep, relieved, breath, so grateful for Shane. For us.

Then I turn to the room myself and clap my hands sharply to get their attention. It works, and they all look at me, still patting at their hair or tugging at their dresses. Yvonne's coach smacks her hand to keep her from messing up the boob tape she just applied.

"Okay, girls," I say. "I know how nerves get before pageants, but you've all done this before and you've been brilliant. You've had to be, to get this far."

There are nods and some smiles. I see growing determination in several expressions.

So far, so good.

"You've got this. I know you do. And more importantly, *you* know you do. Each and every one of you is incredible and talented and has earned her spot up on that stage. So let's go show that to the world."

It's a Southern California beauty pageant, not Miss Universe, so "the world" may be stretching it a bit, but the girls cheer and beam and bounce on their toes excitedly.

They've got this. And so do I.

TWENTY-FIVE

Allison

The music swells, and the audience claps, and Shane strides out onto the stage, mic in hand.

It's a bigger crowd than normal. The large auditorium is packed. Tickets sold out pretty much the minute the press got wind of Shane Beckstrom's first public performance since the accident. The fact that he's only hosting and not playing music doesn't seem to have deterred anyone.

And right now, it doesn't seem to deter him. Despite the fact that emceeing a beauty pageant is new and different for him—and not exactly something he's been thrilled about—the man knows how to own a stage. He flashes that charming smile to the packed audience, welcomes them all to the pageant, then launches into the opening lines from the script, which are now scrolling past on a teleprompter.

The jokes are cheesy as ever—Carlyle can run a good pageant, but he insists on being way too involved in the scriptwriting, and it shows—but Shane manages to sell them, or at least show by his tone that he's aware of how cheesy they are. And the audience loves it.

I want to pay attention to Shane during his opener, but I'm busy making sure the girls are lined up in the correct order and that nothing's out of place with their wardrobe or hair. Their sequined dresses are all basically the same cut, with minor variance in sleeves and straps, and they fidget with the fabric and with the small matching tiaras in their hair.

"Now I know what you're really here for—let's see the lovely contestants!" Shane's voice filters back through the speakers, and the girl-power pop music for the group dance number kicks off.

Shane comes off stage by us, just as the girls paste on their biggest smiles and saunter out in front of the audience, hips swaying in time with the music.

"Hey," I say to Shane, smiling, as he walks over to me. "You're doing great."

"Yeah?" He looks a little abashed, like he doesn't want to feel as proud of that as he is.

"Clearly you could have a future in this."

He gives a mock-grimace. "I might have to. The chance of me having the cred to start a music festival is going down dramatically with every stupid pageant pun."

I laugh, but really it warms me to hear him even joke about the music festival. I think he's starting to really think of it as more than just a far-off possibility.

The first group number finishes and Shane heads back out there for the girls' quick contestant intros—each giving their names and which city they represent. As the girls file off one by one, hustling back to the dressing room to do a quick-change into their swimsuits, I can tell by the grins and even-greater determination that they're feeling more confidence now.

Which gives me more confidence too. I don't believe in Collette's visions, but I sure do believe in the power of self-fulfilling prophecy, especially where pageant panic is concerned.

While the girls get ready, Shane introduces the judges one by one, and they stand up and wave to the audience and the cameras in the back. In addition to the three who actually have significant pageant judging experience but who no one outside of the pageant circle recognizes, we also have three "celebrity" judges. One is a former Miss California, another is a minor-league baseball player I've never heard of.

The third, though, is the pageant's biggest get—before Shane Beckstrom, of course—and receives by far the most applause. Bridget Messler, famous soap opera star from *Passion Medical*. She gives a pageant-worthy wave to the crowd and sits down.

The music kicks up again, and the swimsuit portion of the competition begins. Once again, the girls do great, their turns well executed, their walks poised and yet sexy. Carmen especially nails this mix, and, in true beauty-queen fashion, doesn't show a hint of her unhappiness at being forced into a swimsuit with an actual lower half. My heart skips a beat when I see Yvonne wobble, but she rights herself quickly.

I let out a breath.

The talent portion starts right after, and the nice thing about this part—other than it being the most interesting to watch, in my opinion—is that while Shane needs to introduce each one before they perform, he's not on the stage for the actual talent. Which means he gets to watch with me from the wings.

Heather does some excellent face-painting on a volunteer from the audience, making her look like the scream figure from that Edvard Munsch painting.

"Do you think she could make me look like Gene Simmons from Kiss for the evening gown intro?" Shane asks.

"I think the better question is, could I ever have sex again with you after I saw that?"

"Hmm," Shane says, pretending to consider. "Not worth the risk."

Next up is Sherry and her (fully recovered) poodles, the third of which, I have since learned, is named Ellen Degeneruff. This act is a real crowd pleaser—in addition to the cuteness factor, the dogs are actually impressive. One of them jumps rope with her, another rides a little scooter. They all three dance in unison. Even Shane seems slightly charmed by this, though he maintains that Lord Shelldon could kick their asses at a talent competition if he was ever so inclined.

I disagree, because I have seen Lord Shelldon jump headfirst into a wall to catch a moving bit of reflected light, but I appreciate Shane's faith in him.

I make sure that Gwen's marimba is far away from Becky's camellias (and that Gwen is far away from Becky) while each of them take their turns, and the flowers and instrument all come away unharmed. Carmen sings her aria beautifully, and Angelica's speed-painting (done with glow paint while the canvas is upside down) garners lots of oohs from the crowd when she flips it right-side up and voila! It's Jack Sparrow. Deena entrances them with her scarves, and Collette—whose talent, shockingly, isn't related to her psychic abilities—freestyle roller skates to "My Country, 'Tis of Thee." It seems like a weird combination to me, but the judges appear to really dig roller-skating patriotism. Even Bridget Messler looks a little teary-eyed.

One by one, Shane announces, and the girls perform, and Carlyle—standing on the wings on the other side of the stage—slowly looks less and less like he's about to have a panic-induced stroke.

When the applause dies down for the final girl, Simone, who I'm helping to shimmy into her poppy costume right here backstage due to lack of time to run to the dressing room, Shane launches into his intro for the second pageant group dance number. He even says the tragic line, "And I don't know about you, but I'm looking forward to seeing this"—and here he turns to give me an almost imperceptible head shake and a *you owe me* expression—"bouquet of beauty."

I grin back at him. God, this man really *must* love me.

The first batch of five girls in their glittering green "stem" gowns and their big petal headdresses walk out to the beat of the dance music, and Shane passes them as he walks off stage to me.

"Well," I say, smiling at him, "if you hadn't already lost all your punk-rock cred before, you definitely—"

"I thought you were going to fix that!" a male voice says from behind me, and I turn to see Thomas rushing up the backstage steps toward Collette standing in her still-offstage group, waiting for their music cue. She gapes at him, and I find myself frozen for a beat in shock.

"Thomas, you can't be here right now!" she says. "You can't—"

"You can't wear that slit out there, Collette," he growls, and grabs her by the arm. "Looking like a slut like that, no way."

Oh hell no. He is not doing this, not here. Not to one of *my* girls.

"Let her go, and get the hell out of here!" I demand, stepping between them, trying to physically pry his fingers off of her arm.

Collette squeals as he grips tighter, and the next batch of girls sauntering onto the stage is a beat behind the music, looking back to see what's happening.

Even in the relative dark of the stage wings, I can tell that Thomas's face is bright red, and he shoves me back into Amanda, who lets out a little shriek, and it's all I can do to stay upright in my heels and not take both of us down.

And suddenly Shane's in between Thomas and Collette, and his fists are clenched. I think he might punch Thomas—and I'm generally anti-violence, but god, I think that jerk deserves it—but Thomas is apparently afraid enough of Shane, who has a good six inches of height on him and a lot more muscle, that he dodges back. There's a ripping sound as the sleeve of Collette's dress tears, and Collette yells, "Thomas, stop!"

Shane grabs Thomas by the shoulder, but Thomas twists himself free and darts past him—

Right onto the stage, where the next group of five girls has just entered, joining the other ten. Several stop in shock and then get bumped into by the contestants who keep dancing. Two girls—Chloe and Sherry—fall down, and the audience gasps.

Thomas has run to the middle of the stage, looking frantically back to see if Shane is chasing him, but Shane is watching him from next to me. The girls who had managed to keep dancing all pause, and I hear Carlyle yelling for security.

I think my heart has entirely stopped.

I'm about to run out there myself, maybe with Shane, to drag Thomas off stage, security be damned, but suddenly Gwendolyn's furious voice rings out from her place center stage.

"You jerk! Stay away from Collette!"

"Damn right," Becky yells, in perhaps the first agreement with Gwen I've ever heard her utter. Becky shoves him and he stumbles into Angelica, who shoves him back.

"Yeah, leave her alone!" she cries.

"She deserves better than you!" Carmen says, and oh my god, she's taken off her shoe and throws it at him, heel first. It bounces off his back, and he flinches and wheels around.

But before he can retaliate or even say anything, Wendy and Deena have also stripped off their shoes and are hitting him on the shoulders with them, and Heather and Simone have taken off their poppy petal headwear and are using those like floral whips, and Thomas is curling up on himself, protecting his head from the wrath of the vengeful beauty queens.

The vengeful beauty queens protecting one of their own.

Maybe I shouldn't be proud, but dammit, I kind of am. And I'm also having trouble breathing.

Because there's a huge audience out there, and this is being televised. Poor Collette runs off sobbing, and I hear Carlyle now yelling for the curtains to be closed, and security has finally, finally gotten to the stage.

But Thomas has seen this, too, and he starts to run away from them—only to slip on a fallen fabric poppy petal and land face-first on the stage with a massive thump that makes us all gasp yet again.

He turns just as security parts the sea of angry women to grab him, and my jaw drops as I see him clutching his nose, blood streaming down his face.

Oh my god. My pageant girls have broken his nose.

I can't see Shane among the girls who have swarmed

backstage, some of whom are still jeering at Thomas, and I can't see Carlyle, and oh my god, the pageant is falling apart.

But I can't think of anything I can do to save the pageant, so instead I run to find Collette.

TWENTY-SIX

Shane

As security drags that asshole off the stage, I stare him down. I may not feel protective over these girls like Allison does, but I can recognize a total douche when I see one. And if anyone was going to get a broken nose—shit, did that actually happen?—I'm glad it was him. Several of the girls are standing around looking smug, and others look horrified. The curtain is closed, and I can hear the murmuring of the audience as they wonder what the hell is going to happen next.

What *is* going to happen? Where's Allison? I suspect she went after Collette, but someone has to get these girls ready for the next act, which is—god, where did my script go?

Carlyle comes charging around the scrim at the back of the stage. He'll get it under control, I'm sure.

Except what he does is shove an acoustic guitar into my hands. "Here," he says.

I hold it up by the neck. "What the hell do you want me to do with this?"

"You're a musician, right?" he snaps. "Play!" Then he turns me around by the shoulders and shoves me toward the stage.

Oh, shit. I *was* a musician. Now I'm a has-been who hasn't played guitar in months. It's not that I can't play. I've mostly done bass but I could play lead almost as well as Kevin. I remember how, but the idea of doing so in front of people makes my blood run cold.

Carlyle's shove propels me forward, and I'm at the curtain. I could throw a fit, say I can't work like this and storm out. But somewhere backstage Allison is panicking. Her pageant is falling apart. Someone needs to give the audience something to focus on while she and Carlyle and the girls pull it back together.

I used to love this. I used to live to be up in front of people. That feels like another life, but here goes.

I step out onto the stage, and the crowd quiets, staring up at me. I realize I don't even know if this guitar is in tune, and so I give it an experimental strum as I step up to the microphone. The mic is set high, since I've been speaking into it, but I don't adjust it. If I'm going to perform solo I'd better sing, which was always JT's thing, but I've done back up long enough.

I look out at the crowd. I can see more of them than I want to, even with the lights. They might be incandescent, but they're blinding, and I feel like I'm going to pass out.

Then I see him. There, standing in the middle of the center aisle, is JT. He's looking up at me with this angry expression on his face, his arms crossed. He arches an eyebrow at me, like, *Well? Are you going to play?*

I don't want to play our songs. I'm not sure I ever want to play those songs again.

So instead I play the first chord of Pink Floyd's "Brain Damage." I've played it before but never performed it. Still, it feels like the most honest thing I've ever played, and suddenly I feel like I'm naked.

I play the song slowly and deliberately. The crowd, which was murmuring about the spectacle they just saw, falls into silence. I sing about losing my mind, about having voices in my head that aren't exactly me. My voice chokes up slightly when I get to the part about being in a band that goes on to play different songs and leaves you behind because you're too messed up to keep playing.

I look right at JT, and I try to tell him that I know how he feels. He got left behind in that van. Kevin and I escaped with our lives, but the whole world just kept rolling around us and forgot about us.

Now I'm going to leave JT behind. He's right. I have to take the medication. Not just because I'm hallucinating, but because I'm a mess. Between the nightmares and the lack of sleep, I can't function, and I need to be able to do that again.

I'm not the one who died, and that sucks, maybe worse than if it had been me.

But I'm going to move on, because I have to. If it were me who died, I'd want him to do the same.

JT looks up at me, and he sighs. That's the thing about a hallucination. I don't even have to tell him what's going to happen. He already knows. He looks up at me and gives me a mock salute, and then he turns and slouches up the aisle and out the door at the back.

Allison

It doesn't take long to find Collette sobbing behind a rack of costumes just outside the practice room. I don't say anything at first, and I don't have to; she just throws her arms around me, and I hug her tightly back. There's a low murmur coming from the speakers—the mic on stage is still live and being piped back here, so those off stage can know when their cue is coming up. The audience is coming out of shock and getting confused and restless.

My stress spikes even higher, but I can't think about the pageant right now. I have to take care of Collette, who just got undeniable proof about what a jealous, controlling dick her boyfriend is.

At least I hope she considers it undeniable proof. I hope—

Suddenly a guitar chord sounds through the speakers and I startle. I look back towards the stage, even as I keep my arms wrapped around the crying Collette.

A guitar? Who—

Oh. *Oh.*

When I realize what's happening, my heart pounds harder. Silence follows, a long pause stretching through the speakers.

Shane's up there, and he hasn't played publicly since the accident, and I know for a fact he wasn't sure he ever could again. But Carlyle must have made him, shoved him out there, and now I want to go yell at Carlyle, because he doesn't know how freaked out Shane must be, how this could trigger another public meltdown—

A different chord sounds, one more confident than the last, and then it occurs to me—Carlyle couldn't make Shane do this. He definitely would have told him to do it, but no one *makes* Shane do anything. There's no way he wants to be up there right now, doing an impromptu guitar solo for a beauty pageant crowd. There's no way he's not dealing with all the crushing emotion of being up on a stage again with a guitar in hand, but this time alone, with none of his band mates, his best friends at his side.

He's not doing this for Carlyle or the pageant.

He's doing this for me. Even though I hurt him, even though he somehow thinks I don't need him the same way he needs me—something that is so far from true I can barely wrap my brain around it—he's doing this for me.

A bright warmth fills me, growing even brighter as Shane starts singing. He's not a lead singer, but he's got a really good voice, solid with just that touch of rocker gravel to it. I only vaguely recognize the song—for all that I work with bands, I'm not as immersed in the music scene itself as I could be. It's not Accidental Erotica, though. That much I know.

Shane sings about a "lunatic on the grass," and my eyes burn, thinking of us sitting on the lawn outside the benefit, him telling me about him losing his mind, about the hallucinations.

He was so afraid, I remember. To tell me, to tell anyone.

Now everyone may already know, but I think this is his way of telling them on *his* terms—or at least as much of his terms as it can be, this unplanned concert he's giving to keep his girlfriend's pageant from falling completely apart.

My heart is swelling with so much love for this man, and I want to just hang on every word coming through those speakers, but Collette's sobs are turning into gasping hiccups, and I know I need to take advantage of the time Shane's giving me to be there for her.

"I'm so sorry that happened," I say, stroking her platinum-blond hair, careful not to get my fingers caught in the stiff, hairsprayed curls.

There are definitely things I don't miss about being in the pageants myself, and the sheer volume of hair products is one of them.

She pulls back enough to look at me, her watery blue eyes red-rimmed. "He's such a j-jerk," she sniffles. "Everyone said so, and I kept making excuses for him, even when he made me feel bad about myself. I'm an idiot."

"Hey," I say, holding her by the shoulders. "You're not an idiot. It's always harder to see the red flags when there are feelings involved."

She scrubs a trail of snot onto the back of her hand. I look around for a tissue, but short of using one of the other girl's costumes as makeshift Kleenex—something I very much doubt any of them would appreciate—I've got nothing. But Collette doesn't seem to notice. "I should have seen them. I'm psychic!"

This last part comes out as a wail, and she buries her face back into my shoulder.

I am starting to believe she might actually be. But apparently even visions from dream-Cher don't prevent heartbreak.

"Oh, honey," I say, patting her back, wishing I knew what to say. Shane's voice still drifts over the speaker, his song settling over me, morose and yet empowering—to him and to me.

I think about how I wondered at the beginning if I was being naive when it came to him. Wondered if I was ignoring my better judgment in thinking there was so much more underneath the bad boy rep he'd definitely earned, if maybe not quite to the level everyone assumed. Thinking that the reputation and the attitude that fueled it was all a mask, but wondering if I was going to be proven wrong and left heartbroken.

It scared me, then. But it doesn't anymore.

"I don't think anyone's psychic when it comes to their own love life," I say, gently. "We're all just kind of putting ourselves out there and taking a risk."

She nods against my shoulder.

"But the guy who deserves you," I continue, "the guy who's going to be worthy of your love . . . That guy isn't going to try to control you or make you feel bad about yourself, Collette. He's going to love you for who you are, for your true self, and never try to make you less."

I listen to Shane sing and feel tears behind my eyes.

Shane makes me feel more like my true self when I'm with him, like the true self I've been afraid to be. He gives me a safe space to be that person, gives me a safe place to fall, and I'm more and more confident that I do the same for him.

"Thomas isn't that person," Collette grouses, with an especially loud sniffle, as she plucks at the torn sequined sleeve half-dangling off her arm. I'm glad to see that there's a spark of indignant anger in her eyes, blazing through the sadness.

"No, he's not," I say. "But one day, you'll find that guy. And until then, I think you've got some friends out there who'll be willing to beat down anyone who's an asshole to you." I jerk my head towards the stage, the scene of the shoe and tiara-throwing, and Collette manages a smile and even a little laugh.

"Yeah, I guess so," she says.

"And don't forget that you're badass all on your own. With or without a man at your side."

She nods, letting out a long, shaky breath.

"Now, if you don't want to finish the competition, that's totally okay. You just went through a lot, and it won't affect your chances in future pageants, I'll make sure—"

"No," she says. "I wanted to do this, and I'm not letting some stupid boy ruin it for me." She glares at the half-torn sleeve, and then with a sudden, angry tug, rips it all the way off. "I'm going to finish."

I smile at her, even as the designer in me winces at the ragged seam. "Are you sure?" I ask. Because I know how hard it is to make a choice like that in the middle of all the hurt she's going through.

"I've earned my spot on that stage," she says firmly, quoting my earlier words. "And I'm going to show the world."

"Good for you," I say, feeling more than a little proud. I squeeze her arm. "But if you're going back up there, you might want to fix your makeup first."

She sniffles and swipes at her eyes, smearing more mascara across her cheeks. "Totally," she says. Then she gives me another quick hug. "And in case you were wondering, your aura and Shane's are very compatible. I'm, like, ninety-five percent sure you won't murder him this time."

I laugh. I'll take those odds.

Collette hurries into the practice room to fix her makeup, and I all but run toward the backstage area. The other contestants are bunched up in groups, whispering to each other, and Carlyle is trying to line them up—probably for a redo of the dance number—but I weave through them to get to the edge of the stage. I make it there, hidden by the curtain, just as Shane finishes the last couple lines. He's bathed in the spotlight, owning it, his voice and the notes from his guitar filling the auditorium. His pain and his honesty infusing every beat.

Tears finally slip from my eyes down my cheeks, my heart so, so full of love for him.

It ends, and there's just the echo of his song.

And then the applause. The audience going nuts, knowing they've seen something special, even if there's no way they can fully grasp what just happened—I'm not sure I can. I'm not even sure he can.

But he looks back at me, and I smile at him, wishing I could somehow convey from here all that love. I don't think that's possible, but I blow him a kiss, and from the way he smiles back, I think maybe he knows.

TWENTY-SEVEN

Shane

I finish the song, and I stare out at the audience. I can see several people with their phones out, plus the pageant is being filmed. This is going to be on TV as well as all over the internet, and I didn't have the rights to perform it, so I better keep Parker around long enough to clean up that mess, if there's going to be one.

There's a beat after the last chords fade away, and then the audience applauds. I turn back to the curtain, hoping for some signal about what the hell is going on back there, and on the other side, I see Allison hiding behind the proscenium, peering out of the curtains, watching me. I can't quite make out her expression, but I realize that aside from recordings, this is the first time she's heard me sing. She presses her lips to her fingers and blows the kiss at me, and I smile.

Damn, I love that woman. And while I need to move on and let go for me, I want to do it equally as much for her. For us. For our future. One that will likely be messy, but I hope will also be long and beautiful.

"Thank you," I say into the microphone. I look back at Allison and she nods.

Then I slip back through the curtain just as it parts in the center.

The pageant goes on. The music from before cues up again and the girls start their flower-themed dance number, round two, though several of the headdresses look like they've been through a storm—or, really, a pretty awesome asshole-beatdown. I make it backstage just as the first of them file on, and I sit down on a stool, glad to be out of the spotlight for a moment.

Allison comes over and throws her arms around me so hard she nearly knocks me off my stool.

"Are you okay?" I ask. "Is Collette?" I don't see her dancing on stage with the rest of them.

"Yes for me," Allison says. "And I think it will be yes for Collette, too, at least eventually. She doesn't seem inclined to try to patch things up with that douche."

"Good. Did she drop out of the pageant?"

"I told her she could, but she still wants to be in it. I guess in addition to surprisingly accurate psychic predictions, the girl's crazy tough." Allison looks proud.

I smile back at her and brush her hair over her ear. "Did you like the song?"

"Yes," she says, smiling softly. "I wanted to kill Carlyle when I realized he sent you out there. That was a good song choice, though. You sounded amazing."

I'm not sure that's true in a musical sense. More like passable. But I'm pretty sure that's not what she means.

"Thank you for doing that," she says. "I know you didn't want to perform."

"I think it was good for me," I say. "But yeah. I did it for you."

Her expression softens even further, and she tugs her lower lip between her teeth like she wants to say something, but I think we both realize at the same time that the song is over and the girls are filing off stage, which means I'm back up.

And I sure as hell don't want anything else to go wrong in this pageant.

So I do the announcements for the evening-wear competition, and I stick to the damn script. Collette shows up for this part, and

I notice all the girls giving her—and each other—encouraging smiles. Becky and Gwen even do a little fist bump. I bet Allison is feeling even more proud of her girls today than ever, and with good reason. Pageant girls are fierce, man.

Last is the final interview portion, which they answer without leaving the stage from the evening-wear portion. They are each given a single question, which I read from the updated script I was given by Carlyle minutes before the pageant started, like he didn't trust me unattended with both the top-secret interview questions and the green room garbage can in which they might end up.

I guess I earned that.

The questions are mostly about current events or their charity platforms (is Pennies for Polyps really a thing?), and they all seem to handle them pretty well—I'm especially impressed with Angelica's grasp of international trade politics, and Carmen's dedication to Alzheimer's research.

And then, after a small break where the judges deliberate, I'm handed the envelope with the names of the winners. The girls are lined up in back, some of them holding hands, others biting their lip nervously, and as I open the envelope, I can almost imagine Allison back when she used to compete. I bet she was the fiercest of them all.

"Second runner up, Miss Sweet Orange, Carmen Rivera!" I announce, and Carmen beams and struts out to receive her crown and bouquet.

"First runner up, Miss Grand Meadows, Collette Frey!"

Collette bounces up and down excitedly, and all the girls cheer along with the audience on this one. Allison beams from the wings. I've got to admit, I'm a little disappointed that Collette didn't win. But she doesn't seem too upset about it, blowing little kisses at the judges, who seem charmed by her.

"And the winner of the Miss California Poppy pageant is . . ." I trail off dramatically, because hell, I know showmanship, "Miss Golden Gal,"—seriously, was this supposed to sound like the beauty pageant at a Florida retirement community?—"Sherry Spencer!"

Sherry squeals, and the music swells and a big-ass gaudy crown is put on her head. She waves and cries happily, and I imagine to myself that in the back somewhere her dogs with their ridiculous pun-names are barking in shared celebration.

After that, and some final terrible closing jokes, the pageant is over. I hurry off the stage, but not before I see Nix all but climbing over seats to get an autograph from Bridget Messler—and, judging by the interest with which another of the judges looks over at her, about to get hit on by a minor league baseball star. I shake my head.

It's a huge relief to be done with all this, to have survived both hosting a beauty pageant and playing music publicly.

Maybe even to have survived these last few months.

It feels even better when Allison comes up to me and wraps her arms around me again, and we hold each other for several long moments.

She looks up from where she's resting her head on my shoulder. "I really am sorry I didn't tell you about my investor dropping out. I should have given you the chance to be there for me. It wasn't fair."

I'm pretty sure this is the thing she wanted to say earlier, before I had to run out to host. I shrug. "I probably would have fucked it up. It's all right if you needed to cope with the problem without wading through my reaction, too. If you don't want to deal with me, you shouldn't have to."

"No, I wanted to. I was just scared."

The idea that she could be scared in this relationship baffles me. I don't know how much clearer I could be that I'm in this. She has to be able to see how much I need her. "What were you scared of?"

She's quiet for a moment. "I didn't want you to hate yourself because being with you cost me something. I don't regret any of it. Not for a minute, not even if all my investors backed out. But

I was worried you'd decide you were bad for me and leave me."

"I probably would have decided I was hurting you. But I wouldn't have left. And you could have told me to knock it off and be there for you. You're good at that."

"Think you would have listened?"

"Yeah. Because I listen to everything else you say. You seem to have that effect on me."

She holds me tighter. "It's not true, what you said about me not needing you. I do."

That pit in my stomach comes back. "Maybe. But not the way I need you."

"No, I do," she says. "Every bit as much."

"I believe you want to be with me. But if I was gone, you'd still have your family, and your life. You have so many good things."

"But I wouldn't have *you*. The way you love me—" She shakes her head. "I've never experienced anything like it. You're focused on me. I matter to you."

"Of course you do," I say. "That's what a relationship is."

"It's not what all relationships are," she says carefully. "If my cancer came back, you'd stay with me."

Oh. She says that she wasn't in love with her boyfriend who left her, that she broke up with him when she was diagnosed, and that was for the best. I believe her, but I can still see how it would sting, never knowing if you'd find someone who would want to stay.

"Of course I would," I say. She burrows her face into my neck, and I hold her close. "You're sure it's going to come back."

"No," she says. "No one can know, really."

"I mean emotionally. You feel that it will."

She's still for a moment, and then she nods.

I understand that. This sense of impending doom, that every bad thing that can go wrong will. But I also don't want to be something she's doing because she's scared of the future.

"If you knew that it wouldn't," I say, "and that you were

going to die in your nineties of unrelated causes in a nursing home, would you still want to be with me?"

"Yes," Allison says. "Because I'd want you to be there with me in that nursing home, and for us to have had this beautiful life together."

I can see it—Allison as one of those little old ladies who's always bitching that no one listens to her, and me mostly deaf from all the loud music I've played over the years, pretending that I can hear everyone even though I can't, carrying on my own side of the conversation, oblivious to everyone else.

But I'd know what Allison was saying, what she was thinking. Because we'd have been together so long, we wouldn't even need to talk anymore to be in sync.

And I'd misinterpret her just to annoy her, because ninety-year-old me is probably still a dick.

"Since I recovered," she says, "I've been so focused on getting things done. Too focused. You remind me of all the things I want to do that aren't work related. Like spend time with my family."

Like have one of our own, I want to add.

She smiles at me, and I'm caught in those warm, beautiful eyes. "You make me think about what I really want out of life," she says.

"You make me remember how to want things." I press my forehead to hers. "And you're at the top of that list."

That's something I know will never change.

TWENTY-EIGHT

Shane
Three Months Later

I get my copy of the interview I did with *Rolling Stone* the same day it hits the newsstands. I'm afraid to open it. I have no idea how the interviewers decided to paint me after I opened up about everything. I mostly did it because I felt I owed it to Anna-Marie to set the record straight—about the lies I told, the way I behaved. We're finally friends again, and I want to do right by her. And the rest of it, well. They were saying it anyway. I hope things will calm down now that I'm not treating it like a secret.

Ripping open the envelope, I sit down on my stool next to Allison's work desk. We're sharing our living room studio now, with her fabrics and sketch pads stacked next to my amp and sound board and guitar stand. She's on her laptop responding to her manufacturer, but she looks over as I pull out the glossy cover.

Damn. There's me and Kevin on the cover of *Rolling Stone*. That's a dream I never thought I'd see happen—especially with the headline: *"I lost my mind there for a while." Beckstrom opens up about post-traumatic psychosis, ex-girlfriend Anna-Marie Rios, and life after Accidental Erotica.*

Allison abandons her email and turns to face me, sitting

sideways on her chair. Kevin and I stare up at us from the cover. We look somber, like we've just been to a funeral. And I guess we kind of have.

"Damn," Allison says. "My fiancé is sexy."

I laugh. "You needed to see me on a magazine to decide that?"

She rubs my forearm. "No. Doesn't mean I can't appreciate your hotness in many forms."

I kiss her and then open the magazine, flipping to our article. I knew the reporter was eating up everything I told them, but damn, they were thorough. It's all here, from the real story of what happened between me and Anna-Marie to the pain of losing JT and my falling apart mentally after the accident. It's embarrassing, having that be public, but the rumors went crazy after the last article broke, and I wanted to set the record straight.

Yes, I'm taking anti-psychotics. Yes, they're working. Yes, I still have nightmares, but they're getting better. Yes, I'm seeing a therapist who wants me to try all kinds of crazy things like holding buzzers that alternate pulses in my hands and staring at a pencil while she moves it in front of my eyes while I process old memories.

It makes me feel crazy, but it's helping. I'm feeling more like a normal person every day. Not my old normal, which I think now was just one long fight to avoid feeling, but a new normal, where I have feelings and I don't need to lash out to protect myself from them.

It's weird as hell, frankly, but for the first time in my life, I'm feeling things I want to be feeling. Allison's a huge part of that, and I'm grateful for her every day. I'm also grateful that Kevin and Maya decided to stay in LA, after all—I meant it when I said I would make it work even if he moved, but it's sure as hell nice not to have to.

The inside article has several more pictures of me and Kevin, and a big, full-page one of me and Allison. There's a long section about how we met, and the influence she's had on me. I smile while I read the long quote about how much I love her, and how much her support has changed my life. *I couldn't have done any of this without her*, the pull quote reads. *I'm not sure I would have survived.*

Allison leans against my shoulder. "I think you give me too much credit," she says. "I didn't do any of the hard work."

"You put up with me," I say. "That's got to be hard work some days."

She shakes her head. "Not as hard as you think."

I'm not sure about that, but I believe she believes it. It's true what I said, though. I couldn't have done any of this without Allison. She hasn't done the work for me, but she's given me a safe place to do the work, and a future I want to work through it for. She underestimates how important that's been, but I don't.

Allison impatiently turns the page. "Please tell me they printed the stuff about the festival."

They did. The article ends with a long section where I talk about the plans for the festival—the concept and the process of getting together bands who want to play. Kevin and I have been contacting lots of the bands we know, but I'm hoping that this article will result in some people calling me.

It can't hurt that the reporter caught the rumor that Alec Andreas has agreed to headline my first event. While I can neither confirm or deny that publicly until the ink is dry—something that won't happen until I get a lot more of the particulars ironed out for the contract—I'm glad buzz about that is getting around without my help.

I may have invested money in Allison's business, but she's invested a lot of energy in mine, and I couldn't be happier with the way everything is coming together, for her and for me.

There's a loud hissing sound from the other room, and then Lord Shelldon, Allison's cat, comes shooting into the room and jumps up on her work table, looking seriously affronted. He's followed by the kitten Allison gave me—Sir Snugglesworth—who isn't quite dexterous enough to leap after Shelldon, so he sits down next to Allison's chair and mewls pitifully.

Shelldon glares me down. The love in the relationship between him and Snugglesworth only goes one way, and I'm not sure Shelldon is ever going to forgive us for bringing this little ball of fur into his life.

I bend down and pick up Snugglesworth, who was small enough to fit in my palm when Allison gave him to me, but is starting to be a two-hand cat. I move the magazine and set Snugglesworth on my lap, and then twist the ring on my finger—a simple titanium band.

"Are you worried about the reaction to the article?" Allison asks.

"No," I say. Most of this isn't new information—just my side of the story from a reputable source. People are going to react how they're going to react, and I'm okay with that.

"Nix is coming over later for her fitting," Allison says. "She's going to die when she sees that article. Somehow I think it's still a novelty for her that I'm dating you. I wonder if she'll get used to that before we get married."

I doubt it. Nix doesn't exactly treat me like a celebrity—more like the older brother she never had. But she's also the kind of person who milks all the fun and excitement out of life that she can, and I have a feeling she'll be milking her connection to stardom for a long time to come.

I look up at the dress hanging in the doorway—a smooth, black sheath dress with a skirt that's floor length on one side and cuts up to mid-thigh on the other. Nix begged Allison to make her a bridesmaid dress when Allison asked her to be her maid of honor. I think she was even more excited about that than she was about my idea for the wedding. Since Allison beat me to proposing—tying the ring she gave me to the collar of our new kitten—I'm planning the wedding, and everything except the date and Allison's and Nix's dresses is a complete surprise. I ran the whole thing by Nix to make sure she thought Allison would like it, then made a hefty donation to the Los Angeles Zoo to convince them to let us do a simple ceremony in the giraffe enclosure.

"Nix said she needed to talk to you about wedding details," Allison says casually. "Any chance you're going to give me a hint?"

"Nope," I tell her, and she pretends to be annoyed. I lean over and kiss her, and we get carried away, both moving off our seats to press against each other. Snugglesworth complains as he slides to the ground, claws scratching at my jeans, but he lands on my shoe and then immediately darts across the room, chasing something I'm pretty sure he imagined. The magazine falls to the floor, too, pages ruffling at our feet.

I run my hand through Allison's hair, pulling her to me, completely wrapped up in this woman, who I love more than anything in the world. I still can't believe I'm lucky enough to end up with her, and I don't know how I could ever be good enough to be worthy of her.

But I'm damn well going to try.

ACKNOWLEDGMENTS

There are so many people we'd like to thank for helping make this book a reality. First, our families, especially our incredibly supportive husbands Glen and Drew, and our amazing kids. Thanks also to our writing group, Accidental Erotica, for all the feedback.

Thanks to Michelle of Melissa Williams Design for the fabulous cover. Thanks to Amy Carlin and Dantzel Cherry for being proofreading goddesses, and thanks to everyone who read and gave us notes throughout the many drafts of this project—your feedback was so greatly appreciated.

And a very special thanks to you, our readers. We hope you love these characters as much as we do.

Janci Patterson got her start writing contemporary and science fiction young adult novels, and couldn't be happier to now be writing adult romance. She has an MA in creative writing, and lives in Utah with her husband and two adorable kids. When she's not writing she can be found surrounded by dolls, games, and her border collie. She has written collaborative novels with several partners, and is honored to be working on this series with Megan.

Megan Walker lives in Utah with her husband, two kids, and two dogs–all of whom are incredibly supportive of the time she spends writing about romance and crazy Hollywood hijinks. She loves making Barbie dioramas and reading trashy gossip magazines (and, okay, lots of other books and magazines, as well.) She's so excited to be collaborating on this series with Janci. Megan has also written several published fantasy and science-fiction stories under the name Megan Grey.

Find Megan and Janci at www.extraseriesbooks.com

The Extra Series

The Extra
The Girlfriend Stage
Everything We Are
The Jenna Rollins Real Love Tour
Starving with the Stars
My Faire Lady
You are the Story
How Not to Date a Rock Star
Beauty and the Bassist
Su-Lin's Super-Awesome Casual Dating Plan
Ex on the Beach
The Real Not-Wives of Red Rock Canyon
Chasing Prince Charming
Ready to Rumba
Save Me (For Later)

Other Books in The Extra Series

When We Fell
Everything We Might Have Been

Manufactured by Amazon.ca
Bolton, ON